For

~~Marie Lauterbach~~

with warm wishes
Lakshmi Persaud.

London
March 2013

SASTRA

LAKSMI PERSAUD

PEEPAL TREE

First published in Great Britain in 1993
Reprinted in 2003, 2006
Peepal Tree Press Ltd
17 King's Avenue
Leeds LS6 1QS
England

ISBN 0 948833 71 8

For Dookhni and Ranee
and
for Sharda
with thanks

PROLOGUE

I celebrate myself, and sing myself
And what I assume you shall assume,
For every atom belonging to me as good belongs to you.

Walt Whitman

KARMA

Parvatee Narayan sat cross-legged before the fire. Nothing stirred save falling ash, while incense burnt beneath a pyramid of pitch pine, freshly cut. Pundit Karsi's garland of marigolds held a ripe fragrance and, behind him, a frangipani, overgrown, cast its early morning shadows from white petals. This place is like a temple's garden she thought.

On a turmeric-yellow peerha lay the Sanskrit texts used for birth readings: the secrets of one's destiny, of karma, locked in ancient writ. The piece of paper she had sent read: 'Birth of girl child, 7.37 p.m. 5th October 1940'. On seeing the clear hand of Narayan, the child's father, the pundit smiled. Puffs of pine escaped into the air.

Pundit Karsi had earlier untied the vermilion cotton wraps of texts taken from a sandalwood box. Broken, brittle leaves, skilfully held together. Each was consulted – large texts and small. Now they encircled him.

A fine Sanskrit scholar, yet his forefinger was halting, moving with pedantic solemnity; he, muttering to himself. Parvatee's face began to wear a worry, albeit gracefully.

The pundit removed his glasses; with both hands supporting his chin, he would elucidate the meaning of the text. It was not an easy translation; he had to use his imagination.

'Judging from the time of birth Narayan has here, the most favourable syllable is Sa. It is a comforting syllable, suitable for a girl child. Sati you have already, and Saraswatee is becoming too popular. You will have no difficulty in choosing... yet... I would like to make a suggestion.'

Parvatee moved her head as flowers do in a light breeze.

'Call her Sastra.'

'Sastra, Pundit? That's a good name and it sounds good.'

He, too, was smiling warmly. 'Somehow, somehow, I knew you would like it.'

He had been sitting more cheerfully at ease, pundit-style on the sheet of white cotton, but now Karsi Pundit began to adjust himself, and the sticks of burning pitch pine, and the incense before him. He stretched forwards, uncurling the edges of the cotton spread.

'As to Karma itself. This girl child, while still at a tender age will experience, with great intensity, heaven and hell at one and the same time. This is strange, but here we have two reincarnations. Normally the span of one lifetime is allocated to one reincarnation, but for reasons we can only speculate, from time to time, the unexpected comes – two reincarnations clasped in a deadlock, moving into the same space and time, neither giving way, so together they play themselves out in one time.'

Parvatee did not understand. Didn't death mark the end of one reincarnation and the beginning of another?

'When will the first life end and the second begin, Pundit?'

'In terms of the first life, it will end as I have said, when she is still at a tender age.

'Does the book say anything else? Should she avoid

10

anything, Pundit, to help her overcome this... this... ? Can it be eased, Pundit?... Tell me what to do.'

'It will come to pass that someone will teach her how to... how to... lift... to fly.'

'To fly, Pundit? You mean to fly?'

'The exact translation is: will show her how to lift herself, raise herself above the earth.'

'What can it mean, Pundit?'

'Translations are not easy; interpretations are even more difficult. My advice would be that on a day-to-day level, rather than do nothing, let the child avoid steps and ladders and swings; merry-go-round, chair-o-plane... At the spiritual level.., it is more difficult to advise... I have sometimes wished the rishis, the saddhus themselves, were here to tell us exactly. Yet, at the spiritual level, I would try and prevent her from taking a path that has not been tested, or from a way of thinking that leaves tradition behind and shoots off in another direction without serious consideration for anyone. This way of not thinking through the full implication of an act is the modern way, Parvatee; to think of the self, of the individual, is called path-breaking; to consider the family: a handicap.'

The pundit paused a long while and then, 'Parvatee, the old ways have been tried and not found wanting, they have served us for thousands of years. We know that for every action there is a reaction, that a concern for others, for all things, is the foundation of life. We are connected to everything and everything to us... There is no concept of dharma that has not been thought about and explained in the *Mahabharata,* the *Ramayana,* the *Puranas,* the *Upanishads,* the *Vedas.* If Sastra keeps to the traditional path of honour, dignity, womanhood; if she keeps to the heart of her culture, her life will be secure, content like her sister's.

He closed the text, but its message snapped like a guard dog at the stillness around.

Rising, adjusting his angochar, Pundit Karsi smiled: 'Is the child healthy?'

'Yes, Pundit.'

'And pretty like her sister Sati?'

Parvatee masked her anxieties for her new born babe.

'How is Narayan?'

'He is the same, Pundit.'

'I know, when it comes to karma, Narayan is not a true believer.'

Parvatee was uncomfortable.

'No, no, no, I welcome that, it helps to keep us pundits on our toes.'

'That is his way, Pundit. He has been like that from small; he will never change.'

'I understand. You see, Narayan believes you hold fate in your own hands. Now that way of thinking helps a man to try hard; I am for it too. It is a good belief. But there are too many things outside ourselves, Parvatee, things we do not yet understand, which influence our moods, our ways of seeing and so on. It is not possible to be in control of everything. Is the ocean in control of itself? No, it is pulled here, it is pulled there by the moon, by the sun... '

'Thank you, Pundit. I mustn't take up any more of your time.'

'Ram Ram,' he said, blessing her with his raised right hand.

Seeing this sad young mother walk past his gates, Pundit Karsi was certain he had done the correct thing. He believed in keeping to the text, preferring to uphold a scholar's integrity than to offer false comforts. But in this instance, because of the impact the reading was having on Parvatee, he had not spelt it out... a period of violent upheaval would come to pass – those years between the death and birth of reincarnations – persons close to the child would be gravely inflicted by intense pain and deep sorrow... the faith of one and the life of another would be severely handicapped... such close juxtapositions of death and life ever brought turmoil – volcanic explosions, upheavals of the earth and sea – Tsunamis.

BOOK ONE

CHAPTER ONE

1957

A lone hibiscus flower jutting out from the hedge bobbed up and down and up and down in a measured way; dark clouds were drifting, building up, piling high; Parvatee Narayan knew it would rain. The jasmine buds were opening. She sighed and her mind slipped to another place. By the time she looked up again, the moving darkness above was coming towards her, and the hibiscus flower, twisting and turning faster and faster, had gone amok.

The wind, pushing, driving forward, loosening her coiled hair, compelled her to return indoors with only a spray of tulsi and a single marigold. The sky slipped downwards; she stood staring, transfixed. Once more her spirit, drifting as gently as thought itself, returned to settle at another time, another place, seventeen years ago, when her younger daughter, when her present anxieties were born:

Seventeen years had passed and care had been taken to ensure that the creeping child kept close to the ground. Parvatee had grieved, inwardly puzzling over what she had not told Narayan: that fate had spun a web of singing, dancing light, chased by charred ghosts from the underworld.

Narayan had continued to believe in the power of the mind and of the will. A thinking man, a serious man, he carried himself as if it were his questionings, his alert mind and not his pumping heart nor lungs that gave him life. As a businessman, proprietor of a general store, he was prepared to listen to his customers' idiosyncrasies; even pundits must make a living he said. But in the privacy of his home, he would, from time to time, chip away at his wife's belief in karma, suspecting something was disturbing her, despite her frequent denials.

After a time Parvatee's trusting spirit grasped at her husband's philosophy of hope – the power of the mind and of the will, of people giving a new direction to their lives – and was comforted; but today, her old fears returned. Something was in the air... that falling sky... the threatening rain... something had come, had entered the yard and she was greatly troubled, for what had silently shadowed her thoughts through the passing years was that other phrase – 'when still at a tender age'.

So it was that Parvatee's anxious spirit, sensing a catastrophe was fast approaching, kept guard.

Again, her eyes were drawn to the lone hibiscus jutting out of the hedge and its torments in the slashing wind.

CHAPTER TWO

THE WINGED SLIPPER

That night the skies burst: it rained and streamed all over the land – sharp, piercing, seething sprays. A flaming scalpel flashed across the skies, striking the heavens. On and on across the land a steady pounding fall, a cavalry of the sky, its horses' hooves lifting high, pelting the rain, drowning the voices of the land.

Meanwhile Sastra slept on under a white mosquito net, wigwamlike. And when this frenzied night passed on, the gentlest, softest sounds plopped from leafy funnels; the overflowing drains subsided.

With the early light she rode on the spine of red earth tracks to the swollen stream, sheltered by swaying yellow-green leaves, x-rayed by sunlight.

On an extended branch she hung her frock and left her slippers in the shallows. Warm and trembling, feeling near naked she entered the flowing stream. All night it had drunk and was now full, embracing her waist, then too rapidly her shoulders.

This greater depth and buoyancy thrilled her. She closed her eyes, pretending to be driftwood, but not knowing how to swim, only to float, and thinking she was alone, dared not, would not allow herself to drift into a depth that would cover her.

She opened her eyes after what seemed an eternity, so intense was her pleasure, and finding herself in the shallow, moved upstream to enjoy yet again, the flowing motion of a greater depth. The wind came and the branches bowed deep and low. It was then that her slipper of decorative wood was caught by the current and floated off into the darker, deeper, colder waters.

She tried to catch up with it, but was soon up to her neck, suddenly buoyant, then, losing her footing, pulled by an undertow, sucked into darker depths. Her difficulty grew and in fear she struggled.

Then something – a mighty splash, a fall from above. Over the stream – nothing – only the sky broken by interlocking branches, and the streaming light channelling a golden yellow to green leaves...

Fear returned, not knowing whether it was reptile or mammal. Using her hands as a strong paddle, battling on with difficulty she managed to turn against the current and reach the water's edge.

Safe and wrapped in a towel, Sastra Narayan kept close to a giant warm rock, while her eyes searched the stream for motion. Then a movement, a surging movement upwards – a form – Rabindranath Pande appeared dolphin-like from the water; the slipper in his hand, dark eyes glistening. Sastra was happy, relieved, excited and embarrassed; all at once.

Then, to think he had been amongst the branches, had observed her tidying her shoulder-length hair, the intimate lifting of her frock to reveal her costume beneath, these tumbling thoughts alarmed and disturbed her. Yet, here he was, behaving as if it was all so natural. Her defences rose up silently against him, for he had observed, uninvited, an unfastening of her inner self; she felt undressed, vulnerable. Confused and cheated. Disturbed.

He sat down beside her on the grass, on leaves and broken stems. A comforting hush hovered the valley.

'Do you come often?' he asked.
'Not often.'
'Would you like to learn to swim?'
'No!'
Emphatic, propelled by a hidden reserve of energy, the sound struck him. Why this instant intense feeling? The force behind the word puzzled him. Sastra, too, was surprised by the strength of her response. Here she was with the young student-teacher who, six years before, just after his father's death, had taught her in the college exhibition class. To be here with him, now, not modestly clothed – she felt alert, tense, electrified; the excitement of incoming waves, eager to bathe the land and to retreat – the embraces of departures – welcoming and withdrawing compressed —and how to deal with the intuitive fears… of many things. Again that feeling to protect herself intensified. Why? What a question! She pulled herself together.

'Thank you for my slipper. It's nice to have both… one is of no use.'

He felt her embarrassment, knew what her studied composure meant, but he did not wish to be protected from the enthralling excitement of the moment. Perhaps her alarm was part of his excitement. This girl, now fully grown, his former pupil; how different she had become. Her response – that of an old head – yet he observed a slight quiver, her skin warm, exuding a glow. He must approach gently, he had made it awkward for her; to capture her would require skill… would that be enough? Desire had wakened his imagination.

Sastra could not understand why she wished she was elsewhere. Such a tumult of emotions surged through

21

her: wanting this chance encounter to be held in time; wishing to be invisible yet observing. There was something inviting about his wholesome nakedness, in the sunlight, its fiery ruddy brown, the hair on his legs and on his fine chest. She dared not look at his waist, lest her eyes were to slip downwards. My god what is the matter with me! She sought sanity in words:

'You swim very well. But here… here is not the best place to learn.'

He was not listening, he was thinking what immense pleasure throwing restraint to the winds would bring. And his left foot of its own accord moved imperceptibly closer to hers, then touched.

Alarmed! Petrified that he should be so daring, and as if reading his thoughts, she got up at once:

'I have to go now,' she said. He too knew he must leave instantly, being with her any longer would destroy them both, so intense was this desire, and plunging himself into the stream, he swam swiftly, obliquely, to the opposite bank.

On reaching it, he did not turn around at once, dared not trust himself to look at her nakedness, well, as near naked he would ever see her, unless… He would ask Milly, how best to arrange something special – softly melting cakes, those crunchy, peaked, coconut drops or a flaky pineapple delight… something sumptuous from the oven; or perhaps later, a proper meal, a dinner. He would ask Milly. He would leave it to her. Then the schoolmaster in him reasserted itself as he turned, waved and shouted, 'Have you read Tolstoy's *Anna Karenin*?'

'Not yet.'

'It is essential reading,' he turned around, '…I'll bring it on Sunday …half past two.'

Out of the foliage into the smooth bright open space of the busy Churchill-Roosevelt highway, steadying her bike, Sastra Narayan thought of how much Rabindranath had changed. His first year as the College Exhibition class teacher was her last year, as well as Govind's and Francis' and Chandra's and Harilall's – what a class! They were all so keen and so was he. What had become of Francis? and Chandra? She had returned to teach standard two at the school of her childhood, the Tunapuna Presbyterian Primary. Thank heavens the College Exhibition class was upstairs and standard two was downstairs. A memory of that first day returned. It was after the first lesson; they were outside at play on the savanna. 'Sir is handsome, isn't he?' the confident Chandra Maharaj had said, fluttering her attractive eyes which she had already learnt to use, laughing and popping parched nuts into her mouth.

CHAPTER THREE

BIRDS WITHOUT FLIGHT

It had been in September 1950, three months after Surinder Pande's death, that his son, Rabindranath, then seventeen years old, inexperienced and untried, began preparing himself as if he were a newly ordained priest. It was not only the syllabus and the need for class discipline that occupied him; more than anything he wanted to know how best to introduce the very kernel of things to a group of ten and eleven year olds. What could he say that would excite them, rouse their spirits, lift them far beyond the village thinking? His thoughts came and went like the wash and backwash on a quiet shore.

His father had been everything a son could have wished, and it was his sudden death, a heart attack, for which Rabindranath had been so ill-prepared and which violently shattered his introspective student's world.

Like brothers, father and son had been: Surinder lifting his son shoulder high, making him tall as the village Hosay, when, once a year, the child would look forward to seeing the magic tazzia on wheels, broken off, he had thought, from a palace of richly sparkling, delicate things; of dancing shimmer and glitter. He had wondered once whether it was sprinkled with sweet coconut and crystal icing and had longed to taste it. He did not know then that the Hosay was both a celebration of the valour of the seventh century martyr, Husain, and a remembrance of his death, killed as he rested his gallant head upon the earth to pray, beheaded by Shimar.

And after the Hosay and its trail of dancers and drummers and stick fighters passed on: 'Come, Rabind, let's have a drink.' That was how his father spoke, as if they were brothers. He was five then, and when taken to the rum shop: 'Two drinks, Ram – one for me and one for this slightly taller man.' And so, carried high on his father's shoulders, he was brought into a man's world.

It took Rabindranath two months to muster the courage to pick up the enormous responsibilities left by his late father, which lay about his study in neatly tied parcels, and postpone his going abroad, to University College London to read Mathematics and Philosophy.

While he himself was working for his High School Certificate, his father had planned with care how it was possible for these agile village children (whose spoken language was a mixture of Hindi, Creole and a few African words that had withstood the passage of cruel times, and whose written English was, at its best, stiffly starched), to enter the highly competitive race of government scholarships, to give themselves at least a sweepstake chance, a wider choice, an opportunity to enlarge their lives. They would have to compete with urban children who had libraries at their disposal and parents at ease with English grammar and syntax. Yet his father had not been daunted.

There had been battles on the home front to be fought. At the staff meeting when he revealed his plans, his colleagues asked him to be realistic; arithmetic, they agreed, could be taught – the symbols and logic of mathematics were removed from culture and from personal experience; but English and English composition, indeed the basis of elegant language, were founded upon the social and economic environment. They were nourished by the quality of the home, its furnishings and its surroundings – 'Like eating with a knife and fork rather than with fingers', someone said. 'From whence will come the intimate tinkling of ice and crystal and red wine?' They laughed. 'At best chipped enamel cups, Mr. Pande.' They roared.

'The competition will be too much… Look at that village, Mr. Pande,' they mocked. 'Have you ever tried to walk on those narrow, slippery clay tracks in the rainy season? All your concentration and blood have to flow to your feet, man. The grey matter is starved.' Something as subtle, as sophisticated as expressing thoughts and feelings, needed an urbane, literary environment; one could not find these things in a village. Though they did not say this in front of him, Surinder Pande suspected that some of them felt the very quality, the texture of language used was nourished by roots deep within, the genetic code of races.

Rabindranath knew that his father had set out to prove that the process of education itself was magical; for his own father Gajraj Pande had revealed to him the excitement, the beauty and the music – the spark of every letter of the alphabet – and he had come to believe in the magical process of learning.

His grandfather's story was one of the family's treasures. It was about how Gajraj had begun to look at the alphabet and discovered what he thought was a great mystery. He had closed his eyes, concentrating on the movement his forefinger made as it wrote each letter on an imaginary wall. Suddenly he became excited; he had discovered something so simple and beautiful, the realisation of which he could hardly believe was the key to the entire alphabet: to all shapes, all forms… to the harmo-

26

nious design of everything. Delirious with passion, he rushed to his wife, Rajkumari: 'Look,' he said with pride, 'I am going to teach you to write; sit down, sit down here.' That evening they and their young son, his father Surinder, sat before a sheet of paper in the light of the oil-lamp. 'Curves and straight lines! See! Just curves and straight lines! That is the beauty, just two simple forms! Only two! Imagine, Surinder, you can write a billion words! More than a billion! How many stars are there?' Three year old Surinder did not know. No one answered. And Gajraj had gathered the straight lines from the alphabet and his son Surinder wrote them – L's and T's and L's and A's, X's and V's and Z's – straight lines, consistently moving with only one inclination, in one direction; two such straight lines brought to touch, to meet, to cross over.

The next day, Gajraj drew curves, circles and crescents; the young Surinder drew the same – S's, O's, and C's, and Q's and the common 'a'. On the third day, Gajraj became so excited, could not contain himself, rose early, prayed to the creator of all things and rejoiced. To him the alphabet was an elixir. His enthusiasm knew no bounds. His own father, Ganesh, had once said that the alphabet held the key to difficulties, to problems, even to madness and he had believed, felt it was so, without fully understanding. That morning when his son Surinder came to him, he was certain that what this unschooled child was about to do was so marvellous, so magnificent, that his spirit needed to rise to the task, and what better preparation than prayer. That prayer Gajraj had written down and his father later recorded it in *Tales of the Pandes*:

'Dear God, give my mind and my fingers strength and charm; enhance them both so that working to-

27

gether they will unite two forms that are so different, two forms that are saying such different things. One is straight and linear and unswerving; constant in direction, strong in its upright stance and regular. And the other, Dear God, you know is soft and silent, and swerving; so fluid, will yield, will move this way and that with the wind; will dance, will rise and fall; will leap and curl and twirl as waves do. Dear God, enable me to bring these two magnificent forms together so that I may create still more forms that are beautiful and varied, oh so varied, that there is no limit to man's endeavour.'

On that September morning in 1950, the mountain breeze was heavy with dew. The first rays of dawn, a splash of deep pink, rose from the east, spread throughout the sky, lifting the mountain mist, casting light and shadow on the Northern Range, changing green forested flanks into a sea blue.

Rabindranath felt the urge to visit where his father lay; he would ask his blessing: he, the new teacher of the College exhibition class, felt hopelessly inadequate. To stand at the elongated mound of earth crowned with a headstone was as close as he could be to that hopeful way of thinking, that generous spirit, as close as he could be to reassurance.

He recalled his father's worry: 'The rules are stacked against the village children, Rabind, but I must take it on board, son.'

His father had written to the Ministry of Education, pointing out that with one hundred and fifty marks allocated to English and with only one hundred to Arithmetic, the system had a built in prejudice against children from the village where standard English was almost a foreign language. He made a case for allocating the same marks to each subject: numeracy and literacy were equally important. The Ministry replied: It was time the Indian community came to terms with the obvious. English was now their tongue and facility in this language should be encouraged early. What better way was there than the added incentive the government was providing by these examinations, written and prepared in England by fine scholars. No word was mentioned about the substantial differential in the allocation of marks, no reason was given for this. His father wrote another letter; on this occasion, the Ministry's reply was less restrained: 'We regret having to say that you are unduly, perhaps unwittingly, stirring up trouble.' He was asked to come to the Ministry.

Surinder Pande kept his appointment, and left that government building with a number of things, not least red watery eyes and an attack of asthma, as the neatly dressed civil servant sitting opposite had smoked incessantly, aware only, it seemed, of the cadences of his own voice as he elegantly justified the crooked thinking of the colonial past.

It was evident that change would not come from that quarter, but Surinder Pande had not almost sacrificed his respiratory system wholly in vain; no longer would he be groping in the dark, for in his worn, leather bag were the most recent past examination papers which the headmasters of other primary schools, seeing him as a competitor, had kept close to their chests. With these mixed blessings he set to work, knowing that he was now better able to prepare the children for the difficult task of their trying to rise above the heavy, sticky, slippery clay of village tracks.

By the time Rabindranath faced the burial ground, the soft pink from the east had given way to the golden halo of mediaeval paintings striking the stones, the brown earth mounds and the grass-green graves, spreading an uplifting warmth and energy as if in a celestial rehearsal for the resurrection. On this ground, he walked alone. No living thing stirred. Burdened with misgivings, he approached the raised bed.

'Surinder Pande, Schoolmaster 1900 - 1950 Streatham Lodge'. There on the moist earth bed he sat and remembered the living past. His shadow pointed to nearby headstones: Gajraj Pande 1880 - 1934 and the almost indecipherable: Ganesh 'Baboo' Pande 1756 - 1821.

As he read these three engravings on stone, he became more aware than ever that he was the last surviving Pande. There were more Pandes beneath the earth than above it, and as he sat amongst them, he asked, who really was his father? How did he become a scholar? What measure of things made a man?

Downstairs, two little boys in the kindergarten class were crying out aloud their common wish to return home. A little girl with large dark eyes looked at them a while, then cried with them. The boys, strapped by large, almost empty leather satchels, on hearing her, on seeing her tears, gradually hushed their voices.

Upstairs, the classrooms were demarcated anew with freshly made white chalk lines and green movable screens. Bright new pink sheets of blotting paper, rulers; yellow, red and white chalk; ink pots; sweet-smelling green, blue, cream and salmon exercise books were distributed, checked and put away in strong cupboards that stood like hospital matrons – erect and closed.

Twenty-two pairs of fresh eyes faced him; the watchful school clock stared down from on high. With the back of his knees he pushed his chair clumsily, then rising, came closer to his pupils.

He wished there was but one word, one phrase, a sentence perhaps which would convey all that his father

30

had ever taught him – a lifetime of understanding into a sort of 'OPEN, SESAME, OPEN' – magic words which would help these pupils – something that would enable them to give of their best. He knew he had to take them the long hard road, yet silently wished there was another way.

'This is going to be a special year for you and for me.' He spoke calmly. 'Why?'

Govind Tiwari, tall and slim, full of confidence and boyish energy, put his hand up. 'It is our College Exhibition year, Sir.' The class sighed, some smiled nervously; in the front row, boys giggled, covering their shyness, muffling their sounds with small hands as they bent their heads.

'Now sit up, everyone. Today you are like birds without the power of flight, birds without the knowledge of flight. On the appointed day, ten months from now, when each one of you walks to your allocated examination place; by that day, after much concentrated hard work, after constant questioning and thinking through, you will have grown, spun from within you, a fine expanse of wings, light and beautiful, but strong; wings to withstand gales and storms, wings to withstand lightning. With such wings you could come closer to the moon and stars and the bluest blue of the skies.'

The class began to smile for he was smiling; he lifted his forefinger, then his eyes, like colour moving from light to darkness, were altering; they were the sad eyes of Gonella, jester at the Ferrarese Court. 'Yes, who knows, you might, just might,' he paused, 'with keen eyes, and by being ever so watchful, escape the Hunters, the Trappers, the Collectors and Persuaders of men.'

The class became strangely silent. Still. Not understanding, but sensing he was offering them something important. A gust of wind rattled the windows, the sun

31

bobbed up from a stream of sailing cirrus clouds, beaming through the open doors. The clock blinked and continued to stare. He felt inadequate, dissatisfied. He moved to the centre of the class, and looking around him again said:

'Later when you leave here,' his voice softened, 'by continuing to observe and question all things, by being scholarly in your method and desire to have a better understanding of life, boys and girls, this earth upon which we now stand will grow and expand to become a grander place with room for all to dance and sing.'

Seconds went by.

'We will be working together. The harder you work, the harder I must work. Remember, don't give me second best; it opens no doors,' he paused. 'It is like a key that will enter but not turn. Second best will not work.'

At the end of the lesson, he watched as the class rose and filed out neatly, but on reaching the outer stairs, stampeded down to the open savanna, scattering, as seeds do that burst their pods, flying with the wind. The girls kept together like bunches of wild flowers and the boys raced each other, trying to prove something invisible to all but themselves.

It was towards the end of the first day; again Rabindranath paced round his class, he had begun to look like a pedagogue in the ancient world; his trunk and head carried upright, his excited spirit moving ahead of him.

'Tell me, to achieve what we are setting out to do, how should we prepare ourselves?' Chalk in hand, before the blackboard, he waited. Govind Tiwari, sitting upright in the back row, bobbing up and down, was again the first to put his hand up. 'We should be careful and not get ill, Sir; with high fever you can't work, you miss school, you have to catch up, you are left behind, Sir.' On the black board, the words 'good health' were written. Another hand went up. 'Good pens, Sir.'

Francis Braithwaite, his bright eyes glistening from his strong, dark, alert face, said, 'We may need to lay off a few cricket matches, Sir. The best ones are on Saturdays and Sundays, Sir.'

The class was silent. Each looked at the teacher for some clue.

'There are two words which will bring together all that you have said. Just two words both beginning with D.'

'DDD DDD,' said Harilall, who was small and serious, 'DDD, DDD,' he repeated, hoping this beating of the letter in the air, like a carpet, would bring out something hidden. 'Doubt, Sir?' his hand was up, 'We shouldn't have doubt about our work. My uncle, Dr. Lall, says doubt weakens a man's aims.'

Someone in the back stood up. 'Draught, Sir. We should protect ourselves against draughts.' The boy winked at Francis. 'Old Mrs. Greenidge, Francis' grandma, told me once, Sir, that a single draught can knock you cold, Sir, just like the Devil. She knows people who did not listen to her and if you looking for these people today, she says you have to look in the burial ground, Sir.' Govind and Francis glanced at each other and began to chuckle, trying to contain themselves with hands over their mouths; it was no use, their stifled laughter overflowed and the class, like a chorus, joined their wayward, playful sounds.

Rabindranath waited for this merriment to subside, and when it did, Sastra said:

'Dedication, Sir, we have to dedicate ourselves to our work, like our mothers.'

'Discipline, Sir,' said Francis. 'My aunt Milly says, without discipline, we would all be like beasts. You only have to look around, Aunt Milly says, and the proof is left, right and centre.'

The bell rang.

On the black board two more words were added – Discipline and Dedication.

It had been a long hard day. As Rabindranath was getting ready to leave, Mr. Ramsaran came over:

'I see you are putting in the ground work, man; that's good. Now just one thing, I had this class last year, and I can tell you that the present seating arrangement will lead to trouble.'

'I don't understand.'

'Harilall and Govind, you can't have them sitting together, they will talk and will disturb the class. They make a good team, but not in class. Then there is the sticky one – Francis and Sastra. You can't have that. She is as orthodox as her mother, but Francis is a well-meaning sensitive boy, and it is clear that he likes Sastra. We have to help him save himself.'

'You know, he sometimes stays with his aunt Milly, who, since my father's death, is not only my house-keeper, but my keeper.'

'That may be so. But if you act now, it would be better for all concerned. One thing at a time. You will need all your energy and concentration to show that your father's foundation will produce scholarships. Don't make things more difficult for yourself.'

'I will discuss it with Milly.'

'Some things should be kept even from one's keeper.'

It was the seriousness of his demeanour and tone, and the knowledge that Ramsaran was an experienced teacher that made Rabindranath listen carefully.

'From time to time, I will need some help.'

'You will find the staff had the highest regard for your father, and if you call upon them, they will be only too willing to do whatever they can. You know you can call on me.'

'I feel better already.'

As he walked home on the broad red earth road, Rabindranath knew something essential was missing. He sensed it, felt its absence amongst his pupils as he moved about them, but was unable to say what it was.

That evening as he sat at his desk, he observed his grandfather Gajraj and his great grandfather Ganesh, who carried himself well, a serious contemplative man. Both men appeared to look more closely than ever at him, through their framed enclosures.

Gajraj was smiling; he seemed excited about something... something very special, but what? What could be the source of his joy?

He strolled about the room but, fatigued, sat down in his chair and soon fell asleep.

When he awoke, he knew the source of the joy was not outside the photograph; it was within his grandfather, his way of looking at the world. He knew instantly what was missing from his class.

The missing ingredient had many names, took many forms, but he saw it as lying in the sheer delight of the pupil in what he was doing, an excitement stemming from a passionate desire to understand the nature of things. It was this way of looking he wished to bestow, and knew it would not be easily captured.

BOOK TWO

CHAPTER FOUR

DHARMA THROUGH THE WINDOW

Though a widow for many years, Shakuntala Tiwari still did not like wearing jewellery, though hers were beautifully crafted pieces, ancient in design as thought itself, and when she wore them, even today, as a courtesy paid to her hosts at the wedding of their daughter Devi, perceived the act as one of display. She knew it gave her mother-in-law, old Madam Tiwari, pleasure to see the family's jewellery admired; but for herself, her main concern was with Dharma, the rules of living, the path of righteousness.

Were you to ask a pundit what Dharma is, he might take some time before answering, such is the nature of Dharma, and when he does, he might simply say: Dharma is Truth or the divine values of life. And though some may be unsure what the divine values are, the upright passenger in the back seat – Shakuntala Tiwari – had no such misgivings. Her religious values and her cultural values were one. Her culture was her way of life, it was all encompassing. Dharma was to her the path of righteousness, the way of life handed down, by teaching and example, from her parents and grandparents, to her and her son, Govind Tiwari.

The car stopped before Narayan's house, the only upstairs house in the street, its galvanised roof freshly painted green, a deep purple bougainvillea standing sentry above the brick wall, a douce-douce mango tree towering over all. On the back porch, Parvatee Narayan, sheltered from the setting sun by the shade of two zabocca trees, was taking a nap, cradled in a comfortable jute hammock. At the sound of a car horn and now the voice and the footsteps on the terrazzo tile, she rose briskly, tidied her hair, draped her ornhi around and hurried to the front porch.

Both ladies burst into smiles.

'How good of you to drop by. You went to the wedding?'

'You were resting, na?'

'Let me get you something cold. What will you have? How was it?'

'Thanks, but nothing for me. It was a good Hindu wedding, Parvatee, when you stop to consider what is involved, and Dyal is not a rich man. I heard some guests saying that the music and the classical dance last night was out of this world. But I can tell you myself, today, the women sang well. Pundit's mother has a strong voice, she led the village women. The pundit too, he made no short cuts and the wedding was really what it should be, Parvatee.'

'How is Govind's Ajee?'

'She is an old lady now; we tend to forget that, hardly going anywhere these days; yet, stronger than you would think from just watching; her voice is still good but the body is getting soft.'

'But you, Shakuntala, you are as straight and fit as those new electric poles I see in Port of Spain.'

'My hair is greying fast, but except for that I am feeling very good.'

'The old lady must be about seventy-five - eighty now, na?'

'No one knows for certain and that's the truth; yet every morning in the dark, before the sun is up, when some far away cock is crowing, she is under the shower; she will do puja and wait in the garden for the dawn.'

'That is good.'

'Yes, every morning Mai welcomes the rising sun, she makes it her business to greet it – every morning – that's her way. Sometimes I think the sun comes just to see if Mai is there.'

'She is accustomed to that. The old people from India believed it is bad luck if you still in bed when the sun is up.'

'I don't know about bad luck; it makes the working day too long.'

'Well at my mother-in-law's house, you couldn't be in bed after half-past five.'

'The cows, na?'

'Not only the cows mooing, Shakuntala; all my sisters-in-law too.'

Both ladies laughed heartily, happy they were now their own mistresses, independent of in-laws.

'Tell me about the dulahin na – how Devi looked?'

'They got somebody just come back from India with new ideas. The palms of Devi's hands were designed like a flower, a delicate thing; and her feet, what we could see – fine, fine patterns. The sari dropped well, real good quality, in crimson and gold, very nice. And Parvatee, her face! Well! That was something else, she looked as if she fell from the sky; you would not believe that was the same Devi you and I know.'

'True?'

'Ask anybody.'

'Who made her up?'

'We could always find out.'

She paused:

'There was one thing though.' Shakuntala pulled her ornhi closer around her for comfort. Parvatee sensed that something important was about to be disclosed.

'They had wedding cake,' she whispered.

'Was it good?'

Parvatee had misinterpreted the tone, the softer sound, the lower key, had overlooked the wider spheres embraced by Shakuntala's orthodoxy, and in an effort to mitigate her error of judgment said:

'The cherry brandy was smelling, na?'

'A good-looking girl came round, a neighbour's daughter 1 think it was, with a tray. "Tantie, try the wedding cake," she said. Is this an orthodox Hindu wedding? This passed through my mind, I was very upset, Parvatee, but didn't want to cause any dissension, so I said, "Beti after all that good good wedding food? A little, later".'

'It is becoming fashionable to serve wedding cake, Shakuntala.'

'Parvatee, today – eggs; tomorrow what? Wine? Fried chicken? Who started all this at Hindu weddings? That's what I want to know!'

'What must have happened, Shakuntala, is, you invite a few Christians to a Hindu wedding and they come expecting wine and cake,' she lowered her voice and her eyes widened, 'I hear they have wine in their church too, would you believe it?'

'Why should they come expecting their culture at our weddings? You make a concession to Christians and before you know it, they calling the tune. They are a very forward people, Parvatee. If you went to a Christian wedding, would you expect sohari or saheena, dhalpuri?'

42

'I don't expect anything when I go to a wedding,' Parvatee said.

'I mean a Christian wedding.'

'I have never been to a Christian wedding.'

'Me neither,' said Shakuntala Tiwari. 'But I have seen photographs, though. The bride has a bouquet of flowers in one hand; now the other hand is where? You tell me? With the bridegroom, Parvatee, holding on to him, quite close too, and in public! You wouldn't believe she is a properly married woman.'

'It is their way.'

'All that in public? I ask you, is that called for?'

'They sometimes kiss in public too.'

'Enough, Parvatee! Such things in public! I would die!'

'They don't mind. It is their way.'

'I was saying to Pundit Misir the other day, he will have to put his foot down; soon, I suspect, some bright fool will suggest we have goat in garam massala at a Hindu wedding!'

'Na! Na! Na! How can you have meat at a Hindu wedding, Shakuntala? Flesh? Bringing flesh? Never!'

'Bit by bit. Bit by bit, Parvatee. Who knows? Next it will be English dancing, and then all dharma will fly through the window. Gone! And what will be left? – A shell? – Ceremonies without meaning, without value, without dharma?'

'I hope that day never comes but if it is to be, I hope I wouldn't live to see it. I hope Shri Bhagwan will take me before.'

'We have to protect our ways, all that is worthwhile, all that is good in this life, be on our guard.'

Shakuntala paused, adjusted herself again and said in a warmer, friendlier tone:

'You know Govind will be leaving next year to study medicine.'

43

'I am so glad for you, Shakuntala, you must be very proud. Govind is such a quiet, good boy and so bright, well mannered.'

'You know I've always had my eyes on Sastra.'

'You told me so many times.'

'She is just right for him. No other girl will do. Beautiful, educated, what ways, she really has nice ways. I remember the time that stray puppy was hit by the car and broke its leg; there was nothing anybody could do; besides, a stray pup? To care so much for a stray? You don't know where it comes from, what disease it is carrying. You can't expose yourself like that for a stray.'

'Yes she cared for it too long; it couldn't stand up so she fed it milk and bread with a spoon… We couldn't tell her but Narayan did it when she was at school. She was so upset, she wanted to know how it died, whether we had given it a drink at midday. With tears streaming, she said she would have liked to bury it herself.'

'You think she suspected?'

'She was only six then, she trusted us completely.'

'She was too young; understanding only life and death, not the in between – and most of life is that, na?'

'I was thinking that Govind and Sastra should become officially engaged before he leaves.'

'You mean a proper Hindu engagement, na? Engaging the boy, na?'

Shakuntala laughed.

'Engagement is engagement, Parvatee; both sides should feel engaged. But I know what you mean. Of course I would have a proper Hindu engagement. I like doing things well or not at all, you know that.'

'What does Govind think.'

'Oh he likes her a lot. They have a lot in common. I overheard them chatting many times about films and music.' She smiled.

'They get along well together, I have my own ways of finding out these things, Parvatee. I should get him married or engaged before he leaves for London… To tell the truth, whenever I think of that place, my body trembles inside, something like an ague hits me and I feel really cold, as if I'm dead already. This is not a good sign, Parvatee. Something… something, about his going over there frightens me. Sometimes I think I will lose him.'

'Na man, you just feeling low; how will you lose him?'

'This is why I want him married to Sastra before he goes. I know, I know what you are going to say: Sastra will think it is too early for marriage; well, then, at least an engagement, Parvatee. That way I will know for sure he is safe… my mind at peace… I would rest well when he leaves.'

'It would be like marrying in the family, Shakuntala. You know nothing will give me more pleasure than to see both my daughters so well married. "There is Govind, a good-looking, educated, brahmin boy, from a nice, respectable family." I said this to her the other day, just getting the feel of things, you understand, after what we have been saying for so long. "Ma, you matchmaking. I am not going to marry before I get my degree". That's what she said.'

'Oh, they all say that. It is a phase they pass through and come out of, thank God. Govind will say the same, but you pay no attention. What else can they say? …Anyway, I will be having a little puja for him; you must send Sastra. I'm inviting a few people. Did you hear Rabindranath is giving up teaching? He is going to England to study.'

'I am very glad for him; at last he is thinking about himself.'

'He has done wonders for our community. All those government scholarships – six – seven – every year.'

'He should have gone abroad to study long ago. What a commitment to the village, eh, and he so young. But his father, when all's said and done, was a good man. Like father, like son.'

There was nothing more to be said. Shakuntala stood up:

'You know I was just thinking, if we can get the same person to make up Sastra on her wedding day, she would look like Rama's Sita.'

'You are full of compliments, Shakuntala; wedding food agrees with you.'

CHAPTER FIVE

A GOOD FAMILY

That evening after Narayana had eaten his evening meal, Parvatee told him of Shakuntala Tiwari's visit.

'They are a good family. I am happy that such a marriage should take place; you will need to speak to Sastra. Let her know. It is important for her to know our feelings, but bring it up in a casual way; we must not appear to be pressuring her. She is still young and there is a lot of time. She knows Govind. If he was not well disposed to her, Shakuntala would not have made this important step.'

'What does he intend to study?'

'Medicine.'

'You know, I always felt Sastra should do the same. She likes caring for people...'

'She wants to teach; you know that.'

'There is nothing wrong with teaching, but with medicine you have independence, you could work for yourself.'

'With teaching, she would have the holidays; it would be good when she has a family.'

That night Parvatee related to Sastra the conversations she had with her father and Shakuntala, and ended by saying:

'So that is the situation.'

'Why me, Ma?'

'You know Govind's ma has always had her eyes on you, so it is to be expected.'

'Govind knows?'

'She wouldn't have come here without first talking it over with him. She says you two have a lot in common.'

'We like many of the same things, but I'm not thinking of marriage, Ma. I want to go abroad to study: I've told you so already.'

'She had a sort of Hindu engagement in mind – engaging Govind before he leaves.'

'I am surprised he wants to tie himself down. I thought boys liked freedom, especially when they're away from home... What do you and Pa really think?'

'From a personal point of view and a family point of view, you couldn't do better. They are a highly respected brahmin family, and you know Govind... a nice boy... if he strives to be a specially good doctor, he would need an understanding wife, just as Sati is to Capil. You would be serving your husband and the community... you would live in comfort and your name would rise high in the district.'

'Do you have to give an answer?'

'Not straight away. But if I don't say anything, it would mean that I am in agreement.'

'Let me think about it.'

'Your father and I will be very pleased with such a marriage, but we wouldn't want you to be unhappy. We want you to be just as happy and prosperous as Sati.'

Later that night as she lay in bed, Sastra could hardly believe that a number of people had already discussed her marriage; she turned over, and agreed with her mother – Govind was a nice boy, had always been, from primary school days, but there was Rabindranath, looking and behaving so differently.

CHAPTER SIX

RABINDRANATH AND SASTRA

By 2.30 p.m. on a Sunday, nothing moves except an occasional breeze which lifts the branches, sways the hammock and gently rattles the open windows. The tropical afternoon haze and heat rule over the sleeping land. Men, women and children sleep and doze under shady trees, in hammocks, on homemade cots, or indoors. They have already had their special Sunday lunch and have eaten and in some instances drunk as if these were the only pleasures they knew. At this time of day nothing stirs. All is still.

Into this silence, the creaking sound of Narayan's iron gate, not noticed in the din of the working day, grated and disturbed. Sastra hurried to the gate, delighted yet uneasy to see he had remembered; that something said in passing, which could so easily have been of no account, had materialised punctually. She had yet to acquire the sophistication to veil her feelings so Rabindranath was encouraged by the warmth of her greeting.

She held the gate lifting it slightly – 'Shhhhhh!' she whispered, 'Ma and Pa sleeping.'

'I am not expected?'

'Shhhhhh!' she motioned, 'Come. Of course. Ma is a light sleeper, if she wakes up before 4.30 p.m. she is fretful.'

'Well,' he whispered, 'come over to my house; there is no one sleeping there.'

'Oh I couldn't do that!' She frowned, awakened by his audacity, and became a little reserved. 'Will you have something cold?'

'I had a late lunch… was at the river.' He had hoped to see her there and was about to say this, but checked himself, thinking that some things were best left to lie.

'I was happy about my slipper,' she began to be the hostess again. 'One is of no use, you need both.'

Her eyes had the alertness of a wild squirrel about to dart off in another direction. Her beauty, the quiet untutored gestures of her hands and head, responding naturally, simply, unselfconsciously, aroused him and he wished he could carry her off to his home. Perhaps he'd read too much Hindu and Greek mythology in his childhood. Maybe it was the heat, the dazzling haze…

'On that day at the river, I felt you were in difficulty…'

'Yes anything could have happened. I was frightened. I was being pulled into that deep, circular basin. It was close.'

He smiled inwardly, but he was not going to suggest anything about teaching her to swim, he knew where that got him.

Your face, she thought, …kind…courageous…the strain. Too many years carrying the Government Exhibition class.

'Your face,' she said, 'it has…'

'Grown old?'

'Less boyish.'

'I feel less boyish.'

'You were almost as green as we were that year.' She laughed as children do at play.

50

'I felt it too. I was terrified.'

'It's the responsibility,' she added, 'the sheer weight of it. To feel you're responsible for someone taking one path instead of another.'

So much empathy. He had not expected this.

'If it weren't for your persuasiveness, many a father would have removed his daughter from school. Are you more relaxed, more at ease with the class now?'

'I don't know. I don't feel any less responsible – that remains, but I am more realistic, more aware of the difficulties of my pupils; I hope the things I now say in class are attainable to all. I hope I am more down-to-earth, more practical.'

'I hope not too much so.'

'Why?'

'It's nice to believe all the things you said to us in your first year.'

She has grown so beautiful, so womanly. Was she always like this? Her eyes sparkle and dance; her hair kisses her shoulders, and like me wishes to caress her eyes and cheeks, but she is pushing it back behind her ear as if she would be severe with it.

He said, 'I brought you *Anna Karenin*.'

'Such a large book.'

'It was meant for reading in the long cold dark Russian winters… I'm glad you have joined us.'

'I'm glad to be back. Your father would have liked to see us all now, his first crop of scholarship pupils leaving secondary school, all going our separate ways. I wonder what will become of Francis and Chandra and Harillal?'

'And Govind?'

'He is close by, we won't lose touch… I often wondered whether your father feared his work would come to nothing when he realised he was dying?'

51

'He died of a heart attack; it was sudden, swift. Life then death, instantly. All his painstaking planning, preparation, thought; the source of it all – gone. I don't know what he knew. Perhaps there's an engaging consciousness just before death? Who knows?'

They said nothing more for quite a while.

'But what will you do now?'

'Has the rumour reached you too?'

'I heard this is your last year.'

'I have changed my mind so many times as to what I should do, that the only thing I am certain about now, is that I will do something.'

She left the room and brought two tall glasses of water with crushed ice.

'If I read Philosophy and Mathematics, I might not come back, while if I did Law, I would certainly return.' He drank and said, 'How long do you intend to stay on?'

'A year.'

'Oh so we leave together. What have you applied for? Don't let your parents marry you off, for if you do, that will be the end of your career.'

'My career gets top priority.'

As she sat before him, he felt that Govind already had too many of the good things of life.

'You will have to be determined,' he said. 'Parents have a way of committing you emotionally in ways that are hard to resist.'

'Is that why you stayed back to see your father's work bear fruit?'

That was not what he had meant. Was she deliberately evading his comment? Taken aback he began answering her question.

'It became an emotional commitment but it didn't start that way. It was, I think, something strengthened by reading my father's notebooks, his collection of family stories, voices from his past: his grandfather, Ganesh; his father, Gajraj; and himself. He called them *Tales of the Pandes*.'

'Family secrets?... Can you reveal anything?'

'Both,' he smiled.

'Well tell me one of those things.'

'There is one called "The Ladder".'

'A Jack and the Beanstalk idea?'

'You'll have to read it... It is Gajraj's, my grandfather's tale of how he came to discover the exaltation, the excitement to be found in the art of simple things.'

'Everyday things?... Excited by them?'

'Yes and motivated too. Another chapter is called, "Sunset in 1888". This is the family record and it's an amazing one – of how one of the finest pieces of jewellery crafted, and worn ever since by all of the Pande brides on their wedding night, fell into my great grandfather Ganesh's hands, when he was a humble gardener in India.'

'Have you seen it?'

'I saw it once when I was a boy; it's kept in a bank in Port of Spain, but there's nothing to beat Ganesh's description of finding it, when he picked up its small casket and unfastened the two gold clasps... But to answer your first question, I saw my commitment as being part of a sort of relay, run by the Pandes. I had to reach out for the baton and run my stretch.'

'Would you prefer something else?' He had only drunk a little.

'No this is all right.' He picked up the glass and drank to please her.

'You felt it was your duty,' she said, 'yet on the path of duty one must often walk alone, without either family or friends.'

'That's only when all around you is crumbling.'

'So you recommend *Anna Karenin*? Did you enjoy it?'

She lifted her glass and drank too, lowering her eyes, not knowing where to focus, where to find shelter.

'The essence of the story is if two gentlemen present themselves to you, choose the older, more serious, sombre, and genuine; and leave the dashing, the young, the handsome. Beware of uniforms, the selfish, the undisciplined!' He could have said, for it was the logic of the story: do not follow your heart, follow your head, let reason dictate, but he didn't.

'If both men were presented to me, I would choose neither.'

'Whom would you choose instead?'

She began slowly, 'I would have the serious, the genuine, the handsome and the young.'

'Do you have someone in mind?'

'I am not in love with anyone now, if that's what you mean.'

'Why do you say now?'

'I have learnt an important thing about the nature of love; it is often harboured by the foolish for the blind. I and several others were very much in love with one of our teachers. He was unaware of this, though we told him so everyday, in everything we did.'

He was embarrassed and confused. 'You are being harsh, judging all situations from a single instance.' Who was that lucky blind man? How long ago was all this?

'As you suggested, I shall be ruled by my head and choose a career. I have no intention of falling in love; it will merely get in the way. If you want to get anywhere in life, you have to have discipline and dedication – nothing has changed; it is still true all that you said on that first day.'

He picked up his glass again, wondering about what she had said earlier, whether it was his father, Mr. Ramnarine, or the male maths teacher she had at secondary school. For a moment, a passing spark of a most entrancing thought touched him, but her composed demeanour made him think again.

'That's the spirit,' he said, striking the table for emphasis at her bravado.

Sastra, fearing that he was about to repeat the act, that he would wake her mother, moved Tolstoy's *Karenin* quickly in position to catch his falling hand and, as it came down, it fell partly on her fingers and there rested. This created a strange, new sensation; she was not at all at ease; the feeling seemed to have a power, a life of its own, something not within her control, and this alarmed her. It was affecting the movements of her thoughts, like a fine mesh constraining a butterfly. He lifted her right hand and again that uncomfortable, restless feeling stirred beneath her breast, and she withdrew her hand gently. He, not wishing to disturb her, released it as if it were a captured nestling.

'I have invited Ramsarran and Mrs. Gopaul to dinner next Monday week; it would be nice if you could come along too. I will ask Milly to let your mother know it is a Staff Dinner; they are old hands and you are likely to learn something from them. You are all in for a pleasant surprise though. Did you know that Milly was taught to cook Indian dishes by one of the best of all our cooks, Draupadi?'

'I've heard Ma speak of her. I think she's related to Old Madam Tiwari. Ma met her a couple of times in Chaguanas at *Kathas* and *Ramayanas*. She said that most men were in awe of her.'

'She must have been generous to women, though. Milly will vouch for that.'

'And a strong character when you think that the cooks at *Kathas* and weddings are nearly always men – and besides that, Ma said she came from one of the higher *jatis* of brahmins. You don't usually find such people cooking outside of their families.'

'From what my father told me, she cooked like a true brahmin. For her it was a sacred craft. Milly still has her "Commandments" written on the calendar she keeps in the kitchen. They are Draupadi's do's and don'ts. Each January I have to copy them out for Milly from the back of one calendar to another, so even I can recite you a few: "Control is vital and is exercised in the measured amounts of each chosen ingredient; and in knowing when to add as well as when to remove. Timing itself is control. The harnessing of the two great passions – heat and moisture – are necessary. Heat, because it can either create new worlds or reduce all things to cinders. Keep guard over your moisture. In the case of spinach, do not allow it to enter secretly, unbidden, camouflaged, hanging on to leaves; dry your leaves. Be alert that other properties do not enter uninvited, lest unaware of their presence you are caught off guard, unprepared for the havoc they cause".'

'Are there others?'

'Another that Milly likes is: "Treat every vegetable with courtesy, retain its colour, texture and unique taste. Why should a marrow taste like a pumpkin?" The only other I can at present remember goes something like this – "Know when to put the lid on, to enable breaking down of toughness, and when to uncover, to allow powerful forces to leave, lest everything becomes mush".'

They chatted on in the still heat of what he had overheard and what his father had told him and what he had read in *Tales of the Pandes*. Much later the gate creaked and again she whispered, 'Shhhhhh!'

When her father descended the stairs, he said:
'Who was that?'
'Rabindranath Pande.'
'Why did he come?'
'Ma knows. We were expecting him, but she forgot. It was just a friendly call; we were talking over things about school.'

As Sastra climbed the stairs to her bedroom, she felt for the first time uncomfortable at her father's questioning. It was the tone of his voice. Why should he be frowning so? His displeasure marred the afternoon, transforming this meeting into something prohibited.

Upstairs in the sanctuary of her room, she wondered how someone like Draupadi, from the heart of Hindu Chaguanas, a vegetarian by principle, a devout Hindu by disposition, could have made that Hanuman leap across cultural chasms to reach out to a complete stranger. For this was what had been required of Draupadi when she was told by Surinder Pande, only on her arrival, that it was his housekeeper, a young, creole, unmarried woman – making up his bed, cooking for him – whom he wished her to teach.

Draupadi would only have met black people on the streets and in the market place and passed shops where the hot piercing vapours of brine from the open barrels of meat they purchased – pigs' feet and pigs' tails in brine – would have brought her much discomfort. She would have observed, too, black pudding and souse sold on the roadside and concluded that she had little in common with their ways. She would never have been in one of their homes; but neither have I, Sastra thought, though I have been in Mrs. Greenidge's yard where the smell of pigs and ducks and hen coops and three goats is too strong – to call out to her to come to our home, when Ma's back is in a bad way.

Wealthy Indians employed Negroes, but not as cooks. To vegetarians like Draupadi and old Madam Tiwari, chicken, goat and lamb were the carcasses of once living things; to have meat was to have death on one's plate, a savagery they would not touch. To kill, cook and eat the sacred cow, as well as an animal that wallowed in mud and made grunting sounds was sacrilegious and obscene, especially when freshly picked green, leafy spinach, bygan choka, dhal and paratha were so delicious and nutritious. So, to have the hand that put those meats in its mouth touching one's pillow, one's cup, was deeply repugnant to these brahmin ladies, and this Sastra understood. Milly's employment as cook was seen, therefore, as a sign that Surinder Pande had been on his own too long, and that this was what happened to a man cut off from his roots, his culture – like a cow grazing on the open savanna, alone, exposed, he was certain to be brought low, seduced.

Sastra, however, received much pleasure in thinking that soon she was going to have the pleasure of tasting a meal prepared, if not by Draupadi herself, at least by her student. She had seen Surinder Pande's employment of Milly as his housekeeper as something that had been done for the first time. There had to be first times and the headmaster had tended to be a first timer in several things. She asked herself, 'Could I be a first timer?' But try as she might, she could not see herself defying her parents or her village. I am my father's daughter and my mother's daughter and a daughter of this warm village.

CHAPTER SEVEN

THE VILLAGE WOMEN

A camaraderie, a warmth of feeling, greetings and end-less chatter filled the Narayans' house. It was the cooking night and the village women were with Parvatee preparing the katha food for the following morning, just as they had promised.

In and out they moved from the kitchen through the spacious dining room to the large open gallery, taking whatever kitchen utensils they needed. Some brought their own favourite knives without which they said they couldn't do anything; others had sent ahead of themselves large pots, basins, rolling pins and wooden trays.

These diligent women, all fully aproned, were preparing for over two hundred guests. How many over two hundred, they weren't quite sure but they knew from experience that on the day, come feeding time, it would be all right. The invitations were given by word of mouth by old Sadhu – everybody's friend and helper. He had hailed the busy women from the roadside and offered grains of coloured rice, for the telling of the day and the time of the katha. Each had opened her palm and nodded her head on receiving the invitation. There was no RSVP; these village women gathered for the cooking, had a sense, a feel of things. They had had their antennae raised high all week and had a good idea of the numbers to expect.

From an outstretched pole an old lantern hung, swaying, forming live shadows in the open gallery where the women grouped themselves in small clusters, heads and shoulders gathered like closed petals, except for those in the wider open circle with its spreading centre-cloth, lily white now, but once a flour bag stamped CANADA.

In this larger circle the women's fingers moved nimbly on, taking pieces of fresh dough, smooth and elastic, filling them with dhal – ground dhal with onions and garlic, dhal with turmeric and jeera – until, burnished bright and orange-yellow, it floods the house with its essence, overflows into the yard, evoking a near spiritual warmth, entrancing the imagination, lifting it higher than soaring kites.

So closely bound together these women were, and Sastra was with them, for how else are womanly attitudes, ways, notions and skills passed on? Parvatee was only too well aware of this; her daughter would not be found wanting when called upon to perform these womanly duties: duties of honourable wife, dedicated mother and trustworthy friend.

But it is their fingers which attract: stretching, opening, filling, closing. The mystery is locked within the dough. But unlike bees buzzing into the sweet floral vortex of nectar, these fingers are not programmed by a common genetic code, but by the powerful order of tradition. But like the bees in never stopping to ask wherefore or why, the women's fingers moved nimbly on.

The clock faced the darkness. Ten o'clock.

In the yard, the bright intensity of the large chulha, now a furnace, warms Mustapha the cook and makes his skin glow. His shadow on the wall behind is larger than life and comes and goes like a puppet on a stage.

The heat, the light and red earth colour escape the chulha's fiery mouth, lighting a trail through the surrounding darkness to the open gallery.

From where Mustapha stands the women look like bronze carvings, but they have much to say, and though Mustapha hears some and loses some, the women's voices travel with the wind. Something has happened which disturbs them greatly but they have not yet begun to talk.

The voices of the night come from the canals and the drains and the bush and the open space. Some hear a lament, others a call, a cry. The women listen until:

'Eh! eh! is you? I didn't know it was you sitting there, the door was hiding your face.'

'I heard you, but my thoughts keep going back to that girl Dolly. Good God man, her father didn't have to treat her like that.'

'You expect that from some fathers, but not a mother, a mother has a different kind of heart.'

'You see the father can't keep his head straight any more; how to walk the road now, that is something he doesn't know how to do. But with a woman... it is different. We can take it. We make that way. We can bear up against the shame, the finger pointing, the gossiping. But with a man it's different.'

'When a thing like that hit them, they don't know where to turn.'

'Everybody blames the mother when these things happen.'

'I don't see why?'

'And she not home? She must know what's going on.'

'So the young people don't have a head? They don't know right from wrong?'

'They don't use it, that is plain to see.'

'Her mother did her best, what more could she do?

You know she couldn't let the father catch her taking food to Dolly.'

'And Dolly was his own own child and still, eh.'

No one said anything more; it was as if what was said needed time to settle, to make place for other thoughts not yet dressed for play.

And so Mustapha heard the last gasp, the last stir of the burnt wood from the forest, a part of the forest becoming less than charcoal, breaking off and falling to ash. He added another piece.

'Well you can't enjoy yourself and not pay.'

'You have to pay for your pleasure.'

'That is true. You have to pay. If not today, someday, someday, God will call you to account.'

'To tell the truth, I don't know how it happened.'

'Well it happened, na. That's life. What you go do?'

'Dolly was such a happy, bright, innocent child, before all this.'

'She was too stupid.'

'She didn't have the sense. She was only a child sheself, we forgetting that.'

'It is not easy when they start chatting you up.'

'When it's over, they treat you like saphee.'

'Everybody knows that and still.'

'Is one thing to know; is another thing to experience the abandonment.'

'And she so young so trusting, na?'

Turning to Sastra one of the women said, 'Dood, you knew Dolly, na?'

Sastra nodded, thinking of this sensitive young girl, who hardly ever spoke. Her consciousness surfaced to hear the women's voices:

'But she did not win an exhibition.'

'If… if only she had. Who knows?'

'Who can tell what might have happened with a new

school, a new place, good teachers eh?'

'Only God knows those things.'

'Yet, if you really come to think. Who can win any-thing, pass anything, in such a house, with such a man as a father, eh? Tell me, that man is a father? That kind of man can ever be a father to anybody?'

'She was born to lose.'

Only a week ago Sastra and Parvatee had seen Dolly. By then she was already thin and run down and her time was near: the weight of her burden was more than a slender frame could bear. She had stopped at the shop.

'Give me a cold "Ju-C", Maharajin.'

'Red or orange?'

'Anything cold, very cold.'

'You want a straw?'

'Give me like that.'

She drank until the bottle was almost drained, leaving only enough for flies and bees, and rested the money on the counter.

Parvatee said, 'Not to worry.'

'You have to buy it, Maharajin, you don't get it for nothing.'

Many thoughts surfaced to Dolly's throat. She could not cloak her pain, but neither could she use words; instead she swallowed, returning her rising feelings into the live mound of her belly. She was pulling her courage, stretching it to cover over too much pain, too much ground.

'We have to pay our debts na, in this life or in the next life,' she managed to say, 'One way or the other we have to pay our debts, na?'

In the silence, Parvatee and Sastra wished that an earlier time of innocence, free from pain, could return for Dolly who knew too well the dark futility of wishes.

She was about to leave the shop, had walked reluctantly to the wide open folding door, now creased as a closed fan, and she was moving, moving away.

'Say something, Dolly.'

'Maharajin,' she said, 'It is not for myself, but would you have… ?' her lips trembled. She held her breath, slowly the air subsided as she looked at the bulging jute bags of sugar before her and the bees that had settled on them, but saw nothing. 'I am any time due, you can see, and I don't have much.'

It was agony that could not be spoken. A pain unbearable. The misery in her eyes, her face trying to cover an inner gnawing hell. The child-mother turned and quickened her pace. As she left the shop's outstretched shade and entered the scorching, dazzling sun, Parvatee lifted her ornhi to her eyes and bent her head. 'I will send some things with Sastra,' she said in a broken voice.

It was an abandoned mud house, leaning to one side. It just stood there. Nobody knew who owned it. School children and straying hens and ducks would shelter there from the rain. And it was there Dolly went, when her father shouted for the entire neighbourhood to hear that she was 'not to cross his door step'. A rush of other things stormed out of his mouth – hurtful, ugly, self-deprecatory, self-diminishing things; demeaning things that slashed her nakedness.

When Sastra approached the door, she stood still before it and waited; for what she couldn't say, yet felt it was right to wait a while before the door, the courtesy a stranger bestows to another, something sensed – something too of the preparation of self before the rite. She recalled doing the same before the threshold of the inner sanctum of the siwala.

Time passed. She knocked. 'Who is it?'

'Sastra.'

'What is it?'

'Ma sent me.'

The door opened gently, as if by an unseen hand, for already she could hide without shelter, could hide in the open, become one with the leaning mud wall. Mesh her frame with other frames. As Sastra rested the things, she said, 'Ma glad she saw you... wanted to send them before but didn't know where.'

A wall lay between them. Impassable. 'Ma has an Anchor cigarette cardboard box full with odds and ends booties and baby bonnets, vests and cot sheets and blankets – so she can send other things too if you would like.' Dolly did not hear. She no longer listened to words. The country of words was arid, eroded, wasted into a land of games – mean, deceitful, nasty games.

The lantern dimmed, lowered itself to a silent glow. It needed pumping.

'The funeral will be tomorrow.'

'Even to the last Dolly wouldn't say, who the father was. The most she said was: "He knows".'

'Over and over I keep asking, who could it be?'

'Whoever it is, we don't know, but now, now it is between his conscience and God. He can hide from you and me but he can't hide from God.'

'That's true.'

'What done happen, done happen eh... What could she do?'

'It is better that way, oui.'

'God knows best.'

'Nothing can happen without his knowing.'

'But imagine, eh, so heavy with child and doing all that. Preparing.'

'And while she busy doing that the child was kicking.'

'Wanting to live.'

'The child sensed something.'

'We don't know.'

'A lot of courage that must take, eh?'

'But you destroying yourself.'

'Strong, strong will.'

'Hopelessness if you ask me. Hopelessness.'

'Is true. Is the pitch darkness, like in a tunnel; you hear the train coming, coming and nowhere to turn, nowhere to go.'

'Is the terror of the life facing you.'

'How to live this life afterwards, what to do; to live with the child, to find work holding the child. Who to leave it with, begging this one that one. And you know how people stop.'

'To have to live like that eh.'

One of the women bent her head. No one said anything.

'A lot of strength too, to be able to do that.'

'More like she break down.'

'The spirit collapse, oui.'

'I don't think I could do that. I don't have the heart.'

'You never know until somehow, somehow, you find yourself like she was… With something like this you can't really talk from the outside. When it's you, only you know.'

'True.'

'No one. To have no one,' Sastra said.

'Yes, Dood, she was all alone.'

'What can we do, eh?'

'We could have talked to her.'

'What good that would do?'

'It's plenty better than not talking. We treated her like a stranger.'

'You want to get mixed up with a father like that?'

66

'When he is drunk, he is hell oui, I can tell you.'

'But to be with child and planning and thinking all that, eh?'

The old lady wiped her eyes.

'What can we do eh?'

'She must have climbed on the table.'

The warmth from the chulha was bathing Mustapha's face, yet all around him darkness had settled; the night had moved on but dawn was still far away. No cock crowed.

'Is too late now anyway.'

'We not her father. What can we do?'

'Well it didn't have to happen.'

'She was too young, man.'

'When you young, you not thinking about tomorrow.'

'Well she was trying to choose between the father and this fella and both of them let her down.'

'I couldn't bring myself to do it.'

'We don't know who he is.'

'She shoulda tell somebody.'

'Yes. Somebody. Somebody she shoulda tell.'

'Who?'

Sastra got up and left.

The night was warm and no air stirred. She entered her bedroom thinking she was the last person to see Dolly alive. Dolly's words were like a testament to her short life:

'I believed his words. Try not to believe in anyone, not to care for anyone more than yourself; because, when words prove to be only sounds like air pushing an old tin cup along the ground – you only have yourself to fall back on; if you love another more than yourself, and he abandons you, you become someone loved by no one, not even yourself. Learn this from me.'

Everyone is crowding in, as in a silent movie, only the movement of the wind; only three years old; I am the shortest. What is it? Some are leaving, leaving so soon saying nothing. I need to climb the steps with my hands. They are steep, too far apart. No one is noticing me, I am below their waist. It is dark but now I know. I too look. Now I know it is Dolly so high above my head. I cannot touch her to say I am here… She knows I am here, she is expecting me; I was sent for.

'You are too late, Sastra, too too late.'

'Yes I have something for you. Ma sent me.'

The room is small. The door is closed. I am alone with her. Where are the others? She turns only her eyes around slowly, for her neck is held fast, and speaks only to me.

'Do not believe, Sastra. Do not care, Sastra.'

Where are the others? There is little light, little air. A chink of light is a shower of sunlight filled with fine floating specks of things too light. Dolly's feet are floating: hanging, hanging, without support. No support. Her feet are not resting on something, not standing on the earth. They are alone. Both above, high above the ground. Air could not hold her, could not support her.

Air asked: 'Why was she so heavy?'

Earth did not reply. Earth looked away. Then Earth said, 'I am here, my feet are clay. I know not how to rise; Air couldn't save her… Air is not strong enough… I am, but I am here; couldn't reach her; was beneath her. Couldn't reach her. I am beneath her, beneath, beneath.'

Dolly is a broken stem, a broken hibiscus flower bent on a hedge. Alone up there. She swings alone; opens her circling eyes, and looks at me.

68

'Remember me. Do not love, Sastra.'

'Come down, come down, Dolly.'

'I am here.' She spins herself – a top, a spinning top singing:

'Look, Sastra. I am already here. Here. Here. Too late! Too late, Sastra! Look at me. Do not believe, believe, believe! Do not believe, Sastra! Will you? Will you?'

She smiles and says, she laughs and says:

'Yes you will, you will believe, believe, believe. You too. You too.'

'Let me out! Let me out! Oh God, let me out, out, out!' Parvatee awakens her:

'Wake up, Sastra.'

'Yes?'

'You were shouting in your sleep.'

CHAPTER EIGHT

THE FIRE

There were photographs of the victims, covered. The morning newspaper was full of it. An arrow pointed to the spot where five bodies were found. Only the back wall of the two storey house was standing.

These human tragedies, Rabindranath thought, as he packed his bag for school, follow the same pattern everywhere. Their codes of tribalism have us rallying round like baying wolves, warding off sanity, impeding the meting out of justice to any member of its pack, seeing the injury to one as done to all. Look at this reporter trying to focus our attention away from the victims Mr. Birbal, his wife and three children.

The charred bodies were found bundled together, huddled together.

'Mr. Birbal should have taken precautions,' the editorial said, 'when so many were coming to borrow money in the run-up to the carnival.'

The reporter on the scene concentrated on the victim's interest rate. It was eleven and a half per cent, he said; but when you totted it all up, as he had done, taking into account the system of repayment, it could have been as much as thirteen per cent. The bank's rate was seven per cent. The reporter repeated the difference.

Could the burning down of the house have been an accident? Rabindranath wanted it to be an accident, but from what he had read, he couldn't say. His bag was packed. He looked out into the garden: Interest rates reflect the risks the lender takes. Why didn't the borrowers go to the bank? They must have gone sometime, and the banks would not lend them. To the established banks, they were not creditworthy, people without collateral.

Mr. Birbal, his wife and three children, ages eighteen, fifteen, and five, were found not far from the window. What was once a sheet had become string, inches long, still tied to the bed post.

At twenty-three Rabindranath felt like an old man, worn, eroded, like the pebbles in the stream. He rested the newspaper on the table, picked up his coffee and again looked into the garden. Rain had fallen in the night and was still drizzling. Would this have been told differently were it an Indian reporter? Who was this reporter, Carl Munroe?

Rabindrath opened his umbrella and stepped out; the water in the canal had risen appreciatively, threatening the bridge upon which he stood.

It was early when he arrived at school; four staff members were in a tightly closed circle discussing the deaths. From where he stood he could hear their subdued voices:

'I bet you one thing, they wouldn't find out who did it. Their policemen, their superintendent, their police investigator, their inspector. And it was a bunch of their firemen, in the fire brigade. Boy, I could see them taking they time, to put on them helmets, I could hear them saying, "It's that coolie man house, the money lender, he used to roast we ass, well let him know how it feels when the heat all round".'

An older member of staff said:

'At least when you know what the verdict will be, you

don't waste your time thinking about the law; all you do is make sure you protect yourself from them and their laws. In this country we on we own. Whatever happens they're protected by their policemen. Might is right here, man. We have to fend for we self; they telling you that openly all the time. They spelling it out clear.'

'Eh! Eh! but we pay taxes.'

'Yes, to keep them in cushy government jobs, in pensioned jobs you know, while we people have to tear they ass taking risks in business, in gardening... As a matter of fact, anything that's safe, with a roof over it, they in that; so come rain, come shine, they don't have to worry. When they stepping out, they only need to open an umbrella; man, when it comes to battling away in the open, against floods and drought, bachac ants, diseases, birds and wayside thieves; when it comes to opening a business, starting from scratch, coping with swings in fashion, rising costs, with a thief breaking in, damaging your property, stealing the little profit; child, when it comes to catching your royal, you can't see them.'

'Is true. They take the government jobs and the pensions and sitting cool on a high cushion, telling you to come back, when you turn up at the Ministry. A woman said to me last week, "Sorry to have to tell you, but the fella you need to see on holidays," and I asked for half day off work mind you, and they knew I was coming.'

'Well look at that.'

'Man, they running the show. This is their show.'

Rabindranath heard the pain and anger in their throwing overboard the constraints of standard grammar, in their hollow laughter and their strained, forced smiles.

All day he was unhappy, his mood shifting from sheer frustration and hopelessness to anger. His tiredness sought solace in looking forward to the possibility of seeing Sastra and the certainty of the good katha food he was going to enjoy later; he liked katha food at the Tiwaris'; they always took so much time and care to offer the best.

After his shower, changed into something clean, smelling of sunshine and grass, thanks to Milly, Rabindranath started the walk to the Tiwaris', his head lifted high, though still he felt drained. There was sure to be more talk of the fire.

Education had failed... he had expected too much of it... and could see clearly it was not sufficient... but it was all he had to offer. Of late this admission had unsettled him, was threatening to throw him. So distraught, he had felt the need for reassurance and had reread for the umpteenth time one of his favourite pieces from *Tales of the Pandes*, – the key to all shape and form and harmony.

As he approached, the Tiwari's gate opened and Sastra's sister, Sati, saw him. She is such a beautiful, attractive woman he thought, as his eyes sought pleasure and cheer.

'Mr. Pande, it's you?' asked Shakuntala Tiwari, pleased to see him. 'Come inside and meet Govind's ajee.'

Already the smell and sight of wide, open, clean surroundings bathed in sunshine, the scent of good katha food and of special leaves brought from the forest (to be used as plates), were massaging his tiredness away. This orderliness, this tradition, these ladies, restored and refreshed him; their voices a song stilling his agitation.

'Ma, this is Rabindranath Pande. You know he helped Govind.'

'I remember you well; you were here before, many

times,' Govind's ajee, said. She was completely grey, a healthy, shining grey, in contrast to the dark eyes that once matched her hair. 'I remember your father too, I used to see him going to school. He was always very serious. His feet walked with a purpose. And my mother knew your great grandfather, Ganesh Pande. All the Pandes are good men,' she said, and saw again Gajraj Pande's eyes. Rabindrath had inherited those eagle eyes, with their quality of dream and adventure, as well as his grandfather's strong black flashing mane; and her own small eyes sparkled and teased: 'And good looking, too, na?' Rabindranath was no longer tired.

'First you must eat. Go wash your hands,' the old lady said. 'If your aja had money, he would have sent your father to England to be a doctor. That would have been a great blessing. And you know many people were sad when Surinder became a Christian. I was, too, when I heard. But one morning, I must tell you this, I was sitting over there, come let me show you, right by that Tulsi tree; and suddenly just like that, a feeling came and rested on my shoulder. I was at peace. Then, bit by bit I began to think he did the right thing; how else could a Hindu become headmaster of a Presbyterian school? And when I heard he was starting this new scholarship scheme to help Hindu children and Christian children, I was too too glad. You see we have no one, we are on our own here. We have to keep working hard, no matter what. Sickness or pain, you still have to keep working... In the old days you had to tie your waist good and then swing the cutlass from five o'clock in the morning to when you see the sun go down and touch the sea... But we are a hard working people.' She lifted her ornhi, turned her head and wiped her eyes. 'Who else would stay all day, up to their waist in mud and water and plant rice? Planting rice is a back breaking job. Garden work too too hard.'

'Go to Tunapuna market,' Shakuntala Tiwari added, 'any market for that matter, on a Saturday morning, on a Sunday morning, and what you see – we feeding them, and you think we getting thanks?' The morning news had made her bold. 'Did you see the papers?' Everyone was silent. Rabindranath nodded.

Govind's ajee said: 'A brave man, your father, a man of courage. And all the time we thinking he letting us down, but he had foresight. A good man. You see we don't know the way God is thinking. You will hear many people, even pundits say, well God was thinking this way, that way, but we don't know. Do you know what I am thinking?' the old lady asked, beaming, her eyes twinkling. 'Now I will leave you.' She got up, 'Sati, look after Gajraj Pande's grandson for me; treat him good,' and she moved to the shade of the spreading long mango tree close to the kitchen. As she walked, her age showed; she, too, had been greatly disturbed by news of the fire, the photographs of the dead family and the reporting.

Rabindranath washed his hands. Sati said, 'All the men are in the other part of the house; they are discussing those terrible deaths. Dr. Lall identified the bodies yesterday… Mr. Birbal was his patient before the fire; he was suffering from an ulcer… The whole family wiped out eh, just like that; who would want to do a thing like that? Why so much hate eh? Why us? Why pick on us? What have we done them?'

Rabindranath listened, and seeing him too thoughtful, too sombre for one so young, she smiled warmly. 'I won't tell the others you're here yet, I'll keep you all to myself while you eat.' She continued to smile. 'You must tell me what you like. Don't be shy. We have channa and aloo, pumpkin, karhee, paratha, bhajee; you will have a little of every thing? Oh yes and there is saheena too.'

'I will leave it entirely to you.'

'Your wife will like that – leaving it to her entirely. Would you prefer a leaf, or tharia?'

'I am completely in your hands.'

'No preference? People say there is something distinctive about the leaf, that the food tastes better on it. Do you believe that?'

'From childhood, I've enjoyed eating on a leaf; I always associated it with celebrations. There may be something about the chemistry of the leaf itself on the food, and there is its distinctive leafy scent. To have the essence of the forest with you while you eat: I like that.'

'You speak like your father,' she said as she brought the katha food, in a highly polished brass tharia which she held in both her hands, placing it before him, lowering her head imperceptibly and retreating in such a way that he felt greatly honoured. Uplifted!

She had worked a spell, an enchantment. 'You are a brahmin, doing the work of a brahmin and will be served as a brahmin should. When you are finished, you will have a little kheer? It is good. I made it.' Then pouring ice cold water into a lothar she said, 'Sastra is here, she will be happy to see you. Try a little of the mango achar. Let me help you.'

'I know it will be too much for you to have some mohan bhog, soon after. You will take it home with you? Would your Milly eat some mohan bhog?'

'She will share mine.'

'There is no need to share, I will send her some. Sastra told me about her. You are lucky.' A reassurance emanating from her warmth and goodwill flowed outwards. She wanted to please; the jewellery resting on her neck, on her wrists, caught his attention.

Sati got up from where she was sitting, for she felt he was not at ease with her.

'I was saying to Sastra, you do not have the time, you are far too busy, so we should be looking around for a nice dulahin for you. One good turn deserves another.'

'What did she say?'

'"I don't know anyone suitable". But Sastra has only just left school, she wouldn't know many people. There are good families. One has to be discreet, of course. You give me the word, and I will keep my eyes open: let the right people know the sort of girl I have in mind. Come to think of it, I could ask Capil to help.'

'The doctor must have his hands full. I hear that after ten on a morning, all three of his waiting rooms are jam packed.'

'You know Capil takes his work seriously. He is thorough. I shouldn't be the one saying so but he is really very good. He treats his patients as if they were related to him, that's why his surgery is just overflowing. On a Monday, patients have to sit as far out as the gru-gru palm trees on the lawn.'

'Well tell me, what sort of girl would you be looking for, were I to give you the go-ahead?'

'First, let me start with the most important bundle of things. She will have to be a beautiful, tender, brahmin girl from a highly respectable family, preferably the professions, but successful business people will do, since it is only a matter of time with them, before they acquire a natural grace. She will have to be educated, intelligent, sensitive, willing to adapt, but also to conserve, knowing when to do one, and when the other.'

'Ah, that means she must have a great deal of judgment. So much insight to expect from one so young?' he hesitated, 'and tender?' He teased.

77

'Why not? I'll tell you how.' He had smiled provokingly and this challenged her.

'She will have to get rid of traditional prejudices and modern ones. This is the first and most important thing.'

'Very difficult, an unusually tall order, Sati. I hesitate to say whether such a thing is possible. Nevertheless, your first bundle of things is impressive. I feel tempted.'

'Oh height is also important, but that is in the second bundle of things.'

He said nothing more and waited for her to explain, while she thought he would enquire.

'The ideal height is where she meets you, when she stands before you. About here,' said Sati, pointing in a matter of fact way to her neck encircled by a fine gold chain of leaf buds, 'so that she can rest her head comfortably on your chest when she needs to be comforted.'

But before he could recover from all the images she had evoked, Sastra entered, and he found himself asking, where would she rest? But though this thought was leaping about in his mind like a firefly in the night, he was well aware that he was a guest in the home of one of the old brahmin families and conducted, if not his thoughts, certainly his manner, impeccably.

'How good of you to come. I didn't know you were here. Sati, why didn't you call me?'

'I wanted him all to myself. Not everyday I meet such a handsome, intelligent young man.'

'What will Capil say if he hears you?'

'I will leave you now with Sastra and see if the men upstairs want anything.'

'Have some more saheena,' Sastra said, looking at his plate. 'Govind's ajee made it; you wouldn't find better. It crumbles in the rich dahee.'

'I agree,' he said, and as she approached he lifted his head to absorb her coming and they smiled.

On returning the blue enamel pot to the kitchen table she said: 'The jasmine is out and its perfume is everywhere. Would you like to see the garden?'

He paused, aware of how full he was of all the goodness around, and knew he must decline to enter the garden with her – the Tiwari's garden – the scent of which was so captivating.

Upstairs in the sitting room, surrounded by portraits of the Tiwari family spanning three generations, the conversation was heated. Rabindranath was determined not to enter the fray, but it did not turn out that way.

'To begin with,' Dr. Lall was saying, 'They feel differently than we do about a lot of things.'

'How do we know that?' Rabindranath enquired.

Dr. Lall took a long pull at his cigarette, 'Look around you, man. What do you see?'

'People trying to make a living, Lall.'

'Let me tell you what you don't want to see, man. A people dancing, dressing up in lamé velvet and satin, spending all they have today, without a single thought about tomorrow. They want the best in everything, food, clothes... and they want it now.'

'How many you know live like that?'

'A foolish question. Where you living, man?'

'Well, tell me.'

'Look around. What happens at carnival? You tell me.'

No one spoke.

Govind came and sat next to Sastra, whispered something and she smiled.

'They save up and spend it all in two days.'

'Carnival means a lot to them,' Rabindranath said. 'If we'd been through the years of slavery, mightn't we feel it is an important symbol of freedom. Wouldn't you spend money on something that means a lot to you?'

'Sure. A car. A house. A piece of land. The education of children, a hospital. Not in that order, eh.' And everyone laughed.

Sati said, 'Putting a car, Lall, before a house and a house before a piece of land? Your grandfather must be groaning in his grave.' Everyone laughed again.

'Look at it this way,' Rabindranath continued; 'they are enjoying themselves, it's a release from all the bad times during the year. Wouldn't you spend a lot of money on a good holiday?'

'Not before I had a house.'

'Some of those people, Lall, if they waited for that, would never dance. Imagine their lives without dance.'

'I take your point,' Dr. Capildeo said, 'it is legitimate, but you see, Rabindranath, you can't have your cake and eat it; because on the third day, when the carnival tempo, the music, the jumping up are over; the debts face you. Distress and, unfortunately, envy come to the fore: envy of those who denied themselves two days of pleasure and saved; of those who worked tirelessly serving behind counters; envy of those without debts. And as envy builds up, it becomes a lethal gas and is used by politicians.

'What is particularly vicious about these deaths is that they borrowed heavily, for the carnival; then finding that they couldn't pay, one of them must have come up with this idea of getting rid of the evidence and the creditor. It only takes one lunatic to think like that.'

'We don't know what happened,' Rabindranath said.

'After reading the newspapers, I can suspect what happened.'

'They not like us, they so different, man.'

There was silence. It was as if everyone felt the need for the comfort of private thoughts. 'At one level,' Sastra said, 'the differences are wide; at another level they are nonexistent… ' She lowered her voice, 'Have you ever seen how Govind's ajee lifts a dressed chicken?'

'With the outermost tips of the forefinger and thumb,' Sati said.

'Imagine her having to touch pork and beef. The Indian Mutiny speaks.'

'And carnival?' asked Dr. Capildeo, 'What do you young people see?'

'Gay abandon, a pounding rhythm, a pulsating beat, a stirring up sensuality,' Sati said. 'Compare that with Indian classical dance,' she continued, 'the subtleties of hand and finger movement; also of eyes, head and neck; controlled thought underpins the dance… '

'You are not comparing like with like,' Rabindranath said, 'what about chowtal singing and music at phagwah and the stick dance at Hosay time. Thinking of pulsating beats? Nothing to compare with the tabla and tassa drumming at its best. Have you ever seen those fellas, their entire body moves with their hands and the vibration takes them over… the trunk and shoulder and head, partners the music.'

'Don't forget the unstable family,' Sati said, 'the abandoned women, the disappearing, absent fathers and that brine of pickled meats.'

'Yet we are very similar, too… ' Sastra said.

'That is true,' Rabindranath said. 'We are both loving, warm-hearted people; sensitive, sensuous in our foods and art, overgenerous to our friends. We can harness ourselves together to the same cart – the building of our small island, and get to understand those differences we have talked about, and place them at far corners, not at centre stage; they are not that important. We have enough warmth and generosity to keep us together.'

'I think,' said Dr. Capildeo, 'they have tended to keep to Government jobs, to sports, music and dance, not the hard grind, managing only with your own hard-earned savings to get a business off the ground, like the Birbals last night, and alone, always alone; managing without government handouts, subsidies, knowing that you sink or swim, with no one, no newspaper, no intellectual, no scholar ever seeing your plight or your contribution.'

'Come, come, these achievements, in sports and the arts, don't they involve hard work? You know they require skill, intelligence, dedication,' said Rabindranath. 'To stay at the top means working all out... even if you are gifted.'

'So, you don't think they are different in any way at all from us?'

'I think that what we have in common is more important than our differences.'

'It is good to have ideals,' Dr. Lall said, 'and there will be exceptions; only a fool will put a whole continent of people into one category. Yet let us look at the evidence: Let us start with the obvious differences – Discipline, man, where is the day-to-day discipline, the tightening of the belt?'

'Lall, you know all achievements require discipline.'

'All right.'

'Look at it historically, Lall: to have faced slavery, the destruction of your culture, contempt for your skin, and then to grow in and develop in a hostile environment full of injustices and deep prejudices, don't you think that requires courage, faith, hard work, discipline? How to survive all that degradation, inhumanity, don't you think that took self-control and the patience of Job? And still they dance and still they sing and laugh and love. O God, man, what more you want from a fellow human being that has been crushed over and over again?'

'Dear boy, just look at today, man, not yesterday when poor people everywhere lived in hell. Do you have any idea what life in the sugar belt is today? Those labouring people begin to die by age twenty; by the time they are thirty, their heart and blood vessels have already seriously deteriorated. By age forty, permanent physical handicaps become the norm in the sugar estates. Go to Couva: breathlessness and cough everywhere; children wither like flowers, eyes dull, energy sapped, and why? Dire poverty; they can't get even enough dhal to eat. They not asking for meat, can't get enough vegetables, though their parents labour in the fields all day. Today, in the 1950s, their parents still labour for a mere pittance, and they can't leave, they can't get out. The government doesn't help them. Government jobs are not for them. Who speaks for them? Who works in the oilfields for high wages? Who works in the sugar belt for the lowest wages on the island? Why? Tell me why? Wake up, man! Have you seen the latest official figures? Indians have the lowest median income on the island, and that's not all, there is a large gap, I'm telling you, a large gap between it and the second lowest group – the Negro population.'

'I was not aware that the gap was large,' Rabindranath said.

'And why is that? They don't have power. Urban workers have power and the people in power look after them; the civil servants look after their own. Indians can't expect anything from the Government. They are on their own; they either sink or swim and the majority are too weak; the tides and currents too strong… Yes, we did not enslave them, but they treat us as if it were so. Last night our very humanity was in doubt. We were not seen as humans.'

No one spoke. Each man kept his thoughts. Then Dr. Lall said, 'Birbal was in a high risk business, providing a service – lending money to people the banks didn't want to know; yet, he was seen, we are all seen, as money-crunching machines moving without blood and tears and pain and ulcers. We are seen as perpetual winners. I'll tell you this: for every successful Indian business on the road, ten went bust; losers lose their business, but not their large overdraft and larger ulcers and inner hell.'

'Some end up in the mad house,' Sati said.

Govind began to play with the three gold churias on Sastra's arm.

'There are differences between us here in this room,' Rabindranath said, 'and there will be between people from different cultures, but when you get to know people, all kinds of people, really know them well, you find you are looking at yourself, with only a change of style… Sometimes people change their style… It is our common humanity that matters. What is the shape of the human spirit? What is the colour of human courage?'

No one answered him.

'Yes. But physical differences,' said Sastra, 'in form, shape and colour; or the differences in language and religion often lead to a belief that there are inherent, distinctive differences between us.'

'The problem is,' Rabindranath said, 'when these differences are exploited in times of hardship, mistrust and suspicion creep in.'

'That's true,' Govind said, 'and if it so happens that one group appears to be doing better than the other, even if in reality it isn't so, it is enough for envy and hate

to displace reason. Perhaps the solution is to live apart.'
No one replied.

'You see,' said Dr. Capildeo, 'we must come to terms with the fact that whichever group is in power, once it has a majority, it will keep power and stay there until the resurrection, because, no matter how corrupt they are, what a mess they make of things, year in year out, all the time, at the back of their minds, they know they have a trump card – the strong tribal card – primeval, instinctive. They only have to play it on that deep gut prejudice, that preference for ourselves when under threat.'

'That's true,' said Sati, 'they only have to say, consider carefully, if you throw me out, who will come in? And because of this, the politicians appeal to race, the more sophisticated politicians – those smiling, making pretty little speeches...'

'Dipped in a syrup of covert racism,' interrupted Dr. Capildeo. 'They will get away with murder again and again until the minorities leave. These things happened in Europe, in East Africa and elsewhere. Why wouldn't it happen again? Why wouldn't it happen here?'

'We are inseparably bound together, 'Rabindranath said, 'like Siamese twins and neither of us have the good sense to know it. If either tries to destroy the other, his days are numbered too. The economy works like that too. It needs everybody to pull together; things far apart as the clouds above and the oceans beneath are connected. They hang together, bathing the land.'

'Rabindranath, shut up; you are an idealist,' Dr. Lall said. 'Your trouble is, you have been with books and children far too long, you speak like a man from the moon.'

'I want to live in a place,' said Sati, 'where no matter what the race or religion of the judges and policemen, I will receive a just and fair judgment.'

'Fair judgment?' said Dr. Lall. 'Christ didn't get that, so you shouldn't be going around with these ideas. Look at what is hitting you in the face out there – that is the reality.' His lips quivered, then his voice stopped altogether. After a while, he pointed in the direction of Sangre Grande; his hand remained outstretched, gradually it lowered. Much later he said: 'Reality is out there – that family last night – the Birbals. They and they alone were facing it last night. I hope to God it wasn't for too long.'

He sat quietly for a time and then got up.

'I have to leave. This was a good day for me. Sati, you are looking more beautiful, every time I see you. This husband of yours is a lucky man. If he ever gives you trouble, you know I will be on your side.'

'I have a nice girl in mind for you, Lall, ask Capil.'

'True?' His face lit up with pleasure. 'This man hasn't told me a thing.'

'Lall has to stop drinking first,' Capil said.

'Listen, Lall, I'm serious,' continued Sati. 'I will talk to you about it. And about the drinking too, for when you see her, you will stop drinking. You will want to be sober.' Dr. Lall looked at her and they both exuded a warmth of affection for each other.

Dr. Capildeo raised his eyebrows. He wasn't happy with the easy camaraderie she had with Dr. Lall; he had a charisma that made him special in the hospital, so much so that the nurses and matrons fussed around him, as if he were the only doctor in the bloody place; and women behaved as if he were a god. I will have to warn her about Lall, he is full of high spirits, too passionate a man. She needs to be more circumspect; this warmth of hers will put ideas in his head. I don't want her to be alone on the shore when he is rolling in.

Just before Dr. Lall left the room he turned to

Rabindranath, 'Listen, my family and I never thanked you properly for all you did for my nephew Harilall. He is in Canada, and hopes to do medicine.'

'When you next write, tell him to send me a Christmas card. I like to know what the old boys are doing.'

'Old boys?'

They laughed.

'We can't thank you for a chance like that, an education that changes a man's expectations, his whole life. Your personal sacrifice has been enormous. I hear this is your last year.'

'Yes.'

'Good. And high time too. Another thing. You may not think so, but my God, if you only knew how much I want to believe what you were saying, only the reality out there… is coarse, man.'

He embraced him and said: 'Look after yourself, you are tired. Overdoing it, eh? When last did you have a thorough check up? Come and see me any time, the earlier the better. I mean that, I am serious. Stay well. You're one hell of a fine fella… that I know damn well.'

CHAPTER NINE

ONLY THINGS WEST INDIAN

Through the shutters shielding the kitchen from the morning sun, Milly could see two young men approaching. Her face brightened and she hurried out to hug her nephew as if he were a prodigal son. They were laughing and talking at once until she said, 'Introduce me, Francis.'

'Carl Munroe,' the onlooker said, 'I am pleased to be here, Miss Matthews.'

'Any friend of Francis is welcome. Come on in. What brings you to these parts, Francis?'

'Work and pleasure.'

By the time they had washed their hands and faces (at Milly's insistence), she had put together a dainty spread of homemade biscuits and coconut cake, with pieces of ginger and sultanas and raisins and currants. A whiff of cinnamon escaped as she sliced the cake for them.

'Out here, Mr. Munroe, on the west porch, it's cooler at this time of day. Rabindranath would be disappointed to know that you came, Francis, and he was not here. I told him you were with the Bank.'

'That's right, Aunt Milly; safe and secure, Gran says.'

'I guess that's where all the money is,' Milly said laughing.

'You have a point there, Miss Matthews,' Carl Munroe

said, 'though we all know there are other forms of wealth – like this house for instance.'

'Oh, Gajraj Pande had this house built a long time ago. Old George Greenidge and his son did a lot of the building work though old Gajraj laid the foundations himself. Don't you get the feeling he wanted to build for all times?'

'Sounds to me like the same old story. We Blacks always the builders, rarely the owners. You have to wonder when it will end, don't you, Miss Matthews? First it was the Arabs, then the Whites and now, if we don't stop them, the Indians. They'll take over this country if we don't act. Look around you: big shops, big houses, big cars, land, estates; they buying up every-thing, building all the time. We have to start looking after ourselves; if things continue like this, mark my words, we'll be squeezed out.'

Milly was not prepared for this and, treating the remark like an occasional flare in a coal pot, decided to let it pass.

'Well, tell me what is the pleasurable part of this mission, Francis.'

'We going up to Arouca to see a Shango ceremony.'

'In this hot sun?'

'A bit of sun's not too much to put up with to support your culture, is it, Miss Matthews? Have you ever been to a Shango ceremony?'

'I must confess… in Barbados?… Mind you I have heard of it.'

'Excuse me for saying it, Miss Matthews, but this is the trouble with our people. We need to be much more aware of our traditions, to support those in our midst who against immeasurable odds held on to our African cultural heritage.'

'After this, Carl's taking me to meet some of the

players in the Free Rangers,' Francis said. 'They're the up-and-coming steelband.'

'This is another part of our culture we have to preserve and develop,' Munroe said. 'Otherwise, the writing is on the wall. All we'll be left with are those big drums and Indian music blaring out of every upstairs house in Chaguanas.'

'You mean the Tassa players?'

'I don't know what they call them, but whatever it is, we can't sit back and not exert ourselves. They not interested in our culture, in things West Indian: Parang, Shango, the Shouters, steel band music, nothing like that.'

'What are they interested in?' enquired Milly, as she refilled his glass.

'In things from India.'

'Isn't that natural?'

'I mean they keep looking back to India. They're here, and they should be interested in West Indian things, in things here and now on this island.'

'But shouldn't we know about Indian ceremonies too? After all, festivals like Phagwa, Divali and Hossay have been taking place here for over a hundred years.

'Well, I'm afraid things West Indian have to be my first priority, and then I could turn my attention to foreign things. But they must make up their minds; if they want to live here, they should live as we do. If they want to look back to India, they have a choice. Nobody will stop them from returning. We are West Indians, and this is the West Indies...'

Well, thought Milly, fancy talking like that in this hot sun.

'But you have to admit, aunt Milly, they do keep to themselves and only marry their own kind,' said Francis. 'You just can't penetrate their culture.'

'Work and save, work and save, build and build. They won't relax man – not like regular folks. They just scheming away all the time. One Indian man in the office one day; next day it's full of them. You just can't trust them.'

'If you will excuse us, Mr. Munroe,' Milly interrupted. 'Francis left a number of things here; I need to know what he wishes to keep and what he wants me to throw out. We won't be long.'

'Francis, close that door as you come in. Now, son, I am telling you this for your own good, Mr. Carl Munroe cannot be a true friend to anybody. He's an unhappy man, full of half-truths dressed up as convincing sounding arguments that are emotionally satisfying to himself. Whatever is the cause of his unhappiness I wouldn't know, but whenever he opens his mouth, foolishness comes out. I hope you don't believe what you were saying.' She plumped up one of the cushions, and indicated that he should sit. 'I can see that under his influence, you're not using your head. Well, my boy, use it. You were one of the few in that first exhibition class they were certain about. That first year, Rabindranath wore himself out worrying about all of you. Don't let your aunt Milly down, don't let the late Mr. Pande down and for heaven's sake, Francis, don't let yourself down.'

'A lot of what Carl's saying is true.'

'You mean partly true.'

'Well, look how I was removed from sitting next to Sastra. Why was I removed? …They wouldn't allow a little black boy to sit next to an Indian girl.'

'Listen, Francis, your feelings were hurt, but you must be fair. All the boys sitting next to girls were removed and placed with other boys.'

'That was only done so that I could be moved. I'm not stupid. We can't get close to them, aunt Milly. They keep us at arms length.'

'Look at me, Francis. Did Mr. Pande keep me at arms length when you were here?'

'I don't know.'

'I see. I can't believe this is you speaking. This is Mr. Munroe speaking. His experience is not yours, Francis. Tell him so... Stop looking through that window and look at me, Francis. You have a choice; you can go about with hate and envy and resentment maiming your life, or you can try and understand people, put on their shoes, stand where they stand... it helps. You're young and good looking, but if you let this ugliness build up inside you, you'll hurt a lot of people.'

'Mr. Pande was hardly a typical Indian was he, aunt? Look, the way I see it, our people have suffered and we'll go on suffering if we don't make a stand. If some people get hurt, too bad... '

'Plan to live in a grander world, Francis, not just in your skin. The world is your inheritance. Don't let a mean, limiting vision dictate what is your inheritance.'

'Look, aunt Milly, I have to live in the real world, and out there people don't think like that. It's still white people's power and now the Indians trying to take over. That's what we're up against. You live here all cocooned from everything.'

'Put everything into that bank job, son. Try and get promotion. Go for the good things, try and get yourself in a position to help people, Black people, all people. Grow tall, son.'

'You're not a Black woman, you see the world with Indian eyes; you've deserted your own kind.'

She was stunned and her soft eyes silently welled up.

She was sure she had lived in the real world, not cocooned, but the blow was unexpected and all the more hurtful for coming from someone she loved so much. It struck a vulnerable spot, one she usually kept well covered. But the depth of her affection for Francis also goaded her to resistance. What came to her rescue, surging through her temples and her breasts, were her memories – the delicious crumbs from the feasts they once shared. She recalled when they had both tried to draw a melongene and the laughter they had embraced together, sitting on the grass, looking at that satin purple, succulent form, with its green, closely-fitting helmet. Each was convinced that theirs was the better. And when they had shown them to Mr. Pande he could not recognise either drawing, even after three guesses. And what a shy, beautiful, boy Francis had been, conscious of his body and her touch while she bathed him, how she would hug him and throw him up in the air Whoopeee! and without thinking, her throat said 'Whoopee!' She looked at him and wondered why he seemed not to have gathered crumbs from those feasts, something from the years of their closeness which could have been stored for hard times. Were those experiences only for the time, the place, the moment? Were they so transient? No! No! She refused to believe that.

Time passed between them and as she looked through the window, her pain eased and her badly bruised spirit began lifting itself.

After a while, Milly said, 'Look at me, Francis. In the three years you lived here with me, did I ever make you feel less than anybody, anybody at all?'

Francis did not stir.

'Answer me, son. What am I to make of your silence?'

'No, aunt Milly.'

'There was a time, Francis, when I felt… had been taught to think, that only things from England, created in England, had any value, that Africa was some darkness in the past, destroyed in any case by slavery. I don't think that now, but I can't accept that only things from Africa can be mine… Nothing stands still. We change, our cultures change; besides, as far back as you go, people have been travelling, taking things from one place to another and we don't really know where many things have come from, where the good ideas that stirred people came from. All cultures have been borrowing from one another since the dawn of time.'

'Nobody believes that in Europe or America.'

'But things are changing. The world's becoming a better place and will become an even better place. I know, Francis; I know I can be good at anything, no matter where on this earth it was born. I've stepped out into the whole wide world and have been walking it ever since.'

He looked at her unconvinced, sombre and sad, sorry for the pain that awaited her in the world outside. How far would she get through No Man's Land before the bullets rained down on her, he asked himself.

He's so vulnerable, so young, Milly thought.

'You know, Francis, if I were just a bit younger and had some big money, for every day of the week, fifty-two weeks of the year, I'd wear a different dress – something from the Yoruba or the Twi people or Indian, Chinese, Japanese, Scottish, English, Russian, French, Spanish, Italian – complete with the right accessories – just to show what can be done.' She lifted her head at a mischievous angle and for a moment transformed herself, becoming sweet, desirable and strong, enjoying to the full a world that would one day accommodate such a splendid variety.

Not unmoved by his aunt Milly, his dear aunty Milly and her magnanimity, and her image of a world he knew did not exist, his anger left him. What remained was a subdued sadness and the feeling that he had to awaken her from her dream before it was too late.

'And Arawak? Red Indian? The Aboriginees of Australia and Maoris of New Zealand? How will that help anyone? How did ideas like that help them when the whites cut them down?'

'Listen, Francis. As an African, a descendant of slaves, of men who crossed the oceans shackled in filth, death and disease, you would have had to grow a big heart, just to survive; and today you need that kind of heart, a big powerful heart, to pump oxygen and nourishment to the brain. So, Francis, you either learn to embrace the whole world or you die slowly; becoming mean, narrow, resentful, withering inside, until one day you so dried up, man, any passer-by would bury you for dead. Don't be boxed in, son, by any one culture, any one way of thinking. We have borne daily terror and we don't hate; you have to have a spark of the divine to manage that, Francis, that's why we will grow tall, because Francis, some of us have that spark.' And she smiled so warmly that he smiled too.

Later that night as she rocked alone with a hot cup of chocolate, Milly wondered whether once, deep down inside, Francis had ever fancied Sastra; how first loves had that very special energy and force...

CHAPTER TEN

THE WISE TROLLS OF ANCIENT CROA

'Good evening, Milly.'

'Sastra my dear, good evening. So much rain today, come, come in quick, child.'

'This is cosy, Milly, this is really nice!'

'You mean to say, you haven't been here before? Well, a visit was long overdue, wouldn't you say so? Your Ma was reluctant to let you come, and it is only when I said that Mr. Ramsaran and Mrs. Gopaul were also invited that she agreed.'

'Pa is strict.'

'She told me, "When he asks who will be there I must be able to say".'

'She is right.'

'Anyway you are here and I am pleased.' Milly looked through the window. 'I'll tell you though, with the rain coming down like this, I don't think they'll want to come. But I have laid the table for all four of you... It's the sort of evening that has set up for the whole night. You can't see the sky. It's growing darker and colder; already, you can't see Mount St. Benedict and the Northern Range is fast disappearing.'

'Something really good is coming from the kitchen.'

'Thank you, dear.'

And they both laughed.

'Would he be able to get away from the enthusiasm of his class?'

'Kept back this evening by all those special meetings with the headmaster and parents that go on and on. And now this rain.' She opened the shutters a little and peered through. 'Listen to that rain falling, it coming down with a vengeance... The Northern Range has gone. How is your Ma and Pa?'

'They both need a holiday.'

'Well, well, that will be the day, a businessman going on a holiday? I could hear Narayan: "Milly, go for what? Here I have everything to my liking, whatever I want, whenever I want. What better holiday can any man have, eh?"'

'That's exactly what he says, but a little change is what he needs.'

'Listen to that downpour; the spray is coming through. I'll have to close the shutters real tight... now look at you? Remove those shoes. You need a towel to rub those feet, child... Here give it a good rub, I am sure it is as cold as ice. You have good looking legs.'

'I've always had them, they are not a new pair.'

'Full of cheek today!'

'Do you think Rabindranath would be able to come through that?'

'Relax, he will come through all right... Here, put these on. They are Rabind's. I'm sure he wouldn't mind.'

'And what will he wear?'

'He can wear his father's which is still a good pair. I'll put these in the kitchen to dry. My god, they are soaking.'

Sastra followed her, 'Rabind was telling me how Draupadi came here to teach you. What sort of person was she? You are the only one I know who was chosen to be her student.'

Milly chuckled, 'That's too tall a question… She looked taller than she was; it was the way she carried herself, as if she were related to the gods; very slim, like bamboo, lithe yet sturdy; she always wore a nose-ring of some ancient design; small eyes, with karjal, that made up for their size by their penetration. I wouldn't want to be on the wrong side of her. On days she was teaching something she considered very important, she would be all in white wearing an elegantly simple, silver bracelet; on the days she taught me kheer, gulab jamun, and rasmelai, she wore a sunny, smiling yellow, like rich creamy milk, like the gold crystals of Demerara sugar. She used to say, "A kitchen is where many a divine thought first reveals itself, Milly; it was when the creator was in his kitchen, listening to the throb of creamy kheer, that the idea of the universe came to him." Everything she wore, everything she did, you could sense that concentrated thought went in to it.'

'How did she relate to you on the first day?'

Milly laughed, 'You mean to me, a black, creole, small island, Bajan lady, as the village women call me?'

'Yes. How did she respond to what the village woman sees.'

'She was a master cook and behaved like one. I think having come all the way here with her spices – adrak, ilaychi, laung, dalchini, jaiphal, jeera, methi, javitri, saunf, kesar, massala, turmeric, chili, mustard seed, bottled mango and imli – she decided to go through with it.'

'For women like her and Shakuntala and my mother, that wouldn't have been enough to make them cross the boundary of their religion and culture; there must have been something more, Milly.'

'She was a religious woman, too; but I think most of all she had more than a soft spot for the Headmaster, she was proud of him and respected him. He had a tremendous affection and regard for her. She wouldn't have wanted to let him down. She may have felt it was a real challenge. She had her little ways which, at the time, were odd to me, like the moment she steps into the house, she would remove her outdoor slippers for a soft indoor one; if she was coming from the market place, would wash her hands up to her elbows, and her face, and would drink a glass of water.'

While Milly was busy in the kitchen, Sastra stretched herself out, trying to relax, to allow her mounting excitement to leave her. The pelting rain continued to roar. There was something about the closed shutters cutting off the harsh rain; the richly polished mahogany table, like a still lake mirroring the bookcase; the old fashioned lamp and candle; the stately giraffe making a mighty U-turn with her neck back to the earth to caress her young; the homely kitchen sounds which combined to give her a feeling of tranquil pleasure.

Bang! the door swung open, and in came a gush of wind, fierce sprays and Rabindranath. 'Come, let me take that from you,' said Milly, 'before I have a pool here.'

'Sastra! You braved it too!'

'She is delighted to be here,' said Milly, 'and don't keep us all waiting now.'

'Ramsaran and Mrs. Gopaul won't be able to make it. They said you would understand if once they got home they stayed there. The roads are beginning to flood.' His pleasure at seeing her in his slippers was more than he had dared hope for. 'I won't be five minutes,' he said and hurried out.

Milly was again busy in the kitchen and as Sastra was peering through the glass door of the bookcase to read the spines of the small, dark, reddish-brown books,

Milly came up to her and said: 'Look, my dear, he knows where everything is, he will be a good host. The rain has just eased and I'm not going to stand about here waiting for it to start again, which will be any minute now.' And with that she left, closing the kitchen door behind her.

They need a little time together, Milly had thought. Fancy, arranged marriages in this day and age. Well, I tell you, where can you get to know those close by better? No clubs. No places for young people to meet; this is a big handicap in this community, forcing young people to tie themselves and carry the consequences. She knew what the village women would think – just what you'd expect of a black woman, failing the trust placed on her by the Narayans, but if well brought-up young people couldn't be trusted, then something was wrong. And the Pandes needed to be helped.

Rabindranath came out buttoning his cuffs, 'Now I can do justice to Milly's creations. The shower was as cold as hell must be. Milly,' he called, 'wasn't that quick?'

'She has only just left, you'll be a good host she says.'

'Well, let me start by offering you something daring and dangerous.'

He opened the lower right-hand door of the book-case.

'What will you have? I'll have whisky.'

Except for a little sweet cherry wine at Christmas time at her sister's home, Sastra had never tasted alcoholic drinks. She had observed Sati take a single glass of sherry at parties, so that was safe, she thought.

'Something to warm you up?'

'I'm not cold.'

'Have some sherry.'

'A little. This giraffe with her baby, is a fine piece,' she said and picked it up. 'The black satin wood makes such a grand turn so smoothly – it comes to life.'

Words at that moment were devoid of meaning for Rabindranath; what he heard was a flow of musical sounds. How delightful she is. I must concentrate on being a good host or I'll go berserk.

Milly had thought of everything, even the bouquet of small, sweet-scented roses, their petals still cradling drops of water.

And her feast of piping hot dhalpuri, lamb in massala and crushed mint, steam-fried beans garnished with freshly picked tomatoes, home-grown spinach followed by her special coconut ice cream was a heaven's delight, and it made their cheeks glow and their eyes shine.

Throughout the meal he was as attentive a host as Milly would have wished. At first she said little of her own accord, her eyes silently questioning, but overcome by so much warmth and his gentle attention, she began to relax. Each time they met she realised there was more of him to know.

The table lamp in the corner flickered; a pair of freshly lit candles, fanned by occasional gusts of rain and wind pushing through the partially closed jalousies, were shortening their brief lives away in bold leaps. And so in the midst of lively shadows they talked, less and less aware of the continuing downpour outside.

Inside, the room was warm with the richness of jeera, the fragrance of roses and the warmth and scent of each other.

'A little brandy?' he asked, bringing out a pair of old fashioned, delicate cut-glass goblets of a generation ago.

'No thank you.'

'Have you had it before?'

'No'

'There could be a first time?' He waited. 'Yes?'

He held two glasses of unequal measures, containing the glow of sunsets. 'There is just enough here for two

101

sips. Try it. If you don't like it, leave it. Is that reason-able?'

She smiled.

'Well here's to you, Sastra.'

'And to your good health, Rabindranath.'

'It is an exciting drink.'

'Liquid fire.'

'The first time is special, and this is really special and different. You will feel good in a while.'

'I don't need it to feel good. Milly excelled herself. Already I feel transported... sailing in the sky.'

For a moment he was at a loss as to what to say, yet then remembered that Sunday at the Tiwaris; he had felt world-weary and tired, a little jealous of Govind... of the close camaraderie he and Sastra shared, growing up together. But now he could challenge anything.

'I liked your argument,' he said, knowing she would understand. 'You pointed to the way physical differences may make us overlook how similar we are at root. I often wonder how much of our feelings comes just from the way we think about difference, or how much actually comes from the propulsion of things physical?'

'I'm sure a great deal must come from the physical self. Look at our temples, how the builders and makers of the sculptures in them understand that people need the senses to help them reach the essence of things spiritual.'

'But don't the sculptors of Hindu temples propose that the spirit and the physical may all be one?'

'Well, I've certainly read of the view that the physical and the spiritual are one continuum of differing intensities.'

'Not differing intensities. Not differences really. Simply two forms of the same essence, the same spirit, which at their most heightened, acquire qualities of the other.'

'No! Not at all. I was brought up to believe that they were separate, with the senses definitely the inferior. God the supreme being, the creator of all things, was presented to me by my father as a flame of light, a disembodied, rarefied, abstract power for good.' Almost like the essence of these perfumed roses, she thought. 'The senses, on the other hand, were presented to me as an imperfection: it was as if a fine quality metal – the spirit– was covered over with a sort of heavy green dross – the senses. "There lies a struggle", as my mother would say; our true metal would only shine through if we were taught how to use an exceptionally good polish – faith – with fervour.'

Why doesn't she relax, he thought.

'The roses,' he said, 'are meant for you.'

'Oh no, they are part of Milly's dinner party creation.'

'She wanted you to have them.'

Sastra was overcome by the perfection of everything; though she did not believe what he was saying, and felt that it was he who was offering them to her, not Milly.

'Thank you. I'll have one. Not all.'

'Sastra, will you marry me?'

'I am to marry Govind.'

She replied so quickly and in such a matter of fact way, it was as if he had merely said, 'You may borrow my raincoat', and she had replied 'I've got one, thank you', as if the seriousness of his proposal had not dawned upon her. He was taken aback and a little amused at her innocent, uncontrived manner. Though it was not the reply he wanted to hear, the way she had spoken, as if a proposal of marriage was just another thing that pops up in conversation, made him feel at ease. But he couldn't allow his proposal to be dispatched with such aplomb, in such a carefree style.

'Who says?'

'We are sort of informally engaged.'

'What does that mean?'

'There is an understanding between Govind's family and mine. My mother –'

'Do you wish to marry him?'

'It would be a long time away; sentiments, feelings etc., all that will come gradually, will grow. That is what the older people say. At the moment, I am not considering these things. When the time approaches, I shall focus on what is expected of me and will be a good wife, mother, citizen of the world and so on.'

He came over and sat next to her on the couch. His closeness disturbed her a little and for a moment she lost her concentration; on regaining it she said:

'You see, these things have already been thought out by both families. Our families are close you know, have so much in common. Marrying Govind would be almost like strolling leisurely from my flower garden into his.'

Rabindranath was silent and Sastra felt the need to speak further.

'There is nothing wrong with Govind. I have known him for a long time, from primary school. We did the College Exhibition together.'

'It was a very good year.'

'He is from a fine brahmin family and there is so much trust and good will between our families – essential I think in marriage.'

'What do you like about Govind? What makes him special?'

She had not asked herself this question and was both taken aback and embarrassed by it. For it to have come from one who should have respected her intimate feelings was distressing.

'Why these questions? I like Govind, I don't dislike him. I've already said that.'

He said nothing; again his silence touched her. She felt awkward and it was some time before she regained her composure.

'Come to think of it, Rabind, you are on your own, so you do not understand. I would be inclined to leave something as weighty, as important as marriage, which is such a grave step in life, to people who are older and wiser, more experienced; who, in truth, understand the larger world outside far far better than I, with my limited experience can possibly do. What do I know about the character of people? Any sophisticated young man under the guise of caring could win my affections; but I have confidence in my parents, they make very good decisions about a whole host of things. Sati is happily married to Capil, and that marriage was arranged by my parents. They are not ordinary parents, taken in by the present or the appearance of things. They ask questions too, they think of the tomorrows, of the qualities that will last, of what a marriage needs... and unlike you, they know the present fad, the camouflage of things. They know, Rabindranath, they know what they are talking about from the sheer experience of having lived it.'

'Perhaps because you are a daughter and not a son, you feel this way. There is something about domesticity; it clings on, encourages you to comply with the tradition that has created it. Perhaps this is why people say women are the custodians of culture.'

'Oh no! Were I a son, I would feel the same. No difference. It is not that. Capil went along with his

105

family's wishes too; he was a qualified doctor at the time, and left it entirely to his parents.'

'Didn't they know each other before?'

'Of course they did; he used to come to us so often that we all felt he should marry Sati and give us some peace. And his parents were always inviting her over to puja and katha, and *Ramayana*.'

'They may have wanted to get married, whether their parents approved or not.'

'If their parents had not approved, they would not have got married.'

'I'm not so sure.'

'Do you know Sati better than I, Rabind?… Though, come to think of it, there was a time I thought she preferred Dr. Lall… I have often wondered… '

'Your sister is an exceptionally attractive and accomplished young woman. If I were Capil, I would rush to obey my parents' wishes.' He felt the need to say more, as well as the need for restraint; in this confused state, anxious for himself, he hesitated, then added, 'You may not be aware but there is something, an awakening within, called falling in love. From time to time this takes place between people.'

'I have no intention of falling into a well or in love. Falling in love is a pastime for the foolhardy. The definitive word, it seems to me, is "falling". Those with such an affliction are vulnerable and they suffer so…' She thought of Dolly: 'I intend to be rational and sensible… I hope that brings me strength. And it's not just because I don't want to conflict with my parents' wishes. Love is a painful business. You lose your independence, become enslaved.'

'Speaking for myself I know my own father would certainly have consulted me before he approached any-

one on my behalf, simply because marriage is as important as you say. Now in the absence of both my parents,
I intend to speak for myself.'

'You have no choice but to do so, Rabind.'

'Not quite. I could, by neglect, give up this right to
have an important say in something that will affect me
more than anyone else.' He paused again and then:
'What is bothering me is why you aren't also speaking up
for yourself. Why aren't you, Sastra?'

'Life is far far more complex than you think,
Rabindranath. I need the reassurance and the affection
of my family; they have been like gods to me, they are
older and wiser than I am; they have more experience of
life, of marriage, than either you or I have. My father is
a good husband and father, and a worthy member of this
community; why shouldn't I listen to what he has to say?
What experience of life have you got?'

'This subject is now closed. You have made yourself
quite clear.'

'You are encouraging me to ask different sorts of
questions; they are not easy questions; besides I have a
whole year to think of all these things. Let us not be
angry.'

'Yes, you are right. What right have I to ask you all
those questions?'

Sastra's eyes began to shimmer, she was hurt by the
tough tone of his voice earlier and the way she had been
compelled to defend her parents and herself She turned
her face quickly away, getting up to look out into the
back garden.

After a while Rabindranath stood behind her and she
felt the need to say something to anchor herself, for her
emotions were drowning her.

'Tonight, you can't tell for certain where the moon is

hiding. On a bright, moonlit night, we village children used to play hoop… I miss that happy, carefree time.'

'The moon has better things to do than witness our first row.'

A soft silence embraced them as they stood together.

'Sastra, I care for you deeply, and I cannot stand by and see you behave like most girls your age when you needn't.' He held her shoulders gently with both his hands. 'You are an educated young woman, more educated than most in the village. This should have some effect on your decision-making and your behaviour. Think, Sastra, what do you want out of life? What sort of life would you consider ideal for a thinking young woman? Your life should be different from that of your mother and grandmother. Your great great grandmother's life and your mother's are very similar in their aims and functions. Yours must be different, Sastra. Don't go into a rigid, limiting path, don't allow yourself to jell in that ready-made mould of tradition. Fly, Sastra. Fly.' As he spoke, her eyes became more and more misty, remembering his first day at school, and he was overcome by a strong surging impulse, and embraced her. She rested her head on his chest; there she felt comforted and strengthened by his closeness. Together they were silent for a long time. Now he felt the confidence to say: 'I know you like Govind. But do you like him enough to marry him?'

'How much is that?'

'A great deal.'

'How will I know when I have reached that measure?'

'When the pain of living without him becomes unbearable. When your body, your very being, aches and a sort of mad frenzy takes hold of you and will not let go, will not leave until you are with him.'

'In such an instance I will have no choice but to be with him, but what if he does not suffer so?'

He was taken aback by the simple honesty of her question; and since it never occurred to him that such a thing could happen, that she could give her love to someone unable to respond, he was unprepared and looked at her not knowing what to say. He picked up the brandy bottle instead and offered to add a little more to her glass but she declined. As he poured himself some, he thought, if such a rare fool exists, Sastra, I shall be tempted to teach you to love me, even if I might not succeed. He said, 'In such an improbable situation, Sastra, you would have no choice but to retreat graciously – to let go bravely. It wouldn't be easy. In fact it may be the most difficult thing to do – letting go what you most wish to hold.'

She emptied the remaining fire in her glass and, gradually, as if the brandy was awakening her, said:

'It is so different from anything I have had... difficult to describe my feelings.' She was happy, no, experiencing a rare delight, an exquisite moment, just sitting quietly there with him, warmed by the brandy and surrounded by the scent of Milly's red roses in this neat, pleasant home. She wanted to say something but knew that in being cautious lay her strength and said nothing. But as the rain continued to pour outside, Sastra found herself wishing some things were different.

Their paths did not meet for some time. Then one Sunday evening, a fortnight after the travelling 'Coney Island' was erected on the village playground, she saw him standing alone, deep in thought, looking sombre. He was facing the 'chair-o-plane'. Without thinking, and so pleased to see him after that night, she crept up quietly behind him and placed the soft of her fingers over his eyes, as if it were a balm.

'Guess who?' she said in a deep guttural voice pretending to be a creature from some outer watery darkness. 'Now that you are well and truly caught, your very life depends on your guessing my name.'

He was thinking of her and to find her materialise behind him was enough to make him feel he had drunk a heady wine, for in addition to her own delicious fragrance, she was wearing a frangipani flower in her hair. He covered both her hands with his, saying, 'How many guesses am I allowed, mighty one, for I am but a mere mortal, and there are many things far beyond my reach, so I beseech thee to have patience with me.'

In her make-believe, her voice changed into a Troll's:

'Three you have, weak earthling, no more, no less, and may I remind you, were you to fail, your fate will be an unhappy one.'

'This must be one of the goddesses.'

'Ha! Ha! Ha! you are indeed a wily one, but flattery is not an art form I respect.'

'Bear with me, I am deeply grieved that I should offend thee, for that was not my intent.'

'Hold your peace for I am becoming impatient.'

'Saraswatee.'

'No. I am not Saraswatee, the goddess of Education, though I fear you are coming uncomfortably close to a deeply kept secret.'

'Oh Great and mighty one, thou must knowest how disadvantaged I stand before thee, therefore I appeal to thy kindness and mercy to give me but one clue, after which I will be resigned to my fate.'

'Today, in the interest of that perfect equilibrium necessary for this cosmos to function as it was meant, I say to you that at this favourable moment, in the span of time that hath no boundaries, I have taken the form of a mere mortal.'

'Delilah?'

'You reveal much about the inner workings of your mind, the images you hold are not of the sublime. I am greatly disappointed, but was forewarned by my people, the wisest Trolls of Ancient Croa, that the minds of men do dwell on passing shadows – the less enduring. Throughout the changing tides of time, I have seen them cling to the dust from whence they came. Alas! We the wise Trolls of ancient Croa are weary and wary of men.'

'Sastra Narayana, the most gracious of mortals.'

And they laughed together, enchanted by each other. 'You are funny,' they said together.

She did not know how it happened, but found they were holding hands walking towards the chair-o-plane.

'Have you ever been on the chair-o-plane?'

'On the merry-go-round,' she said, 'but not the chair-o-plane.'

'Would you care for a ride?'

'Are you having one?'

'Will you come too?'

She agreed and he went to get the tickets. The queue was long and while he waited, Govind Tiwari, glowing in health and smiling broadly, the scholarship boy, now a young man, continuing to fulfil the dreams of teachers and parents with ease, walked confidently towards her. He was handsome, charming, delighted to see her. On approaching he said something to her and they both laughed.

They look well together, Rabindranath thought. And suddenly, he didn't feel like having a ride on the chair-o-plane any more. Govind took out a packet of cigarettes, lit one with flair, becoming the most stylish dragon Rabindranath had observed. You have to give the fella that, he is a natural, he thought. It is clear he has her full attention. He is now offering her a cigarette. She is declining. But were I not here, would she have taken it? Govind came closer and attempted to kiss her ear, then he tried to circle her waist, wanting to lift her on to the chair-o-plane. She said something and, turning around, he smiled broadly. This fella has charm, good looks, wealth, family, everything; and he plays the part well. Govind is going to be something very special, and Sastra will help to keep him in check; he will need a firm hand. She has the beauty that he will respond to.

He bought the tickets, returned to Sastra and Govind and gave them to her. 'This is for you and Govind.'

Sastra was confused. Were the tickets not meant for them? Well, he has changed his mind, probably thinks it is silly to be swung around. Rabindranath looked at her and seeing that she accepted this change with such equanimity, not even surprise, still less disappointment, took her casual acceptance, her unruffled pleasantness to be a confirmation of what she had said: 'I am to marry Govind. There is an understanding between his parents and mine'.

And seeing them again, so closely standing there, Rabindranath had to admit that Sastra was right. How perceptive she was, they looked so well together. This shattering disappointment he was trying to accept in much the same way he had to acknowledge, year after year, that some of his nicest pupils would not gain one of the few coveted scholarships, no matter how hard he tried with them, no matter how great their need; but the nature of this disappointment was new and disabling, though he felt he had done the right thing for her on the spur of the moment, and perhaps for himself. Maybe, he mused, she has already shown me how to be rational, sensible and strong, for he also recalled her saying of those who fall in love: 'They suffer so… '

'How are you, Govind?'

'Couldn't be better, Sir.'

'Excited about what's ahead?'

'Yes, Sir.'

'You should know, I may be calling upon your services as a doctor when you return.'

'I hope, Sir, you wouldn't need to do so.

'Thank you, Govind. You'll make a very fine doctor.'

'Thank you, Sir.'

She was still holding the tickets and, seeing he was thinking of moving away, said, 'Thank you, Rabind.'

He acknowledged this with a gentle nod and turning to Govind said, 'Take care of her; and Sastra, don't look down. Eye level is best. No fooling about at that height, Govind.'

He walked away and Govind said, 'Why do you call him Rabind?'

'Milly and the staff call him Rabind; it is shorter.'

'I still call him "Sir". I must admit, I felt awkward tonight.'

After the dizzy ride and while the earth still seemed to be spinning, Govind took her to the merry-go-round and the 'Big Circle' and together they laughed and laughed.

But that night as she lay in bed she was overcome by a gentle sadness, a disappointment and could not understand why of late her moods were so varied, changing far more rapidly than the colour of light at dawn. Was this just 'a part of growing up,' as Sati said; a passing phase – a result of leaving school and entering the adult world of work and responsibilities. She didn't know what to think.

CHAPTER ELEVEN

THIS GENTLE SPIRIT

Time and time again Milly sensed he had not been himself. It started with the far longer working nights, his loss of appetite, his going to the stream more often. His father's death and the heavy responsibility of this College Exhibition work was draining him.

Each year for six years, Rabindranath had yoked himself to this cart, full of young village children, pulling uphill alone. Each year he took a fresh batch of trusting young faces to new pastures and, at the end of the school year, there were winners to congratulate, but also losers. There were always those who tried really hard but did not make it, a small number of marks standing like a bulwark between them and the best opportunities on the island. To them he could only offer the second best schools, though while he did this he would try to convince them that they still had time, that they carried within themselves something uniquely special which he was sure would flower if they cared enough, persevered enough. It was to these he was closely drawn.

All this had taken its toll. There were times when looking back at his first speech, so full of idealism and hope for everyone, he felt saddened, aware that he had raised their aspirations, had offered what their parents wished, what they too wanted for themselves, not understanding then that, were he to work like an ox, he couldn't fulfil the expectations of all. He had been so very optimistic at the beginning, as he had intimated to Sastra, but today his speeches were leaner; now he better understood the harsh realities, for the disadvantaged, of competitive exams.

The bell had just rung. It was a Friday. Lunch break. The children were rushing past him, tumbling down the stairs; Sastra had come upstairs for some chalk; had opened the cupboard, taken the chalk and was about to leave, when she and Mrs. Gopaul saw him fall.

'Collapsed?' Milly queried, as she walked back to the car with Mrs. Gopaul.

'Fainted, Milly. Sastra is with him.' Milly at once took charge, and as they were about to leave, she said: 'Would you two mind dropping in at the surgery for me, please, and make an appointment for Dr. Capildeo to visit him?'

Milly was thinking of his father and was trying to keep calm. These Pandes, she thought, are like birds. They can fall to the ground from soaring high and in a flash – gone.

'I'll wait here in the cool for you,' Mrs. Gopaul said, parking her car under a flamboyant tree. Inside the house, Sastra had to walk through two waiting rooms of patients to reach the reception desk.

Sati smiled. 'Getting the flu?'

At that moment, Dr. Capildeo came through a swinging door and said: 'Love sick; at her age nothing else can be the matter,' before disappearing out of the same door. Sati saw her sister's distress and, asking the nurse to keep an eye on things, took Sastra upstairs.

'Now tell me, what is it? Take your time.'

'Mrs. Gopaul is waiting for me in the car; I have to get back to school. Milly would like Capil to look at Rabindranath.'

115

'What happened?'

'He fell off his chair at school.'

'Fainted?'

'Yes.'

'What do you think is wrong?'

'I don't know.' Her feelings were being choked back and for the first time Sati began to wonder.

'His father died of a heart attack,' Sastra said, 'just like that.'

'Look, you see how busy Capil is. Fridays and Mondays are hard for him. I'll send him over at his lunch hour. Rabindranath is at home?'

'Yes.'

She embraced her young sister. Perhaps there was a lot of rethinking to do. Yet this could just be genuine sympathy for a friend.

'How is Sastra?' Capil asked when he next passed by the reception desk.

'Rabindranath fainted at school; she thinks the worst.'

'You mean like father like son?... What time is lunch?'

'Could you do me a special favour?'

'Tell me at lunch.'

'You should only have fruit today, Capil.'

'I think I get the picture. Is he at home?'

'Yes.'

She came up to him and kissed his forehead, 'You are wonderful.'

'The doctor is still on duty, Miss.'

'Is that what you say?'

'Not so firmly. It's an art, Mrs. Capildeo, to resist while not wishing to discourage.' He smiled broadly, 'You are not entirely unaware of it, are you?'

As he was taking his leave of Milly, Dr. Capildeo said, 'Let him sleep. He needs rest, a lot of it. His blood pressure is low, but nothing that a little care wouldn't put right. That letter should give him at least a month.'

'I appreciate your coming, Doctor.'

'It's my job,' he said.

Later that afternoon at the emergency staff meeting, no one volunteered to take the College Exhibition class. Why should they? They knew the reality of what they would be up against: a month, maybe more, of total dedication, teaching highly motivated bright children, at a crucial time. The material to be taught was exacting, demanding in its content; there was as well so little time left before the exams. And what of the responsibility – not least the inevitable comparison with the young and dedicated master by pupils and parents! Mr. Ramsaran was on leave and Mrs. Gopaul, sitting next to the headmaster, was deputising for him, and though there was none so good with seven year olds as she, what was required for these exceptional ten and eleven year olds was outside her experience.

At the meeting some said they regretted it was not their field, others that there was no time to prepare themselves, they were taken aback, bowled over by the suddenness of it all. One member pointed out that the class had difficult 'elements', though no-one knew exactly who was being referred to. Others sighed, wishing it were otherwise, showing how their plates were full – what with home commitments, family commitments – even with the very best of intentions, it was not possible. Again and again, much concern and regret were whispered all round. Then a silence ensued and members avoided the headmaster's eyes, or those of enterprising colleagues who might have been tempted to put forward names other than their own. Then, Mrs. Gopaul passed the gentlest of nods to the headmaster, who, turning to

Sastra, with a warm and encompassing smile, asked whether she would mind helping the school children and the reputation of the school. She was, after all, the only one amongst them who had taken these very exams, albeit today they were slightly different exams, though really not so different. Besides, she had been taught both by the founder of the exhibition class and by Rabindranath himself, and knew the methods.

On their way back to school from Dr. Capildeo's surgery, Mrs. Gopaul had mentioned this as a possibility. She had said, 'You will really be helping Rabindranath; he needs to have this rest, otherwise he could so easily go the way of his father. You could visit him every afternoon after school, and discuss the work on a daily basis if you wished. You are fresh from school, fresh from preparing for examinations yourself, besides... you have what it takes.'

There had been something about Mrs. Gopaul's suggestion which made the job sound challenging and indescribably exciting, but the way the headmaster had just proposed it, and after all that the staff had just said, it appeared heavy as lead, a relentless grind, a strenuous uphill climb. Why should she shackle herself to this tough task, which more experienced hands would not take?

Then she heard Mrs. Gopaul say, 'Perhaps Miss Narayan could be monitored closely by Mr. Pande; I'm sure he had more than an outline of what he intended to do. Perhaps Miss Narayan could discuss the matter with him, and follow his plan. This way, the class wouldn't be interrupted, the direction and pace would be the same – with the younger driver consulting with her more experienced colleague at the difficult junctions ahead.'

Immediately, the entire staff saw there was much merit in this plan, and wondered why they had not thought of it before. Indeed there must be close consultation with Mr. Pande; it was the most 'natural' solution; meetings on a daily basis were recommended, but of course Miss Narayan and Mr. Pande would, they were sure, work out what was best for these well-deserving pupils.

Parvatee was proud of her daughter; after all Sastra was one of the younger members of staff; this must mean that many in the school already had confidence in her; had felt she could be of help to the village children, a task no one else felt able to take.

When he was told, Narayan only listened, but after he had eaten said: 'It is an honour to be asked. But let me say from now, it is not going to be easy. It is the kind of job, if she does it well, you wouldn't hear anything, yet if it proves too much for her, all will know. Under the circumstances, I don't think a choice was open to her; we must therefore be supportive – that's the least we can do, and if she wishes to teach later, the experience will be valuable.'

When Govind heard, he said the stress would be too much, that the headmaster, like Mr. Surinder Pande before him, should have taken it on himself. 'People have a way of shirking their responsibilities. After all, who gets all the fame and the glory, when the results are out? Doesn't he?'

Sastra had discussed the staff's proposal with Milly, who said that Sunday afternoon would be a good time for her first meeting with Rabindranath. 'Child, just knowing that something is being done about his class will act like a tonic, for I am sure he must be worried out of his mind. Yes. Come, my dear, about half past four, by then he would have had a little rest.'

She prepared herself as well as she could, by checking

the exercise books of three of the pupils, also managing to obtain the exercise books of a former pupil, better to ascertain what was ahead, what was yet to be done.

As for Rabindranath, the weakness and tiredness, the pent up emotional stresses and intellectual strains were all beginning to pour out of his system. He was absorbing sleep as the parched earth would the first rains. He had let go, Milly felt, allowing himself to become dependent, almost like a child again.

She made him chicken soup with young green 'figs' and pumpkin, and fish broth served with homemade bread. She made his favourite dhalpuri and lamb in massala. She visited the early Saturday morning market to fill her basket from that oasis of plenty – mounds of green, purple and yellow, cream, white and red vegetables and fruit – so that by the time Sunday afternoon arrived, Rabindranth ought to have been feeling thoroughly refreshed, revitalised.

But when she told him in the morning of Sastra's impending visit, and having read Mrs. Gopaul's letter explaining the staff's decision, he felt turmoil inside. Nothing was making sense. He felt as if the staff were dispensing with him and his concerns for his pupils, taking away his class without even consulting him. Why hadn't he been consulted? There was something thoroughly displeasing about the ease and speed with which it was being taken from him and 'managed'. He must make it clear he was not ill. Just tired. And she had been avoiding him, deliberately avoiding him, and now she was coming here at their request. Well, I am not ill. Sympathy I do not need. Capil did not say… I am not an invalid. But his weakness was such that, angry though he was, sleep overcame him.

He was still asleep when Sastra arrived. She said she could return later, but Milly would have none of it and so she found herself comfortably seated with freshly-made lemonade in her hand. An old family rocking chair built by the late George Greenidge moved to and fro and Milly with it. From her sewing basket she picked up a circular wooden crown, its cream Moygashel linen held firmly in place. A quaint, tall side table was smiling through its polished face, a fancy crocheted piece hanging from its sides. Framed embroideries on the wall, large ixoras on the coffee table. Everything in its place. Her cat, Tom, entered and curled himself at her feet on the faded rug.

'You don't mind cats?'

'Not at all. Is he lucky for you?' Sastra laughed.

'You feel that too? I was with another Indian family, the Bharats, before my Gran told me of this job. They had three black cats. I learned if you wanted good luck to stay with you, the cats had to be black all over – not even a touch of grey or white. They also had a parrot with a yellow-orange crown. That brought good luck too. I think the more yellow it carried on its head – or was it blue – I can't remember now, the better it was.'

'You have a parrot too?'

Milly laughed out. 'Child, you are something else. Now tell me, they had a large brass elephant with its trunk raised so high it fell backwards...'

'We have one, but it is in beautiful blue-grey china. Its significance flows like this... the raised trunk... the energy, the conscious determination needed for such a feat... an uplifted trunk curled high above itself, onto itself... that upward, captured trumpet movement...'

'Yes...'

'Held above the head forever...'

'Yes...'

'Brings good luck.'

'Well,' Milly chuckled, 'fancy that. I'll need to get one.'

She got up. 'Look at it this way, I need good luck… Rabindranath is still sleeping. You know, one incident I'll never forget. The Bharats were having a puja and old Madam Bharat whispered something to Mrs. Bharat. The lady was so upset, she almost began to tremble, and the St. Vincentian girl they had in the kitchen was fired on the spot. I later heard from Sabita the cook that Christina, that was her name, had gone to the pot and eaten a good pot-spoon of that real nice deep tangerine-coloured pumpkin, before they had offered some of it to the pundit for the ceremonial fire.'

'Yes. Well, you can't eat before the gods. They should have told her.'

'It was like this. She wanted the job and Sabita needed the help, but was sick on that day, and you know she had got that job in the first place because she was Indian. She looked Indian, but Sabita told me later that she had lost all her Indianness, that she didn't keep any of her good good culture, and that was her trouble and that was the long and the short of it.'

'So after that, the Pandes must have been…'

'Heaven sent.' She rested her work and said, 'Purusha was very frail when I came to do the washing and the cleaning. I remember my first gulabjamun, that offering of a lightly-burnt brown, sapodilla-shaped, syrupy rich, moist cake. I had picked out the almond nuts and sultanas from its centre. It was a mouthful of warm delight. I can see her even now carefully removing one from its warm cardamom syrup and offering it to me. "Taste it, Milly", she said. When I asked what it was: "If you like it, I'll say". Surinder came in and said, "Milly, let all cultures be your inheritance; be like a bird not a tree. A culture is like a forest, it stands in a certain place for a certain time. Those that are bound by their culture are like trees, but why not be a bird, Milly, and dwell in all forests". It was Purusha who was going to teach me how to cook Indian dishes. When she died, he called upon Draupadi, exactly one year after the cremation.'

They sat in silence for a moment.

'That embroidery you have up there, may I have a closer look.'

'Ah, that's my aunt Jenny's painting with threads.' As she lifted it down from the wall, she heard her aunt: 'There is much more to colour, Milly dear, than you can see with an untrained eye. These neat parallel lines of blues and greens I have here, convention says will clash, collide, cannot embrace; yet look closely, the true colour, the inherent colour is inside – the depth is there'. Aunt Jenny had then taken her work to the window and said, 'See how light changes everything, it shows up what your eyes missed, dear, what you didn't know was beneath. The fine quality of the thread with the play of sunlight throws up feelings which some call tone, others warmth and shade'.

Sastra said, 'Look how the light is carrying over, spreading one colour onto another. This white has become a Forget-me-not blue because of the deep ultra-marine here … That sea gull can hardly move.'

'Yes, it has had too much of a good time for too long… These two sea-green serpentine pieces behind this warm granite are vibrant. Alive.'

'Their shadows are almost threatening the deep.'

'They want to leap out and shout at this sparkling gneiss which they don't realise is radiating more than it is receiving… We have to go now. Rabindranath is looking at his wristwatch.'

He was all in white, dressed as if waiting in the pavilion to bat.

Milly said, 'Rabind, Sastra has come to see you. Sit

down, child. Would you like another drink?'

'Nothing more for me thanks.'

'Are you sure?'

She nodded, and with that Milly left.

'How are you, Rabindranath?' she asked. It was a soothing balm, a cool hand on a fevered brow. And for a moment he pretended they were engaged, for this is how he wanted to feel. He would have preferred not to speak, just to sit there with her alone on the lawn. The yellow and white hibiscus flowers fencing the lawn bent forward to listen. She noted his hesitancy and said, 'If you would prefer me to come another time, maybe Tuesday? I would understand.'

'No I am perfectly all right. How are you?'

'Pleased to see you out here. I've brought you some laddoo.' She had meant to say, my mother sent this. But suddenly something had happened; she wanted him to know a little of how she felt and having handed him the sweets, got up and started to stroll to the edges of the lawn, the two tones on the spirally arranged leaves of the calabash tree engaging her. 'You have quite a large lawn here.'

On returning to her chair she said: 'I want you to know that I could not do this for one week, let alone four, if you were not going to control the class, direct it from here. I'll discuss what I need to do, but I have no experience and you must draw the important aspects of the work to my attention. Please make no assumptions. You must tell me everything I need to know, for I am aware that these weeks are crucial. You'll continue to teach your class from here and I'll do my best to assist you.'

He was listening, wanted her voice to continue to sing, but when she stopped, awaiting a response, he was confused.

'You are making it so easy for me.'

'Easy for myself too. The responsibility is too much, I couldn't shoulder it alone. How have you, all these years?'

The thought reminded her of his plan to leave and she decided all the more to enjoy the present.

Each day she came punctually and discussed the day's work with him. She was thorough and he was happy. Each student was discussed, and their progress and weaknesses noted. She would ask his views on the method of approach; exercises were examined, past papers studied; it was as if they were preparing themselves and not their pupils for the same examination. At times at the end of their session, in order to keep her a little longer, he would offer tea, because it took a while for the water to boil, but she would decline, preferring to leave as punctually as she had arrived.

One evening he tried to delay her departure by engaging her in a conversation, but she moved to the door, saying, 'I must leave now, Govind is coming.'

You shouldn't keep your guest waiting, he wanted to say, but dared not trust his voice, its tone, its emphasis; he wasn't sure what it would convey; for he had become... it was a gradual thing, their working together, thinking together, being together, motivated by the same feelings, climbing side by side towards the same stupendous height, along a path chosen by him.

He had passed along this way before. Only this time it was not a lonely sojourn to the cloud-covered summit, this time he had a companion. This time he had become so hopelessly in love not with the mountain and what it stood for, as his father had, but with her, and the ascent itself because of her. And so, fearing he might betray deeper emotions which even carefully selected words might not well mask, he just stood up and walked with her to the door.

She hesitated. 'Good night, Rabindranath, I'll see you tomorrow… At the same time?… Would you prefer me to come later?'

'Is it convenient to come at this time?'

'Yes. I was only thinking of you.' She stepped outside and then, 'I am embarrassed to say this, but I haven't even asked how you are.'

'You are not expected to be a doctor as well,' he smiled. 'You know how I am, you see me at work.'

'You look so much better, I hope you feel more rested.' It was her eyes that gave him hope. And leaving her warmth with him, she ran, and he lost her to the night.

As he gently closed the door, Rabindranath was overcome by an overwhelming weariness. Perhaps for his own peace of mind, his health and for his future relationship with both families – the Narayans and the Tiwaris – and to be able to keep her friendship, he would ask her to discontinue their working together. He would have to think of a good reason… Yes… Govind… they are better suited to each other. He tried harder to convince himself: one day Govind would become a doctor and a good doctor too. His pride would assist him to do the best he could. He would want to be known as a fine doctor and would be prepared to work for such a reputation. Wealth, he mused, is important; it helps to cement difficulties – it provides choice – immense choices – books, space, travel, servants, pleasurable surroundings. Look at Capil's grand residence!

She always left promptly, but tonight had stayed a while. Professional all the time! Why did she have to be so? … Yet he knew that her very manner protected them both. He should be the same, should be as professional.

126

Yet on more than one occasion that evening he had been tempted to say something about the stream, he didn't know what exactly. How would she have responded? He wasn't sure. And so in his thoughts, her imagined responses varied a little and then too widely, for he had created a strange unpredictable Sastra of fantasy.

The cost of being as formal as she was towards him was more than Sastra had anticipated. She had cloaked herself with the pressing problems of her students, and their welfare was her saving grace, though she did not know the extent to which this was true. Occasionally, her emotions would rise above the rim of reason and overflow, like on that day she had with such daring (it had taken so much out of her just thinking it through) stopped by on her way to the stream to take Milly flowers; she had hoped he would be at home, and would see her intent – had approached his house with so much throbbing excitement; and when the realisation came that he was not there, the stream had lost its lyrical enchantment, all its delight suspended.

She stopped running and simply hastened her steps. That delay over parting might result in a warning, a scolding. She knew her mother kept her eyes on the clock. Didn't he know the only reason her parents allowed her to go there was because Milly was there; and because she came and went as clockwork, carrying herself as a school teacher should?

Govind was, as ever, well dressed. He remembered the small niceties – gifts of favourite things – Julie mango for her mother; *pehnoose* and *gulab jamun* from his mother to her. He was a natural winner, winner of school prizes and parents! They loved him. Tall as a sweet cedar, open to the sunshine, and yes, she must be fair, he was lovable: attractively handsome – those laughing eyes with that innocent disarming smile. So gentlemanly dressed, a sort of natural engaging formality. Everything he wore looked well. He was the best of springtime – that film she saw 'Springtime in Canada': Blossoms and freshness and colour. Yes, she liked him. Of course she liked him. His parents and her parents approved of them both.

She said, 'Come, let's sit outside on the porch; it's cooler,' and offered him chilled soursop juice topped with ice cubes, the colour of Angostura bitters. She was enjoying his company, learning to appreciate him, understanding better the need to prepare herself mentally for the future.

'Hope that schoolmaster's plan is not wearing you out,' he smiled warmly at her. 'You are working too hard, much too hard. Ma is having the puja in the morning and she wants you at least to come over, and have lunch with us. Sati and Capil are coming too.'

'Of course I will come. Your Ma spoils me too often.'

'Not at all. She thinks not often enough and I agree.' He spoke rapidly, trying to sound matter of fact: 'I would visit more often, but I know you have a lot to do, and the very last thing I would want is that you should look at my coming with anxiety. Ma didn't like you taking on so much this early. It's the responsibility you have to carry that frightened her, having to concentrate on school work out of school, not being able to turn your mind to other things – constantly on the one thing. She thinks it may even be harmful for a young lady.'

Sastra laughed: 'It's not that bad.'

'You know her views: "If Sastra doesn't live up to the expectations of those parents, you will never hear the end of it; and every year parents are expecting more and more – an ungrateful job".'

They laughed.

128

'Pa feels the same. Will Dr. Lall be there?'

'He is away in Canada, getting the feel of Toronto, may even be thinking of living there.'

'I would miss him if he leaves for good.'

'The hospital would too. Capil says he is really the best.' Govind paused. He got up and walked about, looking around. 'You have a very good view from here. I see you can tell whether Rabindranath is burning the midnight oil or not. How is he?'

'Far more tired than he thinks. He should have given up earlier, let someone take over two years ago at least.'

'How long has he been at it?'

'Six years.'

'Crazy fellow. Should have read the signs… seen it coming.'

She let it pass. Caring fellow, you mean, she wanted to say, but could not. She would have been embarrassed to be seen defending him, especially in the presence of Govind. What was happening to her judgment? She felt awkward, confused. Unsure.

'Capil is seeing him.'

'I hope it's rest he needs. I noticed the way Dr. Lall was looking at him.'

Govind didn't stay long and she was unhappy when he left; she wished she had welcomed him with a greater warmth, a greater openness, had encouraged him to stay for a while by expressing her interest in him, especially as he was so considerate; she also wished she had said something, just something, in acknowledgement of Rabindranath's dedication to the village children. She could feel a terrible headache coming on.

CHAPTER TWELVE

NARAYAN AND PARVATEE

'That young man, Rabindranath, has improved a great deal; frankly I was surprised at how well he looked.'

Sati said nothing to Capil's observation, for what was there to say.

'He is in love with your sister.'

'I am sure he is not the only one.'

'He has it badly. I enquired about his health and all he did was talk enthusiastically about Sastra and their College Exhibition class.'

'His work is uppermost in his mind. It is just like you, Capil, to hear sonnets when you're taking a pulse!'

★ ★ ★ ★ ★ ★

Her parents were out on the front porch, just sitting quietly, not speaking. Forty years of marriage had woven their thoughts. Theirs was a comfortable old fashioned marriage, blessed with good health and more than ample means and a most satisfactory companionship.

Sati was hoping they would say, 'Sastra isn't here,' and give her the opportunity to raise the topic. But neither spoke of her, so she said: 'I see Sastra is helping the College Exhibition class.'

'They asked her,' Parvatee said.

'She had no choice,' Narayan said; 'it entails a lot of work and I have yet to see people put themselves forward for more work, more worries, increased responsibility with no additional pay. Who will do that today? The question is, was it right to ask her?'

'Sastra was asked by the headmaster to help out the school,' Parvatee explained.

'Ramsaran is away, you see,' Narayan said. 'Normally, he would have had the class.'

'I hear he is getting married,' Sati said.

'He got married already,' her mother said. 'It was a small thing. The girl's parents did not agree.'

'Why, Ma?'

'You know, he walks with that limp.'

'One of his legs is shorter than the other,' Narayan said. 'The girl's father and mother were only trying to carry out their duty as parents – simply pointing out the pitfalls to their daughter and trying to help her to negotiate a new route. But today children think they have more sense than their parents.'

'Is Sastra coping with all that extra work, Ma?'

'She is working very hard. When she comes from school, she has her shower and dinner and then settles back to work; later she discusses the following day's work with Rabindranath.'

'I don't want to say anything,' Narayan said gravely, 'but your mother goes along with whatever Sastra says. I am not happy with this arrangement. I ask myself what is there to discuss every evening? Every evening? I can understand two evenings a week for the most; but every evening seems to me something else.' He paused, reflecting on what he had just said, but, not wishing that his older daughter should think any less of her younger sister, and not wanting to sow the seed of suspicion, he

131

added, 'Of course I am in no position to dictate; I don't know all that is involved. Maybe the best way to look at it is to remember she has only, what? Another two and a half weeks?'

'There is nothing to worry about. What is there to worry about?' Parvatee asked. 'It is Rabindranath's class; he helps her with the correction and preparation… That is what Sastra told me when I asked her.'

'Nothing is that simple. She is a young girl; he is much older – was once her teacher.'

'Just for one year, and that was some time ago. Listen to how you're speaking. Rabindranath is not a vicious old man.'

'I didn't say that… He is not well… Sastra will feel sorry for him; that alone makes her vulnerable. Look how she behaved towards that hopeless case, that stray puppy. Common sense alone should have dictated…'

'My God, she was a child then. You will always find something, something to say, no matter what the situation.'

'You can say whatever you like, I am looking at it as any father should: our daughter is a young girl, inexperienced; fresh from school. She has everything to lose. I shouldn't need to say this: we live in a Hindu community. We are brahmins, what example are we setting? How does it look, her going there every evening. Every evening. What is the village saying?'

Neither woman said anything.

'It doesn't look good. That is the long and short of it.'

'Milly is there. Everybody knows that, Pa. Besides, Sastra is a teacher; she is there because of a special request from the headmaster. The children know Rabindranath marks some of their exercises; Sastra tells them; they know she is helping them. They know she is working hand-in-hand with their teacher; it helps her with the discipline of the class, and it helps her to complete the large amount of work on time. There is nothing secretive.'

'And I'll say this,' Parvatee joined in, 'she goes on time and comes back on time. I am telling you there is nothing to worry about. You worry all the time.'

'The Pandes are a good family, Pa. You remember Rabindranath's father, Surinder. You couldn't have found a finer man, a gentleman through and through; and you know when his wife died, he brought up his son alone. They were very close – father and son. Good qualities rub off from parents to children.'

Narayan listened, but mother and daughter knew that what they were saying he considered naive and irrelevant. Nevertheless Sati continued: 'Of course, people will talk; what can you do? That is the world. But there is nothing underhand in what she is doing; she walks there with the approval of parents and pupils, remember that.'

'Let me come straight to the point,' Narayan said. 'Do we know how the Tiwaris are thinking? What does Govind think? Have they said anything to Capil?'

'I don't think they mind, Pa. They understand the situation. Shakuntala knows the importance of the College Exhibitions to the community. They know Rabindranath and his father and they know Sastra.'

'You have to learn to trust your children,' Parvatee said.

'Well, soon it will end; and after that, there will be no more going over there. If Rabindranath wishes to see her about anything at all, let him come here. I hope I am making myself clear; I don't want to have to say this again.' And with that, Narayan stood up, stretched himself as a tiger would, and left.

When the outer gate creaked, Parvatee whispered, 'Is he suffering from an illness that could spread to Sastra? How very sick is he?'

'Ma, he is very very tired from overwork and stress. He is just run down.'

'Good. That's what Sastra said too, but a mother can't be too careful. He is going abroad to England, London, na? And Sastra is going to Ireland; they won't be seeing each other. I don't like saying this, before you, but sometimes I believe your father is suspicious of God even.'

Sati smiled, remembering Capil had said something similar after his first meeting with her father. Seeing her mother's discomfort, she said: 'Ma, you know Pa likes Sastra a lot. She resembles him so much. He is just being overprotective, that's all… When he looks at her, he sees his younger self.'

Parvatee wanted to ask: Do you think there is anything between Sastra and Rabindranath? But she held back. I am fast becoming like Narayan, she thought. I, too, am worrying needlessly. Soon they will be as far apart as ever and Govind is such a nice boy.

CHAPTER THIRTEEN

AT THE MARKET

The following morning Sastra met her sister at the market, a place of turbulent waves of ripened smells and sounds and scents of life and death; of the cries of those brought to the slaughter; of buyers and sellers weaving amongst mounds of vegetables and fruits.

Sastra's attention was caught by a half barrel of crabs. Their legs were effectively bound with blades of grass, but one crab, unlike the others at the bottom, kept trying to crawl out. Whenever it approached the rim, the vendor would, without ceremony, hurl it back into the crawling darkness beneath. The steep angle of the tub made the long journey to the rim hazardous. The crab would lift its eyes like antennae, and slip and slide the tight blades of grass making movement near impossible. Yet, again and again, it would attempt the painful, near impossible feat.

'Thinking of having crab and callalou?' Sati asked.

'The luncheon – nothing serious is it?'

'Serious?'

'Yes.'

'You mean like an engagement ceremony?'

'Yes.'

'Oh no. Just a family lunch that's all. Besides if it were, they would tell you. The Tiwaris wouldn't pull you into their fold, Sastra. You join them willingly or not at all. Govind's mother and grandmother are like that. What's the matter?'

'I'm so confused.'

'Are you all right?'

'So much has happened without my knowing, without my wishing anything.'

'You look tense and tired.'

'Really?'

'It's that examination form isn't it? Try and give it up as soon as you can. It's taking far too much already out of you. I hardly see you. I dropped in twice. And each time Ma said you were at Rabindranath.'

'You too? I have to go. Don't you see I have to go. I can't manage the class on my own; it is a difficult specialised syllabus. And it is for such a short time. I would prefer not to go. Don't you understand? What can I do?'

'Oh *that* I understand.'

'Nobody, nobody understands what's really involved.' And Sastra embraced her sister, wishing to bury her eyes and face and throat. Both sisters absorbed each other and Sati was surprised at the amount of tension her sister had bottled up within her. Sastra, hurt by the tone of Sati's voice, found her trembling lips had lost touch with her voice.

'I do believe you Sastra,' Sati said, trying to comfort. A choking anguish came out in gushes.

'You need a rest from school and exams. You had your own to cope with only recently, and now this, so soon after. Come after the puja, come and eat with us, if you can't manage the ceremony. Ayisha and Arjun haven't seen you for a long time.'

'How are they?'

'Growing too fast... Fighting and making up, what else is there for them to do?...You are too conscientious. I don't think I could have taken it on. But I hear the parents are saying you are doing a good job; it must mean the children think so.'

'It's not me. Rabindranath is really guiding...'

'Nonsense. Now, Sastra, don't give him all the credit. Be fair to yourself. Capil went to see him.'

'What is really wrong with him?'

'Rabindranath just needs rest, Capil says. His pressure is back to normal. He looks much better but he should stay away for another month at least. I think he should have a thorough check up with a specialist before he leaves.'

CHAPTER FOURTEEN

A PUJA

It was the beginning of the day of Govind's puja – half past four in the morning. Old Madam Tiwari couldn't sleep; it would not be long now, she thought, before he leaves us. She was convinced she would not live to see his return; this made the Puja especially important. Last year she and Shakuntala held a Satnarine Katha for him. That had been her idea too. It was now a good time to have the puja; she had checked with the pundit.

She pushed the door; it sighed. The parrot opened one eye, saw her and closed it again. The cat did the same. Slowly she entered the yard crowded with shadows. She looked in the direction of the siwala. Were it midday, its beautifully whitewashed outer walls and glittering, brass-coloured dome would have flashed and flared, but darkness veiled everything into an indecipherable dark grey.

With her hair still damp, the old lady unlatched the siwala's door. It opened and revealed the decorated stone images of gods and goddesses brought from India. They looked frozen, lifeless without allure; the siwala cold and dark.

But when she lit the camphor in her brass tharia, it offered incense instantly, its flame made the faces beam, and as its strength increased, the rhythm of its dance

leaping outwards, the gods, becoming warm, smiled
unguardedly; then warmer and resplendent.

Later that morning, Dr. Capildeo's car swung into
the Tiwari's yard. His two children like cooped hens
could hardly wait to get out; they jostled at the door, and
as soon as Capildeo pulled up the hand brake, tumbled
out. Ayisha and Arjun ran towards their ajee; then Arjun
stood still. It was all over in no time – a relief and an
embarrassment in one. Ayisha looked back with fury,
'Arjun! Look at that! Look at your shoes and socks! And
in the yard! Stupid! Mummy! look at Arjun! Here
Mummy, look here!'

Arjun started to cry. Old Madam Tiwari hugged
Ayisha who was always first, and then, lifting herself
with difficulty from a peerha, moved towards Arjun.
She picked him up and kissed his wet sweet cheeks.
'Never mind,' she said, 'this is nothing. You wanted to
go in the car, na? Well what a brave boy – you waited too
long, na?' Arjun nodded in quiet agreement. She kissed
him again. Ayisha said, 'Govind's ajee, put him down; he
will dirty your clothes.'

'That is nothing; there is soap and water, Ayisha.'

'Mummy look at this!'

Sati and Capildeo came and hugged the old lady and
asked for everybody. Arjun and Sati went upstairs and
after he was cleaned and dried and changed, regained his
confidence to run down the stairs and look for Govind.
Everyone was now in the large dining-kitchen room.

Capildeo asked, 'When is the pundit due?'

'In an hour's time,' Govind said.

'Have you prepared yourself mentally for this?'

'I hope so,' Govind replied, unsure of what was
meant.

'Mai spoke to him, I spoke to him,' Shakuntala said, 'and now it's your turn, Capil; you take him in the garden and have a little talk with him too.'

'Not too long now,' Sati warned.

'I bathe already Ma. I only have to dress. And Capil will help me with the dhoti.'

'You have to learn to tie your own dhoti, man,' Capildeo said, smiling mischievously. 'These are some of the skills a good brahmin should have.'

'Ajee, you know what Arjun did?' Ayisha quietly asked.

'Shhhhhhhhh!' Sati said.

Arjun walked as a man driven and pushed Ayisha; she shoved him back so forcefully that he fell headlong.

'Ayisha, that is not nice. Say you are sorry,' Sati said.

'No! He pushed me first.'

'Say you are sorry, Ayisha.'

'You always take up for him; nobody likes me.'

'You should know better, Ayisha.'

'You are older.'

'I don't want to be older.'

'Yes you do,' said Arjun feeling stronger now, and wiping away remnants of drying tears.

'You invited many people, Ma?'

'No it is just a small family thing, for Govind. Sastra is coming, Dr. Lall is away and Rabindranath is still not well. Only the neighbours and a few people from the village; one or two others, not many people... They will come, when they can make it. I told a lot of the old people, and I asked Narayan to tell all the beggars by the shop to come. They will come. Not altogether; but one, one, they will come.'

'That's the best thing,' Sati said.

'People have a lot to do. Some are working far away, they have to come from work, look after the house, the children; you have to make allowances. I told them if they can make it, I will be too glad, but if they can't, well, what to do.'

'Who is sitting with Govind?'

'Only he. Mai says it is better that way. Just he and the Pundit.'

'Mai,' Sati called out, 'this idea is good. When Govind gets to London, he must have something holding him to his culture; to his family too, otherwise they all become English men and we lose them.'

CHAPTER FIFTEEN

THE SANTOOR AND THE FLUTE

The luncheon was an exciting feast: kalownjee slowly done in massala, silky soft dhalpuris that bathed you in a warmth of jeera and dhal and pepper when, with the help of your fingers, the enclosed warm air bursts out. Baigan chokha – melongene stuffed with garlic and pepper and onions and grilled; delicious shataigne curried lightly and gently, with firm, sweet-smelling garden tomatoes. Dhal chaunkayed with jeera, garlic, onions, sweet and hot peppers; spinach steam-fried in a little butter with garden peas; followed by gulab jamun in warm cardamom syrup, and rasmela sprinkled with roasted pistachio nuts.

It was the time spent in the preparation, the caring, the affection displayed by everyone that deeply moved and disturbed Sastra for she could not help thinking that there was a deeper meaning to this feasting, as she was seated next to Govind.

Often in the Tiwari house there were times like this – when incense and sweet milk mingled with cardamom and warm ghee and the uplifting tulsi fragrance and the house seemed afloat with human warmth, companionship, and friendly chatter.

From next door the passing breeze brought the music of the santoor, and the flute. It was a sad, stirring harmony of sounds and made her want to leave this abundance, with its comforting goodwill and expectations, to be alone with nature's stillness, its delicate rhythms on faraway hillsides and distant shores.

After lunch Govind walked with her along the path to his ajee's well-kept flower garden. The old lady had already retreated, as was her custom at this time of day, and was sitting where earlier she had greeted the sunrise. Now, partially hidden in the shade, it was shelter and solitude she sought. All around her the sunset-coloured cacao leaves, enflamed by the overhead sun, made her look like some ancient goddess of the forest.

Throughout lunch, Sastra's reticence had puzzled her; once more from where she sat, the old lady observed her, smiling with lips, mouth and cheeks, while her walk, her eyes, were of a spirit troubled. Some pain, some anguish abides with her, the old lady thought, but tried to dismiss what she saw. I am an old woman, my eyes are growing dim, maybe this is why today I see everything overcast; this outlook comes to me from a dark feeling visiting me and staying too often. It is my age. My time is near.

He brought her to a circular bed of fragrance and asked which sweet scent she preferred and while Sastra inhaled the perfumes of the shrubs, he moved around her saying, 'Are you looking forward to returning to your former class?'

'Yes. I would be more at ease.'

'Is Rabindranath better then?' The question sounded unnatural, she didn't know why.

He waited.

'He should have more rest but as all will benefit when he returns, he will he back at school soon. His class will greatly benefit.'

'I will be going to San Fernando to spend some time with my kakah and meet all my cousins; when I return, I'll be getting ready to leave.'

'Are you looking forward to becoming a doctor?'

'Yes. And I'm pleased about that, because you know how these things happen; your mother and ajee and father and uncles, and after a time the neighbours too, tell you that you'll grow up to be a good doctor. And if you think about it, besides doctors and teachers and lawyers, our family doesn't really meet anyone from other professions. So it is a great relief if your deep gut feelings correspond with your parents' expectations and ambitions. Problems arise, of course, when they don't.'

He stopped moving about and, from the shrub she chose, picked a deep crimson rose, its petals not fully displayed.

'This is for you, Sastra,' and he held her hand in both of his. 'You are very beautiful, Sastra. Perhaps I should have said this earlier; I believe it may be too late for me. I know I treated you in much the same sort of way I accepted the idea of becoming a doctor. Initially my mother and my ajee wished it; and then I did. I felt that you would always be there, in the same way I am still here. Now I know that thinking in this way was wrong. If by some good fortune, however, I'm not too late, you must let me know.' He hesitated, not sure how to continue, and then decided to keep to what he really wished to say. 'Were we to become engaged before I leave, I would encourage you to come to London in the summer; it would be great to be together this summer. I'm hoping you would agree, but I want you to know that if later you wish to break the engagement, you will not be held against your will.'

He had spoken gently, hesitantly, seeking refuge in a

formal style; and for the first time she saw a side of him she had not realised was there, and wondered how it was she had not known him better. He had come every week to visit her, had come punctually, on the same days, at the same time, showing in his own way a concern, a respect for her time, never overstaying. She, too, had taken him for granted, had behaved as if he would always be there.

The music, the roses, the feast, the warmth, the friendship of this family and now this: it was easy to imagine that the gods had blessed this day, that fate had arranged this meeting, this prelude to their engagement. Seeing the swing which was erected for Ayisha and Arjun, they approached it hand in hand. He tried to persuade her to sit down; she was hesitant, did not wish to, but, lifting her gently, Govind placed her on the swing.

'Now,' he said, and pushed the swing higher and higher and they were both brought a little closer, relaxing more with each other, enjoying the motion. It was nice being with him. They laughed. They were happy.

After a while, she said, 'We must go now,' but unheeding he began to push her higher still and higher. She rose well above the reddish-orange frangipani, and the poinsettia bushes, enjoying the thrill of being aloft. 'It's wonderful,' she cried, stimulated by the wind on her face and the sparkling, glittering sunbeams bouncing off galvanised roofs, piercing lush Rose mango trees. Then she closed her eyes better to enjoy the movement and tenderly, like a soft breeze, a memory from her night at Rabindranath's encircled the swing and captured her. So when the swing slowed to a standstill, Govind felt that something had happened, not the exhilaration he had wished, something else; something had taken her, he knew not what; and they strolled along in silence, leaving behind the rose so warmly accepted a moment ago.

The path led from the roses to the vegetables, and there they saw the old lady, catching the shadows around her. Sastra remembered: 'The rose, it's near the swing.'

'I'll get it.'

'Come sit here,' Govind's ajee said, and the two were lost in their own thoughts under the arch of vines. When Govind brought the rose, his ajee said, 'Let her sit with me a little.'

He was disappointed, unhappy, but such were his genuine good manners that he left graciously and his ajee felt for him.

Old Madam Tiwari looked at Sastra and knew she was responsible for this young girl's dilemma. She saw her own self at the same age, in another time, another place. She decided she must act.

Once she had said to Shakuntala, many years ago, that Govind and Sastra would make a good match, and so they would, she had reasoned then. Look at Sastra's sister Sati, a good Hindu wife, then a good mother and a modern mother, after all. Look at that family, everything going for girls from such a Hindu upbringing – respectable behaviour, good education, knowing how to behave to suit every occasion. These were girls who would put their family's wishes before themselves; their parents and husband and children would always come first, for if a family was to prosper, 'you cannot have two drivers on a train'. Her own mother had said this to her when, just once, she had wanted to please herself.

'This is Demerara gold, na?' the old lady asked as she held Sastra's hands, examining the fine filigree work of her bracelet.

'Ma will know.'

She is so quiet, thought old Madam Tiwari; it is as I suspect.

'You have nice hands. You are doing a big job I hear.'

Yes I am right, any thought that calls him forth disturbs her.

'I am only helping.'

'How is Rabindranath, feeling plenty better now, na?'

'Yes.'

'I knew his grandfather, Gajraj Pande.'

'Did you?' Oh look how she has brightened, she is so interested. Now I believe.

Capil offered to drive her home, for the sun was still too hot, but Sastra wanted to walk, and Govind would walk with her. Umbrellas were offered and two dwarfed circular shadows moved out of the yard.

'Sastra was very quiet,' Shakuntala said, 'usually she makes us all laugh, goes to chat with the girls in the kitchen.'

'Taking on such a scholarship class may be a real strain for her,' Capil said.

'She shouldn't have been asked in the first place,' Shakuntala said.

'Rabindranath is far from fit, but he will be turning out in about two weeks time,' Capildeo explained. 'I advised him against it.'

'Like father like son, Rabindranath is dedicated,' Sati said.

'I was thinking, Mowsee,' Capil said, 'it might be a good idea to postpone Govind's engagement until he returns. The medical course is so long… he could easily meet a nice brahmin medical student…'

'What is this I am hearing? You joking? I want no

other daughter-in-law. For years I have said this, everybody knows this. So Capil, I don't want to listen to any supposing this, supposing that. Besides, if he is engaged now, he will feel committed, Sastra will feel committed. I will expect them to write each other weekly... they will exchange photographs every year. I have given plenty thought to this.'

Capildeo knew it was he and not Sati who had to say these things to his aunt. 'You see, Mowsee, the time is too long. People can change their minds after one year, never mind five, six years. Out of sight can be out of mind.'

'Are you listening? Did you hear what I said?'

'Yes Mowsee... but...'

'You are speaking as if you are not listening.'

Sati brought ice cold water and offered everyone. After they had all drunk, Shakuntala said: 'I met Govind's father only once, once mind you, and that was enough for both of us... Out of sight...'

'Mowsee, times are changing. You did what was expected of you,' Capil said. 'You were a well brought up Hindu girl...'

'And so too is Sastra; and Govind is like her. Look at our families; we keep to our traditional values and ways. I didn't believe I would hear something like this from you. Think. Think carefully. What are you saying to me? Parvatee and I have an agreement, we will honour it.'

The old lady heard what Capil was trying to say and reflected that Shakuntala could not hear and see what she had not thought about, what she did not believe could happen – not only that someone might take Sastra away from her dreams and plans, but that Sastra might wish it. Old Madam Tiwari was in no hurry to enter the circle of controversy which threatened and grieved her.

Age is seldom in a hurry when it knows there is time.

It had been from that day of the Satnarine Katha, when Dr. Lall was there, that Govind's ajee had felt there was a bond between Rabindranath and Sastra. Sati had left them to attend to the men upstairs.

Both were happy, oh so happy, to be alone, and the scene returned. There was tenderness and affection between them; that fragile, delicate play of head and eyes and shoulders; that dance of laughter and smiles, their hesitancy and meaningful silences – an unspoken tenderness in their loving of each other. Sastra in the way she offered him sweets; he having more only because she was offering. Sastra would understand his dilemma and though she had already offered more, would stay his hand as he attempted to lift his spoon. 'Don't have more. Come, I will show you the garden before we join the others.'

But he had not trusted himself to be alone with her in a garden of flowers. The house had been filled with incense then; maybe he was affected by its sacred scents, by everything.

With Govind, the old lady pondered, it was like being with childhood friends, good neighbours of long standing – a warmth, a friendliness were there; but that delicate play, the caress of eyes and hands, that gentle courting, its unspoken tenderness were absent. She, too, was young once and the beautiful serenade she witnessed on that day of the Katha had reminded her of her own adolescence and Gajraj Pande. It alarmed her that her memory of him still had so much life and light, withstanding time and defying death.

But first she must have a quiet word with Sati, and the opportunity came. Capil, with newspapers in hand, went upstairs and Shakuntala was having her mid-afternoon shower.

'Tell me,' the old lady said; 'it is Rabindranath, na?'

Sati was relieved; thank God, someone else besides Capil had come to realise, had seen the changed situation. It was the very gentleness of the enquiry that gladdened her; the tone of voice carried no animosity, no grudging disappointment, no reproach; it was a combination of a confirmation and acceptance.

'Yes. How did you know?'

'Both of them were telling us when they were last here at the Katha. But we were not listening, we were looking another way. I was thinking of the Katha and of the meaning it should have for Govind. It was his day. All eyes were on him. I was so busy with getting this ready, that ready, in time for the pundit, that I couldn't see clearly what was right in front of me.'

'I too... when I recall my conversation with him... In fact it was Capil who realised we were all on the wrong track. My Ma, too, had her suspicions, but she was in a difficult position.'

'The Pandes are an unusual family. I didn't know his great grandfather Ganesh well, but my father did.'

'True? How come?'

'I knew his grandfather Gajraj; there was something special about him. A good man. My family was better off than his. He married Kumari Ramlakhan but she died young and he didn't want to bring up Surinder without a mother. After that I met him once or twice. He first asked me, he was modern in that way; and then he approached my father, but Govind's grandfather was from people of means, of high standing, and already you see there was a certain understanding between our two families. So my father did not agree; I can understand that. How could he? It was my mother who told me that Gajraj had asked for me, my father didn't. I think she wanted me to be on my guard just in case I met him alone. Once or twice before my wedding I did meet him by chance in the market. But he was always very polite and upright. After I got married he avoided me.' Madam Tiwari was wiping her eyes. And it was Gajraj's eyes which after all these years still haunted her. They were clear, alive, undaunted, saying to her what his voice could not. 'I got married to a good man. Both pundits agreed – our pundit and the Tiwari's pundit – that the marriage would be a prosperous one. I was happy in my marriage,' she said, 'and look, today Tiwari's grandson is going to be a doctor, only he is not here to see this.'

That night as Sati was putting Arjun and Ayisha in bed, she thought of Govind's ajee. Here was this old lady trying to prevent Sastra from having a marriage she thought might be without passion. It was clear that after all these years she kept a place in the deep recesses of her being for someone who had asked for her, who loved her and whom she, in her own quiet way after all these years, still cherished. And Sati saw her own mother and all those upright conservative Hindu mothers and grand-mothers for the first time, as having once been young and vulnerable and not unacquainted with passion, despite the many veils of tradition and the passing of time.

CHAPTER SIXTEEN

PAINFUL PATHS

In the cool, quiet of the evening, after the sun dips below the horizon, leaving a warm glow in the sky, when chulha smoke curls and drifts from spacious yards, at this hour, old Madam Tiwari prepared herself to tread a painful path.

She left the siwala and took the cup of milk Shakuntala had warmed for her; at this hour it was all she had. She drank, washed the cup, turned it over to drain. Both women sat in silence until darkness fell. Shakuntala rose and lit the diyas before the framed painting of Krishna and Radhika and said her evening prayer, then she lit the kitchen lantern.

'It was a busy day for you,' the old lady said; 'everything went so well. You worked very hard.' Shakuntala said nothing, she was not expecting such words from her mother-in-law; it was simply her duty, a mother's duty, to do all that she had done for Govind. These compliments sounded foreign, outside her way of thinking and she became a little wary.

'Where is Govind?'

'Look, Mai – the light in his room; he must be reading.'

It began to grow cooler and darker outside. Seeing her mother-in-law fold her arms, Shakuntala fetched a shawl and placed it over her shoulders.

'That is good,' the old lady said, as a gust of wind blew past, attempting to put out the old lantern.

'It is a dark night, Mai.'

'Yes. It might rain tomorrow; the clouds building up again.'

'Govind and Sastra look so well together. I think Sastra is even more beautiful than her sister.'

'Govind and Sastra are beautiful children.'

'Mai, my mind would be at peace if they were engaged. A good Hindu engagement, that would be best. It is the right thing for Govind; it is what his father would have wanted. I know you feel so too, Mai. You heard how Capil speaks? The young generation doesn't understand. Without your support, without Parvatee's support where would I be now? The young only understand what they can put in a glass and measure.'

The old lady inhaled deeply and held her head in both hands as if she was about to remove it. A long silence ensued but at last she said softly: 'Shakuntala, my daughter, you and I, but more so I, must from now be careful about planning things. We have to be watching what is moving about us; I more than you. Try and remember it was I who brought Capildeo's attention to Sati; and as you know I have always been happy with the thought of Govind and Sastra together. Then it looked to me as such a good match – a natural thing, a beautiful thing. I told you so many times. Many, many times I said so. I am trying to remember when was the first time. Shakuntala, it was I who encouraged you with this idea of engagement.' The old lady bowed her head low.

'Is something wrong, Mai? Has Govind, has Sastra said anything?'

'Sometimes, Shakuntala, what appears good… natural even, to parents, to me, to you, to Parvatee and

Narayan, may only be half so. Time has passed, a lot has happened since I first spoke about my grandson's marriage. Sastra would be happier with Rabindranath: that I can see now. She hasn't said so, to me or Sati or Parvatee. When I got married... Do you remember when you got married, no one consulted us about anything; no one asked if we had preferences; in those days we just obeyed quietly. It never came to us to direct our own lives, to do something different from our parents' wishes. We were obedient daughters; later, obedient daughters-in-law and good wives; we tried to be even better mothers than our own. At each stage of our lives we obeyed, we listened to everyone; our own feelings did not matter, so we put them away so far from ourselves that we lost them. Those were our times, Shakuntala, those were very different times.'

The silence Shakuntala heard came from a world that never knew sound. She saw the darkness before her; everything had disappeared and she, left stranded on a planet with no revolving suns, a planet of no light; a hissing sea raging high; she stands alone and cold on the back of something slippery that has begun to move. All around a vacuous blackness; only the sound of water rising, encroaching upon her waist, lap-lapping; nothing to hold. Nothing. A cold darkness rising

'Shakuntala, for me, too, this is not easy. Imagine my state of mind, when I began to see this change. Doubts and more doubts started to grow painfully inside me. At first I was not sure, I did not want to be sure; then I did not want it to be as I suspected, and when you don't want something, Shakuntala, and it knocks at your door, you sit still, waiting for it to leave.'

'Mai, tell me, I must know. Did Sastra say anything?'

'Neither Sastra nor Sati. Not Parvatee. No one.'

154

'It is the first time I am hearing this... this way of thinking... what kind of thinking is this? It doesn't sound like you, Mai. How come you know all this? Why now? How many nights and long evenings, Mai, you and I sat right here and talked about how suitable Govind and Sastra were for each other? How many nights we chatted about the two families until late into the first crowing? It was so comforting to me, so satisfying to know that such an important thing in our lives, valuable to you, to me, would turn out well. We talked about this wedding, this marriage for days on end... and all that I am still hearing inside me. But now, Mai, now... this new sound you are making, listen to what you are saying, it doesn't make sense.' She wiped her tears for she was truly shattered. The earth on which she stood was moving.

A long hell, a quivering silence, a smothering of anguish; the outer darkness was leaving the ground outside the yard to swallow her.

'Mai, you must tell me. Did Parvatee say something?'

'Nobody. Only I. You must believe me, Shakuntala.'

'Well, then, how can you tell all this from here?'

'Look at Sastra today. Afraid and sad. She reminds me of myself. She likes you and me, she respects all of us, she wants to please us. She will marry Govind tomorrow if we pull her in that direction; yet in her own way, in the only way she knows how, she is trying to tell us she is not happy.'

Happiness? What is that? Shakuntala trembled. What if Sastra is unhappy to start with? What is this unhappiness... this happiness people talk about! What is the difference? If you are lucky there is only quiet satisfaction, I should know. I have lived. I want the engagement. Now! Yes I will pull her in this direction. Mai says

155

Sastra will marry Govind if we pull her, yet she wouldn't pull her, Capil wouldn't either; yet they must know it is the right thing for Govind to marry Sastra. It is difficult now because Sastra is young, her emotions strong! She doesn't know how to handle herself. Some learn this art only when they are ruined. Ruined. When it is too late. We should be trying to help her, not allowing her to drift, to be lifted by a high swell and then dropped in a cold, inhospitable place. She has been seeing him every day... I should have seen this coming... But these kinds of feelings are like the mountain wind and rain, coming in sudden bursts from any direction. Some are stronger, like thunder storms flooding the land in a flash, drowning people and cattle and crops, leaving behind grief and loss and dried mud everywhere... But even you, Mai, can't see everything. It could just be something that blows over.

Shakuntala began to breathe slowly to allow a rapidly rising rage within her to lose its oxygen. Much time passed, for much time was needed to smother its smouldering, volcanic core.

'I worked up Govind about this engagement, Mai. After saying over and over how important it was, after saying for so long what a fine girl Sastra is, after comparing her with everyone else and finding she is the pick of the crop, what happens now? How can I face him? What to say now?'

'Govind is your child, he is my grandchild. He was born in this house. He was brought up here by you and by me. You taught him the alphabet; I showed him how to grow things. He knows us maybe even better than we know ourselves. He is a sensible boy, intelligent like his father and grandfather. Don't you think he too must have sensed something? Leave it to me. I will tell him.

It is only fair, it was my idea in the first place. I put it there, now the time has come for me to take it back.'

And late that night, in her ascetic room, with its walls bare except for a framed picture of the god Hanuman carrying a whole mountain in the palm of one hand, flying high across the Gulf of Mannar, intent on carrying out Rama's bidding, old Madam Tiwari looked at this picture from her bed and rehearsed what she would say to her grandson.

'At nineteen you are only a child. Besides, when you come back from England, you could be so changed, she could be so changed. It is better to leave as school friends…' And Govind, like her own father, on hearing something that displeased him, said nothing for quite a while… until a voice came from her grandson, but the words were not his: 'Why do you think like that? Why should I wait? Why wait? Everyone is sure except you!' Then Govind left. She did not see him return but he was standing there before her, so unlike himself, pointing at her, and he seemed to have her father's eyes and he was saying: 'You! you!' Then she was standing on a deserted platform, a train coming round a bend towards her and Govind running up the platform. 'Stop it, stop it for me. Help me,' he cries. And she heard herself say: 'Do not rush into this, Govind. Do not hurry. You will be sorry. She will be sorry. Miss this train. Let it pass. Do not get on the train, Govind. It is the wrong train. Look it says so.'

'Sastra ate over there. Ma knows, she sees it in Sastra's eyes; obeah is showing in her eyes; that black woman is confusing her. Sastra is losing herself. Round and round everything is moving. The train is going, leaving, leaving me. Why wouldn't you help me, Ajee? Help me, Ajee. You prefer Rabindranath, but I am your

157

grandson. Why? Why? Tell us why? We know why. Sati told us. Why? Why? Wicked! Wicked! Call Aja. Tell him, tell him... Aja! Aja!'

She heard Shakuntala's voice reaching her through a haze of revolving cycles of time where present and past meet.

'Mai, are you well?'

Shakuntala Tiwari could not accept that Rabindranath Pande should come between herself and Sastra. She had always said that Sastra was going to be her daughter-in-law. Everybody knew that. She had come out and made a claim openly. Everybody understood that. How come Rabindranath didn't? Why didn't he keep his distance. He must have known. Sastra and Govind are the most natural match you can think of. What kind of life can he give her? A teacher's salary? That never comes to much. He's just in the way. Poor Sastra having to go over there each day and consult with him. Parvatee was far too lax. And that Bajan woman!... One never knows what these people would get up to! Sastra says that she cooks Indian food better than many Indians. Who has ever heard of a thing like that? How can that be? It is unnatural! Parvatee should never have agreed to such an arrangement. I wouldn't be surprised if that black woman encouraged this, boasting up Rabindranath before an unsuspecting Sastra, saying an arranged marriage is an old-fashioned, foolish thing. That's how they think, but I know better. Govind is just the right age for Sastra, even a blind man can see that. Rabindranath took advantage of her. She did not understand that older men are not to be trusted, they use their wider experience of life to trap the innocent. How will she live on a school teacher's salary? Doesn't he think of this? Selfish. Self!

Self! Self! Self is gasolene today, everything runs on it… Besides, is he a Hindu? Nobody knows. She is right for Govind. They will live together just like Sati and Capil. That house in St. Augustine, a little lower down Dry River, that is the kind of place Govind will have, and patients will come from everywhere. He will be a good doctor, as conscientious about his work as his father was. Who knows? He may even be better than Capil, for he will be more up to date, newly qualified. And Sastra will keep him in check, keep him on the right path. I have to consider speaking seriously to Rabindranath myself, I cannot allow him to spoil Sastra's life. I must ask him to consider her future, not his own. That will be the test of true love.

After two days, with her inner tensions growing, Shakuntala could stand it no longer and called on Parvatee, who felt both anxiety and relief on seeing her.

'Parvatee, you probably know why I am here.'

'It is always good to see you, Shakuntala.'

'Mai tells me that she suspects Rabindranath has been courting Sastra. Is that true?'

How direct Shakuntala could be when she was angry Parvatee was learning for the first time. She knew she had to be careful, to walk gently. This old friendship she valued.

'Sastra has not said anything, except that it would be better to postpone the engagement until Govind and she are both qualified.'

'Does Sati believe that Rabindranath is a good match?'

'Oh Capil and Sati were here. They talked about this and that, but when they came round to Govind leaving to study medicine, Capil thinks that if Sastra and Govind were to become engaged now, they would be unhappy. He thinks they both need more time.'

'Sometimes I think Capil needs more time to rest his tongue.' There was an uncomfortable pause.

'Sati says that Sastra will marry Govind if that is what everybody wants…'

'I was under the impression that that was what both families wanted.'

'Govind and Sastra have been good friends, Shakuntala, from before they went to school. I would be too happy to see them engaged, as you had said. But Sastra…'

'This is what we agreed, Parvatee. Why is there a "but" now? I told Govind. Didn't you tell Sastra? I was under the impression that everybody understood what an engagement between families of long standing means… But now Parvatee, you are going back on your word. I am hearing something dishonourable. Honour! Doing the honourable thing has no place in this house any longer. What one pledges in good faith, in this house has come to have the same meaning as kicking an empty tin cup by the roadside.'

'I told Sastra, Shakuntala, I told her straight away. She understood. Narayan too. He is like me, we want to see her engaged to Govind. Nothing would please us more. But I must speak the truth. I will try and tell you some of my own worries… With things of the heart, no one really knows… Parents are often the last to find out. I can't help feeling Sastra is grieving inside. Maybe going there everyday… I don't know how to put it; may be there was something there between them even before she was asked to take his class. How am I to know? You are asking me and I am trying my best to tell you what I see; what I think happened. But at her age, nothing lasts for long. What is true now, in six months time may seem strange. You and I were once young too, Shakuntala;

160

give her time. To enter an engagement with so much doubt, so much uncertainty, cannot be good.'

'Once I told you, Parvatee, how I had a premonition that if Govind is not engaged now, he will be unhappy, I will be unhappy. That feeling you have no respect for, and it gets stronger daily; the pain in my stomach and my throat is unbearable. I see clearly the hell that is waiting for Govind and for me. I am saying this to you now, bear it in mind, I, Shakuntala Misir Tiwari have been humiliated. If you go back on your word, if Sastra doesn't become engaged to Govind, she will never marry him, she will lose an opportunity to live a happy and prosperous life. And I predict that this unbearable pain of loss Sastra is now causing me, she will experience too. She agreed and now she is withdrawing. She promised; her words and those of her parents, who are there to guide children, have come to mean nothing, dust in the wind. The pain you both bring me will visit you too, as God is my witness.'

'Shakuntala, you are very angry and very hurt. You should not speak in anger. I have been so troubled, I have not been able to sleep for worrying. Do you think I find this easy to do? Don't you think I am hurt too and disappointed? I am taking some comfort in looking at it another way: Sastra will be away from Rabindranath soon. All this will help her. Govind is a sensible boy, mature for his age and he understands more than we think. Good could come from this trial. Sastra and Govind would enter marriage as adults not as children, their affection would have been tested.'

When Shakuntala left, Parvatee wept for her daughter; what she heard reminded her of Karsi Pundit's readings so many years ago. She was unhappy that Shakuntala was so unreasonable, so hard. Yet she was glad she had kept her true feelings about this onslaught under cover; she had to, for she was only the mother of a daughter. But she couldn't help feeling that Shakuntala showed no understanding, no sympathy for her predicament, had behaved as if she had courted this outcome. My God Shakuntala was bitter! How hurt she must be. May peace come to her. If her anger rages, the desire for revenge would eat into her and into what is around her. She would be wasted and Govind's ajee too would slowly suffocate. O God help us.

Shakuntala's opportunity to speak to Rabindranath came sooner than she expected. He was there, crossing the railway line on her way home, but he smiled so naturally and greeted her so warmly that she found it difficult to pursue her initial cold stance. It would have looked coarse. She couldn't say why, but today she thought he looked more than ever like his father. That same gentle tiredness was coming through his eyes and his smile.

'How are you keeping?' he asked. It was more than the conventions of courtesy. He wanted to know. 'And Govind's ajee, how is she? A sturdy old lady you have there. Govind tells me he leaves soon for London. He will make a very good doctor, one of the finest this island will know. He has what is needed and you have every reason to be proud of him.'

'I hope so.'

'I wish his father and mine were alive to see him qualified. You mustn't worry about him; he is bright and he is disciplined; you don't often find these qualities together in a healthy, handsome young man.'

As she looked at his gentle eyes, she couldn't help thinking that to continue her indifference would be brutally unkind. But she did not know what to say, was confused, until her past voice – her habit – rescued her. She found she had said: 'Your father and you helped him a great deal. You, too, are leaving soon I hear.'

'Govind is what teachers call scholarship material…'

'What are your plans when you return?'

'I haven't firm plans about anything just yet. I postponed going for such a long time that now it is taking me longer still to orient myself to leaving.'

Old Madam Tiwari saw what was before her and, to give herself solace, to find courage to face the next day, she went to the bottom drawer of her chest, placed her hand beneath her voile ornhis and white saris and brought out an old sandalwood box; she removed her jewellery – the heavy gold necklace of sovereign pieces – and, from beneath it, took the neatly folded letter from Draupadi, her dear old family friend. Sitting on her bed she reread the letter; the ink was changing colour but the Hindi letters were well formed:

Dear Bahin, Ram Ram Sita Ram.

Forgive me for not coming to see you when I was at Surinder. I kept postponing it until it was too late. My spirit then was greatly troubled; it was not the right time to come. There was the strain of being a teacher with limited time – trying to impart a lifetime's considerations of our cooking in a timespan only a man could envisage. But what was even more important, Bahin, I had to remove a lifetime of thinking that had become part of myself, and in digging it out, for the root was deep and so strong, I had to pull out chunks of my own flesh. I cried out in agony to Brahma and Vishnu to show me the way, for I was being submerged in darkness. Help came to me but in a strange way; it was as if I was walking in a maze, but each time I made a wrong turning, I was given a helping hand until the trial was behind me. At first, Bahin, I could not sleep and it was not the frogs croaking in the nearby canal, the stray dogs rummaging in the dustbins, or the voices of late cinema-goers trailing through the night which disturbed me. I kept saying to myself that had Surinder remarried a nice Hindu girl, and with the expectation of daughters, my presence here to lift the standard of cooking would make sense; but to give all this to a complete stranger – a black creole lady, who could leave any time, to what purpose? A waste, a sheer waste, Bahin. These last words – now coming from my own lips – startled me – words long lost that had come from my uncles' and pundits' mouths when they heard my father was teaching me not only Hindi but also Sanskrit to a high level. 'To a girl child? What will she do with Sanskrit? To what purpose? A waste! A waste of your time, Punditji.' My father replied so simply: 'Why, she would enjoy reading the sacred texts just as we do. Reasons should be required only when denying someone a splendid thing, not when offering.' It was his warm gentle tone, Bahin, I would never forget this, God bless him. 'If my daughter is not taught, if she does not know how to read the sacred texts, they don't exist for her, and though she is younger, she would be living in a darker age than you and I. Why deny her? Why deny?' And then, Bahin, with those words my nightmare began: My restless spirit returned to times past – carnival time – and I am clutching tightly at Mai's dress, afraid to cross the road of devil masks and Jab-Jabs with their beads and bells, lashing the road, swinging the long whips and themselves from side to side. We are about to cross, our way is blocked; a Black man smelling of tar and perspiration, almost naked, his shorts wet, his body black and sticky, the perspiration streaming down him; he is a tar man, Bahin, so sticky, bare; he has horns and a tail and a rope around his waist; a boy is holding a rope, a long rope and walks behind him beating a pan; faster and faster now, louder and louder. He puts his hand out to me, then to Mai, and dances before her! Disgusting! His tail moving round and round, faster and faster; his body is wet and hot, streaming. Mai quickly opens her purse and drops something in his palm from a height; she does not want to touch him, her aim is hurried, the coin drops off his palm. He gets it and moves away; the boy follows, beating the pan. I awoke, Bahin, you can well imagine, after this! And then I slowly recognised my strange surroundings, and remembered what was being expected of me in the morning. Then I slept and dreamt again. A damp cold wind surrounds my spice basket, shaking it, tumbling it over, scattering spices on the floor. Two paper bags are intact but when I opened them, one has gone mouldy and the other has weevils. Another wind comes through the shutters with the face of the man with tail and horns; he laughs and laughs, whirling and jumping, running backwards and forwards into corners and cupboards. I manage somehow to save a little of the spice by collecting what has spilt on the table, but it is no use, Bahin; the spices become charcoal in my hands. I awoke shaken from this nightmare and ran to the kitchen to examine my basket of spices – I had taken great pains and paid good prices for the finest grades. To have them all lost – of no use to anyone – greatly disturbed me. My anxiety came not only from the nightmare but from a feeling of guilt, that instead of treating these good quality spices with due regard, by putting them away into tightly

165

fitting jars, ensuring that they maintained their essences and aromas, I had instead spent the entire evening expressing grave misgivings to Surinder at being asked at my age to cross cultures in a moment. How can one attempt to communicate a spirit, a thought, to someone who knows nothing about its source, its vessel? But when I discovered that my neighbour's daughter, whom I had asked to get the basket ready for my journey from Chaguanas to Tunapuna, had not only protected my basket from dust and sand and rain by an outer tarpaulin cover and two layers of silver foil underneath, but that each paper bag was further reinforced with jute twine and the aromas sealed by a protective cellophane – the kind used over chocolate boxes – at last Bahin, I understood what Bhagwan was asking of me. I had a choice of becoming a spice that was fragrant, rich, exciting, a warm spice that had not lost its essence or aroma for this young black student, or of becoming dust, charcoal, of no use to her. While I was still breathing, while Bhagwan was performing the miracle of life through me, I was opting to be of no use, fit only for weevils and mould. And the more I thought about it, the scales of ignorance, of meanness, of my narrowness, fell from my eyes; for the very spices that I had all my life treated with great care, these minuscule grains and buds, were now showing me such a large, magnificent way. I never would have thought, Bahin, that this could have happened, that I, Draupadi, would one day be so obligated to my spices. I was truly humbled, as a child before the sparks of light in the night sky.

I trust you will forgive me and give me your blessings, your choti Bahin, Draupadi.

CHAPTER SEVENTEEN

THE WHISPERINGS OF TWO FLAMES

When Friday came her mother said, 'This is your last evening over there.'

'Milly has invited me to stay for dinner, Ma. I couldn't say no. It wouldn't look nice.' She dressed as if the evening was special, yet wondered whether she was overdoing it. Her mother noticed.

'Now don't be too late,' Parvatee said; 'it doesn't look good.'

'Milly or Rabindranath will walk me back home, don't worry, Ma.'

Your father, Parvatee thought, and was about to give Narayan's views; instead she said, 'Try and leave early.'

Sastra took her briefcase as camouflage; it looked incongruous; it did not match her crimson crepe de Chine blouse; she was afraid to use perfume lest its fragrance brought another strained response from her anxious mother. Suddenly, she was confused, frustrated and angry; angry that she had been put into an uncomfortable situation by those near and dear to her. How did it come about? Had she formally agreed to it? She had no idea... Well, she'd had enough, and a hundred yards from her home, she opened her briefcase and caressed herself with an exciting scent; round her neck, she clasped a gracious, elegant piece of filigree jewellery in burnished gold, a birthday gift from Sati and Capil.

Rabindranath was not sure what he could hope. For weeks Sastra had been serious, businesslike and professional; as soon as the discussion of class work was over, she packed her bags and left. But as the days became weeks, she grew more relaxed. Then their laughter joined. And by the third week, they had become such good friends that he had begun to hope. But because of her integrity, her deep affection for her parents, and the traditional conservative manner of her upbringing, he wondered whether she would still move with conventional currents and marry Govind… seeing it as the honourable thing, keeping faith with the family. And when the last week came too quickly, and he noticed how quiet she had grown, his hopes had begun to fade.

'These are for Milly,' she said, standing before his door, her appearance immediately restoring his optimism.

'I heard my name call,' Milly shouted from the kitchen.

'For you, Milly, some anthurium lilies.'

Smiling broadly, she appeared, wiping her hands on her apron. 'My goodness, how lovely, Sastra. They will light up my sitting room. I would feel it is Divali.'

'Think of all the trouble I have given you. This is only a small token of my appreciation.'

'You are always welcome here, my dear. These weeks have been a real pleasure seeing you both at work.' She did not want to make her self-conscious, but Sastra was looking so beautiful.

'Rabind,' she said, 'bring me a kitchen towel.'

When he left, she said, 'You are looking very beautiful tonight. Treat him gently, he is a fine man.'

'You are like a fairy godmother.'

'You are paying me too many compliments in one night, and you have not yet had my sorrel wine! Aunt Jenny's special.'

'Not too strong I hope.'

'Strong enough,' she said, smiling, teasing with her eyes.

When Milly took her leave, Rabindranath was again the perfect host; he lit the candle and there, with only its upright shadow on the wall for company, they chatted and laughed and enjoyed a meal that would have brought tears of pleasure to Draupadi, for it did indeed tempt the gods. After they had coffee, he brought over the candle and by its soft light poured her a little brandy, and came and sat near her on the sofa. For the first time they just sat, neither wishing to speak. Every evening for four and a half weeks they had talked, and now it had all come to an end. He got up and poured himself some more brandy and despite her gentle protests poured her a little more too.

A comforting hush stayed with them and he remembered how Govind had kissed her ear and played with her bracelets. But here and now, he just wanted her sitting with him in the quiet of the evening for the frogs could not yet be heard and only the soft movement of a candle flame stirred. He longed to embrace her, but was not sure of her and this sweetness of her company he would not mar, would not interrupt for an uncertain outcome.

The rosewood bookshelf and the side tables glowed with the warmth of the candle flame. Sastra, too, grew warm, uncomfortably so, her ears beginning to burn.

In the garden the air was far cooler than either had anticipated and the sudden change of temperature made

169

her shiver, so he removed his jacket and came closer to shield her; and as he was placing it around her shoulders, she gently caressed his face, saying, 'I am all right.' Her fingers were so close to his lips that he kissed them and she allowed him and his delight grew, but she continued to tremble and they returned to the house.

'I have something special to show you. *Tales of the Pandes.* No one knows of them.'

'I remember.'

He brought her a neatly home-bound book, its cover kohl and vermilion in colour, a simple chakra decorating it. As Sastra looked at it, the chakra was changing at the speed of thought from cartwheels to spiders' webs, to sunflowers, childhood paper windmills, floating wisps of cotton, a twirling leaf, a rotating planet, Sudarshan Chakra, hubs of rotation, change. At its back, a number of blank pages remained – fine rice paper, the texture of silk sheen. The detailed, minute pattern of each page varied – combinations of broken crescents, bamboo slivers, drops of pollen and fishes' eyes. She recognised the clear upright handwriting of his father, but would not read – felt it discourteous to do so – and handed it back to him. He returned it to her open.

'I have chosen this piece from "Sunset in 1888". Please read it.' He left the room.

'It was hurriedly hurled over the high palace walls of the Maharanee's garden and now this fallen white disk lay on the bed of soft earth I had prepared for the fragrance of a frangipani. All this while I, too, did not stir, but when I could no longer hear the chase, resting my rake against the wall, I approached the disk. For some time I stood wondering whether it was an explosive. Returning with my rake, and at arms length, I touched it, turning it gently over as if it were a carcass, but seeing it was something wrapped in cotton, I was encouraged and raked it carefully towards me. I don't know why, and even to this day, cannot say why I placed it in my tattered gardener's bag and hurried home, knowing my wife and son would be at my mother-in-law's. And there in my house, cluttered with lowly shadows of baskets and jars and bundles and the scent of jute bags and dried gobar (I had closed my one window as a precaution against the prying eyes of nosy neighbours) I saw an amazing wonder, an incredible thing… first the velvet pouch and the casket. In all my life I had never touched such a thing, nor seen such colours. I felt honoured, exhilarated, blessed; and knew it was from another world, another existence. Another reincarnation was before me in my modest room; such a constellation of stars held together by a vine of gold, formed in the sun. I was sure I was dreaming. For how long I was in this entranced state I cannot tell; but when my neighbours' voices came through the many chinks in my window, I knew this was no dream, that it must have come from the palace, though the palace's insignia was not there. Could it have been a piece specially requested, yet secret? Some royal passion? My delight gave way to a deep anxiety when I realised my predicament, for I couldn't part with it. I couldn't. I couldn't. I had become attached to it, though I could see that were I discovered I would be thrown into prison and allowed to rot there. Who would believe I was not in league with the runner? Supposing he had planned to do this and call for it later; or had arranged with someone from the palace, a collaborator, to pick it up. What then? I knew I could trust no one. This find must remain with me, or I would be robbed of it and be imprisoned too. No one would vouch for me.'

As she closed the book, unsure of turning the page, of trespassing, he entered with another lighted candle.

'Now I want you,' he said, 'to close your eyes until I say.' With boyish tenderness and care, he removed the jewelled casket from its deep ultramarine velvet pouch, which looked simultaneously like the heavens and the ocean deep. Slowly, gently, he opened the casket. Magical, overwhelming; the beauty before him fired his veins and stirred his soul. And he found he was caressing her eyes, whispering, 'Now, Sastra.'

She was dazzled. The delicacy and the power, the magnificence of form and colour and light; it was as if the candle flames had entered the splendour of what he had put before her.

'Wear it tonight,' he whispered. And though her entire body ached as he had once said it should, she knew that were she to do so, she would become his for the night and for all time. This was what she wanted, but that strong tradition of restraint for women folk brought from the land of the *Ramayana*, her nightmare of Dolly, gripped her youthful spirit, formed a dike of fear holding back the surging spring tides. She heard herself say, 'Not tonight.' And then it was that they saw this master craftsman's celebration of the senses singing together, held by outer and inner rings – beauty and ecstasy – each absorbing the other, moving into a dance of whirling light; then dividing, separating, scattering, becoming freshly minted suns, a new universe whirling, enlarging itself; pulsating anew. And after a while he blew at one of the candles, lifting the jewellery from her lap; gently, and by the warmth of candle light, embraced her with his entire being, and to his delight, she welcomed him, at first hesitatingly, until in the warm comfort of his arms they gave and received untold joys.

And for the first time she thought that marriage was a wonderful thing, not merely a duty, a tradition, a family ceremony, an honourable thing, but a thing of joy an intoxication to be shared.

CHAPTER EIGHTEEN

WHAT MADNESS DRIVES THIS WIND!

The wind howled, tumbling waves and crashing rocks, mad drunken sways of massive trees bending to breaking, blinded by a force unseen, whipping the land into a frenzy.

A strange stirring moves within her.

Her restless mind, a frightened bird, seeks shelter in this circling, raging storm. But where? Rabindranath had said he was going to go to Chaguanas early the next day, to say goodbye to his mother's people. His father's side were all gone. A pain, at times unbearable, came upon her at the loss his absence would create.

All evening she had tried to soothe this fire within, and now it was consuming her. A night without stars, dark angry black clouds hanging as if near the sea shore.

Narayan and Parvatee slept, but she could tell Rabindranath, too, was awake. Maybe he was preparing for tomorrow. How could she go to him at this late hour? What would she say? How to describe this ache within her? What if she were seen opening his gate, uninvited? What of her parents and Govind and Shakuntala?

The more she thinks, the more she feels incapable of any action. Thought and Reason and Custom are now effectively tying her feet. Sastra tosses about in bed: her feet clamped down... yet she escapes, by wishing it, thinking: I must not die, I will not die and later in the night floats down the stairs, easily buoyed up like a balloon. The gate is closed. She sails over it as on a witch's broom; over the deep purple bougainvillea, its thorns raised as a sentry's spear; then drops to run and run, fighting with the wind, moving against it as it pushes her back, angrily and with ease. This wind, the village wind, with the eyes of Karsi Pundit, will not hear of this.

'I must go on,' she pleads to the giant samaan trees, 'If I don't, something within me would die. I would die.'

But they too have the eyes of Karsi Pundit, multiplying like dew drops.

Even as she approaches his gate, standing there to catch her breath, to stop herself from falling, the village wind pulls her back. Again she runs forward, approaches the iron gate, lifts the clamp and runs up the path. It becomes steep, then steeper; she is struggling upwards, sliding backwards; the path rises to an angle of seventy degrees; she stalls; then eighty degrees. The border roses reach out, pulling with their spikes, their arms outstretched, overreaching themselves, blocking her path, jabbing in. Ru in! Ru in! Ru in! they chant like a Greek chorus, shaking their heads in unison, in utter disbelief. Rue! Rue! they shout; an old woman from the village pops up and whispers, 'Shame' and lifting her hands like wands above her head, which becomes antlers then antennae, cries out, 'Rue! Rue! Rue!'

She stands before his door, ripped; torn; bruised; but cannot call. The thought comes that he may already have left and it is Milly who has just turned in. What will she say to Milly?

Then his voice; his voice! What sweetness! 'Who is there?' he asks, so at ease as if this were a retreat for troubled minds, as if it were the breaking of the day and

175

not the closing of the night. 'Sastra?' he whispers. Holding the oil lamp, seeing nothing, light shines only through his eyes, flickering its warmth on part of his face, neck and shoulder; the rest of him lost... Gradually he sees her form; no one else can; she is veiled by the night. 'Come in,' he says. 'What madness drives this wind. I am so glad you are here, Sastra, I was sure I would go mad. I was about to come to you, but it is difficult at this time of night to meet your parents, to come merely to leave some book. I am grateful to you. Are you really here?' A small lamp rests on his desk; there she could see his handwriting, the ink still wet on the paper; and as the leaping flame settles down, she says, 'You once told me... You once said, I should only marry someone if my life became unbearable without him.'

'Yes, Sastra, when the pain, the ache of separation becomes unbearable. I do remember well.'

'Yes... I have found such a man, should I let him know?'

'Yes, tell him tomorrow. Tomorrow, Sastra. Tomorrow will do. In the meantime have something.' He walks to the cabinet and pours that sunlight, speaking softly. 'I understand,' he says, 'but won't you stay for a time and share this with me?' He stands alone at the mouth of an abyss and does not wish to turn around and face her for his eyes are beginning to express his loss and fear that he will fall inward with this internal tremor. But she has come close and whispers, 'Rabind, I wish to tell him now, here... This minute.' Slowly he turns and there in the shadow of the dancing, leaping lamp, pours on her head rich, sweet libation which cannot trickle down her soft neck, for he has embraced her as a man possessed, without restraints; and there, two human beings give and receive so much ecstasy, so much maddening joy and pleasure, that their moving shadows do not stand as sentries but remain with them and neither hears the wild wind, nor sees the dark night leave. At last, Rabindranath rose from her side and whispered to her closed eyes that dawn was approaching. And from his desk shone the words written before she had dared to end his night and face the howling tides of wind: 'My dearest, Sastra, I call to thee from the depths of the earth, for there is where I am entombed.'

In the early morning, her dream, so real, lingered on and she blushed. Were it not for the fact that neither her hair nor her pillow were bathed in his warmth, nor her skin torn, nor bruised, she might have thought otherwise. When Rabindranath brought me home, my spirit returned to him, she thought, amazed and embarrassed at the strength of her own feelings.

The bright morning sun entered her room and she was happy that such a fever, a madness, had left her; for she now felt calm and reflective, trying to separate in her own mind dream from reality. She was thankful, relieved it was a dream, and anxious to recover a detached composure during her last few weeks at school, as a member of staff and teacher of standard two.

Now she was beginning to see, to understand, she thought, that there was a certain comfort and protection in wearing the simple maiden's apparel spun by custom, the ancient lores carried by her mother and the village women. She felt peaceful, calm, and did not stop to consider whether her present tranquillity, her composure, might not be the aftermath, the ebb of heightened, consuming emotions.

CHAPTER NINETEEN

JUST PASSING THROUGH

When Rabindranath left, a feeling of deep sadness came to Milly and stayed with her. All at once she felt she was alone in the village, was without friends and suspected that the Narayans and the Tiwaris were thinking that she had abused their trust. This thought gnawed at her. The engagement of Govind and Sastra, long wished for by their parents, had not taken place. No one had said anything to her but she sensed a strain, a tension she could not cope with, taking the form of silent politeness or quiet withdrawal by the families and the village women.

She knew their suspicions were not without foundation; in truth, she had encouraged the warmth and affection between Rabindranath and Sastra to grow. In the eyes of the village she had failed to stay at her post of duty. 'An abnegation of trust', she could hear Narayan saying.

She did not regret her conduct. Rabindranath needed all the help he could get. In the village they were happy to take from him, to accept his sacrifices, but could not see his needs as she did. How could they? They were attuned to their own ordered harmonies.

But it was not just this new coldness which prompted her decision. For over a year she had thought that with

Rabindranath's departure for London would come the time to take her leave. He had said that she could stay in the garden house for as long as she wanted, but she knew she couldn't. Too many changes had taken place both around her and within her. With Aunt Jenny's death and the selling of her plot in Barbados she had cut her umbilical cord, had unfastened an anchor. Francis was now in Atlanta and she wondered what influence America would have on him. She sighed, remembering all that he had revealed of his own hurts and the bitterness of Mr. Munroe touching him. Of course, as he had intimated, she knew that here in the village she was an outsider. Before the present situation, the village women were polite and friendly and would share a joke with her, but she could not marry their brothers, and there was always the danger that too much friendliness on her part might make their husbands think of her what she was not. Thinking of Francis she could see the impatience of youth and of the times. There was now a continuous clamour for instant change as if it could be had as easily as instant coffee. Life, she knew, like good recipes, did not work that way. With life you first had to cry together and pull together before you could gather an understanding, a trust – and she saw the difficulties.

Rabindranath had left with such sadly smiling eyes, embracing her as if they would not meet again. A feeling of desolation had crept upon the place; now she couldn't cope with the emptiness, the silences of only the wind passing.

No voices, no stirrings; too many memories locked in jars and pots and vases, captured in corners, of Purusha and Draupadi and Surinder. The day before she had seen a light from her window; it rested for a while at Surinder's desk. It must have been a passing motor car, but for a brief moment she had become elated and anxious, wondering whether Rabindranath had returned. He had looked so vulnerable on parting.

Aunt Jenny had once said to her, 'Go South, Milly, go South.' She had continued, 'And when your feet have grown strong, walk the whole wide earth,' Now Milly knew she had just been passing through. It was time to pack for Boston.

BOOK THREE

CHAPTER TWENTY

WHERE ARE THE STARS

Parvatee and Naryan read the cable: 'Arrived safely. All is well. Will write soon. Bundles of love. Sastra.'

Two days later Sastra wrote and knew without thinking what she must say for she wanted her mother to stop worrying, to give her peace of mind. Everyone should have peace of mind. At the end of the week she wrote again to her parents and later to Sati: the vastness of the library and its stock room; students from Malaya, Nigeria, India, Fiji, everywhere. Societies – studious Bible Unionists full of certainties, daring, hazard-seeking cliff-climbers, so unlike anything that could be envisaged at home – the clawing boots and the tough harsh rope, the enlarged photographs on display portraying perpetual strain and stress. What an endeavour! So much toughness needed to scale heights, so hazardous! Why seek it out? To lose one's life climbing a cliff?

Seventy-eight girls were in her hall of residence. They were awakened at seven and called again by the gong to breakfast at seven-thirty. No one could miss its recurring seven beats, a call from another age to begin the day. No showers here, a bathtub of cold white enamel which she filled too much on the first day and had to mop up. How does one soap oneself? Should one get out to do it properly?

It was difficult to rinse oneself as the soapy suds were all around and after this she still felt the need to rinse. What a strange custom. Oh for showers that did not encircle you in your waste. The bed was made up differently too. She was shown how by the matron; it became a tight casement and she looked like an Egyptian mummy tightly held in place... Restraint and control all round – the shadow of the war lingering.

But there are letters Sastra writes to herself in the quiet winter evenings, looking through a northern window at the grey, heavy bleakness, or as she walks alone along a path, shivering, unaccustomed to being outside the orbit of the overhead sun.

The feeling of being an alien closes upon her, an outsider to the morning oat porridge and Irish stew at lunch. Only beef! Not a place for Hindus. And here, the sun is so tame; it is unimaginably cold. The whole place is a fridge. You don't need one here. Just leave dairy products out in the back yard. But the backyards of terrace houses are drab, unhappy places. The walls of the buildings – soot. She has the urge to scrub and rinse them with an enormous brush and powerful hose until all is clean. Nothing is white here. Nothing can be. All day it rains drip! drip! drip! and ice cold. Her feet are ice. Why am I here? Where is the sun, where is the blue sky? Are there stars? She smiles, recalling how in her village she would play games – counting the stars. They were everywhere, above her house, over her neighbours', looking down into the open savanna – the village ceiling was a sequined sky – spiked raindrops on a calm sea.

There is no colour here. No orange, no vermilion red, no deep crimson here; only greys, dark greys; no cheer here; dark browns, a sadness, a severity, colours of toughness, colours of wear, a people weary of war, their sweetness rationed, having faced too much sobriety too long. No laughter in the skies, no blushing clouds.

The wind that pushes her with such ease was born over the vast primeval ocean, and still moves like that. One day it will take everything in its path. She can feel its gigantic force, its potential power. Today the rain is restrained to a fast pitter-patter, pitter-patter; later it becomes a drip, drip, drip, a continuous fine song played on paved paths. But this soft cold drizzling chorus does not enter their cocoon, their hall, their fort. They have storm doors, their windows are high. 'I am on the north side. I cannot ever see the sky from my window. What a weird feeling to be cut off from the skies. I am part of the earth but an earth with no sky feels alien. In the two grand, heavy interlocking doors I encounter defiance solidified. It is only when I open them that the sky oppresses. It is raining and I must return and fetch my umbrella. We need a sky on earth.'

The walls are thick. The hall is strong, its corridors are wide. The architect of the hall – his philosophy was durability. Stormproof. Forbidding and heavy. A fort in temperament and strength, built by men for men, with that ocean-born wind in mind. And she sees and smells the soft earth walls of village houses and thatched roofs and rafters low, and knows that she is in another place.

Two weeks come and go. A desire to be fair, honest, guides her and she believes that to write to Govind might convey the wrong messages and so she says, 'If he writes, I will write and if he doesn't, he understands.' But she writes to Rabindranath: of the university and Societies; of subjects that excite her – Economics, Geology, Archaeology, Psychology, Geography. Each measuring time differently, giving a perspective that reminds that we are but one variety of infinite life forms. The

Hall. It is a women's hall, way up on a hill; all around the grounds slope into woodland. A site meant for castles of old. On the south circumference, hemming the land, lies a lake. These rolling, grassy grounds are beautiful in the wind. She follows the movement of its passing energy from wave to wave, meeting and departing. Tall pines are wildly dancing, clouds are retreating. Coal fires in the library; in the sitting room, log fires. No central heating. How are you? What is it like in London?

She gives herself a week and then, each morning, looks at the mail certain that there would be a reply. She waits two weeks; the hurts of the morning bruise are later soothed by the greater likelihood that tomorrow will bring what today had not, and in this way, each day, hope is recharged, relived. Three weeks pass.

There are lectures, new faces, so many. The students' union always a crush. On Saturday nights, the door bell of this fortress keeps ringing. A name is given, then the call of that name, the sound of that name rises to the second floor, for which someone anxiously waits. 'Miss Monaghan... Miss O'Maley, Miss O'Reiley... Miss Donaghue, Miss Flemming, a visitor for you.' The reply comes. 'Thank you.' Footsteps. Joyful steps down, down, down the stairs. The huge door bangs shut. Again it opens, again the call – the hurried steps, the excitement of sweet affections readily displayed in smiles and embraces, again and again the music of youth is played.

The hall empties itself, except for a young woman from Nigeria and one from Thailand and there is Sastra too. There are Bible meetings on a Saturday for those who prefer this to the hop.

Dear Rabindranath,

It is Saturday; there is a stillness that is comforting in this grand hall. Coal fires in the library, a log fire in the sitting room and I become a moth circling a tropical flame in this bleak wilderness. How must our earliest ancestors have danced for joy on seeing flames for the first time. Or do you think they were frightened? And then later to have had the power to conjure it up when needed. What wholesome magic! What an excitement it must have been as control became more refined: to toast, to roast, to kiln.

On a day like this I make believe I own the place. How are you? Is the study of Philosophy what you had expected? I am looking forward to seeing snow. What is advanced mathematics like? What can it be likened to?

The weeks pass and the months. She has written four letters all told, and now knows he wishes to be alone; or to be with another. But why not say this? Is it so painful to say? He is hoping that his silence will speak. Sati writes but never once mentions him. Why? Of course her parents write. Business is not what it should be. Govind's ajee is not well... slowly deteriorating... Old Mrs. Greenidge may not see another Christmas. Sastra writes too and though her allowance is small, says nothing, afraid to cause hardship; she will look for a summer job. Now, only now, she resigns herself to what is clear, to his silence.

Govind, too, has not written and she accepts that he may wish to have a clean break with the past and welcomes this.

And now in this new, colder environment, Sastra is at last at ease with herself. No longer the strain of expectations – the turning and turning over and over in her mind, searching for the answer to the question people have asked from time immemorial – Why? Why should this be so? Now she accepts. It is so that people change with a change of place, with time; maybe it is a natural law – the inevitability of old feelings giving way to new to survive in the new land.

Work. Work. Work. The library, the main library, the hall's library. Essays and study. Field trips.

'Come home with us for the weekend, my parents would like that.'

'Thank you. It is kind of you but I do like to be here.'

'Come with us. You will love the country.'

'Thank you, but I have the habits of a monk.' I prefer, she thinks, the protective walls of solitude of this grand hall.

Human relationships she avoids. It is safer alone. One is certain only of one's self. Discipline and dedication are essential requisites. Why tears? I must make myself strong. Concentrated effort. Energy focused directly on what will lead to a better, a deeper understanding of one's studies. Become knowledgeable, skilful, dependable. Become someone you can rely on in tests, examinations, seminars and talks; enjoy your essays and class contributions. Grow in stature. There is nothing else. Question: What is love? Answer: A figment of the imagination. An emotion without foundations. Like the wind, it comes, goes, passes; nothing flutters. All is still. All ebbs. Oh Dolly. Silence.

It is Sunday, and the high tensions of the busy week have eased as chimney smoke rises tall, drifts and is gone. The hall is quiet. Many have left to spend the weekend with parents and friends. Others are in church.

Alone she stands looking through the window at the green fields, the nest of hillocks, the sloping lawn, the distant lake. But look. Look. Silver parachutes are tumbling, laughing in the wind. Twinkling stars are whirling past, circling in the air. Chased from above. Glistening, frolicking crystals, innocent and free. Mysteriously spinning till they lie stilled upon the earth; rearranged; absorbed.

Is this snow?

A tropical bluish white above. Shattered glaciers in the sky crumbling, crumbling. A magic wand enchants the land – ice crystals sparkling, spinning. A fairy land is born. Trolls dancing.

She wants to be closer to witness this transformation; she wants to absorb it, to be part of it, and rushes to her room. Winter trousers, jumpers, gloves, scarf, woolly hat, so much to put on! Hurry! Must get to it before it is over. How long will it last, this dance of the icicles? Is it less frenzied now? She cannot see the sky.

Opens the heavy storm door. Oh the beauty! Cold crisp air rushes to overwhelm her; she greets it with laughter and absorbs the sparkle, the perfect skill; the master painter's song! She climbs, feet hidden, to the top of one of the cluster of hillocks and looks around. A Christmas card has come to life. A Pieter Bruegel painting. A land for snowmen, fairies and elves. A place for a child's imagination... the wisest Trolls of ancient Croa... the minds of men do dwell on passing shadows... she blinks and the moisture is soft and warm, born in the Tropics. She hears his voice. Does it come from within her or from the pine trees waving to the sky?

She lies down, not feeling cold, just wanting to be closer to the earth, to embrace all of it; she is a part of it, and happily rolls down the hillock, hoping to absorb the wonder of it all, the wonder in its entirety, with all of self.

Knee deep in places. She holds a piece of wood and walks as a hunter; descends to the lake. It is softly frozen. Not yet hard enough to walk on. I will not risk it. Look at the ice pattern on that pile of rotted wood. Dead wood. Uncanny, bizarre patterns like worms, veins glistening. The sunlight imparts an energy, a life, a movement. She steps on it and breaks the fine pronged icicles. Glass. Fragile. Splinters. Crunched. Her steps alone mark the earth. One pair of steps. You need both slippers.

The silver-sprayed trees whisper to the wind; her tongue tastes the snow. Again she wants to embrace, to envelop the entire landscape; stretching out her hands, cradles the air. The evergreen shrubs carry neat lines of silver white on all their stems. Stalactites hang from window sills; pathway lamps are snow men, helmeted; the patterned brickwork now pieces of finely chiselled sculpture in an ordered row. The fort, the hall, has gone; there a snow palace stands, sparkling, strange.

In the night, out she goes again, quietly, quickly, unnoticed; like a child entering a garden of secret delights. It is the company of the cold air, the hillocks, the pine trees, whispering, enfolding, reassuring. They will stand there with her; will not move throughout her time. Will not change their scent nor their stance; will stand and rest there, fall there, faithful to the last – forests, not birds.

This is a magic dream of fairyland. Cold, bracing, beautiful. Sastra stands alone. Her shadow, a giant's, races across the jewelled lawn. Icicles are falling. The wind whispers again; she dares not listen. The branches sway. Thud, thud; snow flies and falls.

A weird glistening life comes to the climbing ivy creeping along the wall to the bedroom light – six inches more and it will become a Peeping Tom. Parked cars shrouded in white – a funeral line silently waiting. It is getting colder, the mist sits.

From the porter's lodge smoke rises, the chimney puffing a signal. She sees the puffs but hears the engine of the merry-go-round spluttering and puffing. The operator is tugging at a pulley. Smoke rises; the old engine growls, is tired, reluctant to start; splutters, picking up lazily, then healthily and off it starts, going fast, then faster and faster. Wheels go round and round, harnessed to the engine. Meanwhile the chair-o-plane tightens and lifts, circles twice, and is off the ground. 'Eye level is best, Sastra'.

From the porter's lodge, from its chimney, smoke rises and puffs out of columnar control; disperses lost in its journey.

The years go by so quickly. Three years! At the end of the final examination, she walks back to the hall slowly, and for the first time in six weeks notices: people stand and wait for the cinema, the buses and the theatres; buses are running in a world outside lecture rooms, libraries, seminars and dining halls.

It is time to pack up and leave. This room, its desk and book shelves, threadbare carpet, a two-bar electric fire six inches long. She smiles when she thinks of the flood of sunshine that awaits her. Thank God for the sun… Suriya, ripening and colouring even earth's canyons and its ocean deeps. All things at life's temperature.

The results are out. It is what she has at moments, bathed in the morning sun, dared to wish. Others say it is what she has earned. Sends a cable home, applies for a job, visits the travel agency.

Now she is ready and walks past familiar things which stare a silent adieu. Past the lake, the nest of hillocks, the chimneys, the storm doors, the clean cool grates, empty craters dormant in July, that will rise again in December and, with crackling log fires, again capture the imagination of new arrivals and make them believe they are nearer the sun and dreams of homelands far.

Across deserts and oceans.

The libraries have emptied themselves.

A silent goodbye to this Northern world, to the sound of gongs, to upright steeples, our fat, red-cheeked cook, to Irish stews, marmalade and scones; delicious Sunday trifles, the starched matron and inscrutable warden; goodbye to the soft continuous pitter-patter, drip-drip; to gale force singing winds, red bricks and rapid rebirth of ivy; and the magic of snow, way up on a far hill.

The taxi is here. It descends the rising ground so smoothly. 'Goodbye' she whispers and takes out her handkerchief. She wants to return to the lake and its surrounding woodland; feels the need; leans forward to say, excuse me, would you mind, but he says,

'The railway station isn't it?'

'Yes.'

'Ireland is a blessed country,' he says.

'Yes.'

BOOK FOUR

CHAPTER TWENTY-ONE

FOR WHITHER THOU GOEST I WILL GO

Sastra did not expect a homecoming party. Three years of silent soliloquies had left their mark. No longer did she perceive friendship as a natural thing growing wild around her, and because of this was deeply moved by its coming.

Her hermit's life of dedicated study, with its loneliness and the loss of Rabindranath, had left her more susceptible to human warmth and affection than even she suspected at the time. In particular she was overcome by the gentleness and the magnanimity of Shakuntala Tiwari. Both women embraced, their closed eyes covering their hurts.

She recognised Ramsaran and his young pregnant wife, shy and blushing; also four of her former pupils, grown in height and confidence out of all recognition. Her parents, she thought, had become shorter. Sati and Capil, blessed in their good fortune of each other and in their material goods, showered her with warmth and generosity. Ayisha and Arjun were disappointed to learn that English apples were not the deep red of Canadian apples, that apple trees were not as large as mango trees, while 'green' apples could be ripe. 'When snow falls could you collect it into a snow ball, add syrup and condensed milk as with shaved ice? Does snow fall

thump thump on your back, or is it as soft as butter?'
Arjun wanted to know. Old Mrs. Greenidge and Govind's
ajee had died and their absence had left spaces in that
circle of friendship. Parvatee explained that Govind's
ajee had lost her mind at the end. 'It was a gradual thing,
Sastra. Slowly she reverted back to being a young girl;
shy, withdrawn. It was strange, Shakuntala said. From
time to time she would say, "Don't tell. Don't tell." In
her last days I don't think she knew who I was.'

Throughout the day, aged relatives and stalwart friends
came to express their gladness on her safe return, on her
having 'completed her mission abroad'. The old are so
generous with their time, she thought, giving away
much of theirs, yet knowing they have little left. But this
concept of time she had learnt abroad: it was still new to
her, and was certainly not known in the village where
'time left over' from housework was simply there to be
used up, to perform yet more family duties and courtesies. Here the needs of 'self' were too enmeshed with
family and community, too interwoven to unpick, to
separate; but she had seen another pattern.

The village community was proud of the village
school: one of its pupils had a university qualification;
this they would talk about; and yes, she would be
teaching at the new secondary school.

'Now Parvatee, we have to get a nice dulaha for
Sastra,' one of the neighbours suggested. 'Maybe next
few months, na, we could have a wedding?'

'Oh Sastra's wedding!' said another; 'that will be
something eh! A grand wedding, na, Parvatee? Nothing
to match it.'

Parvatee and Shakuntala avoided each other's eyes;
they too, at one time had hummed this tune.

With the coming of dusk the guests left; her tired

parents, emotionally drained, retired indoors, and so for the first time both sisters were alone together. On and on they chatted about all manner of things except what weighed most heavily upon them. It was as if each was hoping the other would broach the subject; but neither said anything. The pride of one was mauled; the other was afraid to touch that impermeable bandage, not knowing the wound.

Sati rose and embraced her sister, looking into a calm face with deep sad eyes. She was trying to say she understood, but instead she said, 'I left a large brown envelope for you from Rabindranath. It is on your dressing table.'

Twelve letters strung together as beads and shaken to form a sound, a name. After three years someone else had remembered that there was such a sound. Here it was being made by another outside herself; so it was not a dream, a creation of her restless mind. She was not prepared to hear it called, this sound made outside herself. It stunned her, like an unexpected blow on torn ligaments. Her ear was playing tricks.

'From whom?'

'Rabindranath.'

Within her the gates of anger and pain opened wide their hinges and raged. She struggled within herself. An intense battle waged until once again her disciplined self rescued her. But despite this there was something about his name, its very sound, and the way Sati called it, which was soothing. And to have heard it twice – it was as if she were sitting, parched and dry, high up on the beach and this sound wave had the force to sweep up to her and bathe her, refresh her twice over, before its surge was spent.

'Rabindranath? Who is he? Thank you, but my days

for reading letters are over. I am older and wiser, Sati. No longer an infatuated schoolgirl. There is something about travel; it widens your perspective. You see the limitations of small islands and small places, but most of all the foolhardiness of youth.'

Sati looked at her sister and saw the repressed pain behind the mask that defied and protected.

'Don't judge him too harshly, Sastra. It couldn't have been easy for him; remember that. He did what he believed was the best thing for you. I happen to agree with him. Ma and Pa do too.'

Sastra did not hear, she was looking at something in the distance. Sati said, 'He arrived three weeks ago. Ma got him a good servant. Like you he will be teaching at the new secondary girls' school – Mathematics. He said his father's philosophy helped him to hover above his problems, otherwise he would have been engulfed, gone under; and yet if you look at him his eyes tell – it isn't as he says. He doesn't want us to feel sorry for him so he will say anything. I don't think he knows how to handle sympathy, but since you will be seeing him daily at school, you should at least be civil. Be courteous, Sastra. Read his letters. That's the least you can do.'

Sastra knew Sati was speaking, had said something about him but what? If asked, she couldn't say. She was left with a vague notion that something couldn't have been helped, that it was not his fault.

Having fought against loneliness, drab streets, grey skies, the cold, the wind, and an inadequate allowance, Sastra's willpower had grown in strength.

She undressed, saw the large brown envelope sealed, sitting, waiting to be read, but went to bed. My life now, she thought, is clear, not weighed down by soft feelings. My rational self will make the decisions.

But her sleep was restless, her spirit still abroad. The humming mosquitoes, the net, the heat and the humidity, made her too uncomfortable, too enclosed, hemmed in. She decided to have a cold shower and tiptoed to the bathroom.

Cooled, she went downstairs and sat in the hammock trying to catch any passing breeze. After a while, her mind became active and restless, and having grown accustomed to be doing something with her hands whenever alone, she took the large envelope and opened it at the very table at which they had once sat together, and where in their own shy way they had courted each other.

It is addressed to me; it is my duty. But her fingers for a while had forgotten how to function; and when they did she found a parcel of neatly tied letters.

Twelve letters in all. Folded with care, the earliest at the top.

'My dearest Sastra'. His voice, his hand, his declaration. These first three words were an affirmation of – it was a reply to her first letter, and there before her was a reply to her second, and third and fourth; and when she had ceased to write, he had continued to do so, eight more, until he too stopped. His handwriting, his honest clear prose; his case stated so simply:

Three weeks before you arrived in Ireland, an extreme tiredness came over me and stayed. I thought that in the absence of Milly, I might have been neglecting my meals too often, but as this feeling persisted I visited the Students' Health Centre and was told by the doctor that he suspected leukaemia. Once this was confirmed, and the likely duration of my life span given, I realised, that it would be unfair to you to continue as we had both wished. I was as confident of your affection for me, as I hope, my dearest Sastra, you are of mine; and with the knowledge of this blessing, I was strengthened to take the difficult and painful path. I know you as well as I know myself and had I told you, I feared you would have wished to abandon your studies, you would have wanted to be with me. Our fears and our love might have made us self-indulgent, and neither of us would have committed ourselves to our work as we have both now done, you so admirably, for much was held from you. Forgive me the pain I must have brought you, my dearest. Believe me when I say that there were times when my mental anguish was more than I could bear, and that there were days when I desired to be with you, wanted to come to you, to your Hall, in disguise, just to soothe my wretchedness. Often I whispered your name to the wind, hoping it would carry across the channel so that you would know I was with you, thinking of you. Was there some way you could know the truth and not be distracted by it, I would have gladly taken that path, but I knew of no such way.

Yours always

Rabindranath

p.s.. Let us be friends. Forgive me. I appeal to your generous spirit. This tiredness I may have recognised earlier for what it was, but because I was so close to you all of that last term, your spirit buoyed me up and I did not come down to earth until we separated. Dr. Lall, I believe, suspected.

And there were Rabindranath's other letters. To hear

his voice rising from the pages, declaring his love openly, so honestly expressing his innermost feelings – his deep affection for her, made her think that she was dreaming.

He had captured in those pages the variety of lives in the great metropolis, one she had not known. His thoughts, his ideas on so many aspects of alienation, his mind growing, developing, becoming stronger in unfamiliar surroundings, all the while knowing leukaemia was speedily taking him to the end of a line, greatly affected her. But more than anything else, to know that she was still loved by Rabindranath was a mad joy. She embraced his letters.

Her parents knew her dilemma: she had intimated before leaving that she was not sure whether she wanted to marry Govind. Her father had replied, 'When you both return, we will be in a better position to decide.' They knew whom she had in mind, but did not wish to bring to the open such a controversial thing before she left. However, on hearing of Rabindranath's illness and its nature from Capil and Sati, Narayan's feelings were confused.

Would Sastra be so overcome by sympathy that she would tie herself to his plight or would she accept this unforeseen tragedy and offer him friendship and consolation, but not marriage. The latter course he saw as being both humane and sensible, especially when the alternative before her was so overwhelmingly attractive.

Parvatee thought differently. She could see that Rabindranath's personal tragedy would become a fence over which her daughter would climb with ease, or at least scale over to have a look.

Early the next morning, Sastra dropped a note through his door.

Dear Rabind,

I will call to see you at five this afternoon.

Sastra

It could have been a note from a government official, for now that the stillness and the shadows of night had passed, the strong light of day had affected her mood and she found she wished to be formal, to create some distance, for her emotions seemed to have received a jolt, an electric charge. She was confused, moving from tender feelings to cold reserve. All day her mood changed direction as swiftly as the paper windmills of her childhood. Her spirit had been in solitary confinement for three years; and now a burst of sunlight. She was dazzled. Dazed.

That afternoon as she walked slowly to his house, the memories of her last visit were refreshed, and every step of the way came back with vivid familiarity: the wild-currant bushes; the nettles and the short castor oil plants like sprouting umbrellas on the railway embankment; the grassy verge; the red earth drains; the outward spreading branches of the huge Saaman tree, its fine leaves nodding a greeting to every passer by; the railway line; the red gate at the cross road swaying, striking its iron stopper on and on. The road was empty. It showed the way.

With the sweet glow of sunset on her skin and hair, her body at ease in soft petal pink, and wearing a new, more subtle scent, she walked up the path to his house.

The roses, which in her dream had pulled and tugged, were standing still, witnessing her coming.

Before he opened the door, Sastra wished for Milly, who would understand and absorb and protect her from what was strained and awkward.

Then there he was, like the first dawn smiling through the branches. She wondered what the earth had done on first seeing that vast, glowing, fiery disc coming towards it from its furthest horizon. What did it do on witnessing its first awakening, its first dawn?

What had she expected? She couldn't say; here he was, alive and looking well. Truly the work of some hidden force, some mystery and for her, a resurrection of life itself. The Rabindranath of old, handsome, intelligent and compassionate with his pupils, his hair played with by the wind, standing here with her, so close as of old when she would say good night. Surely he cannot be dying? She smiled, wishing her smile could heal. He had changed a little. It was not his contagious smile that had changed, nor his strong hair; what was it? She couldn't tell. Her eyes spoke. 'You are beautiful,' they said.

He did not think it possible that she could be more lovely than his memories of her, and yet, so it was.

Together they radiated so much warmth and affection that when he closed the door and she felt him standing behind her, something cracked inside and a deep longing overwhelmed her.

'I have brought you these. I wish Milly were here.'

'I have missed her too.'

'Let me put them in some water.'

She walked to the kitchen, and he followed her, trying to absorb her presence. In a large glazed waterjug, she arranged them saying, 'They are for you. The last time, they were for Milly. Have you heard from her?'

'Yes. I have photographs to show you. What will you have – Tea? Coffee? Something stronger?'

'Something stronger.'

'Have you eaten?'

'Yes.'

'Milly is a busy wife, mother of a little girl – Jenny – and is teaching part time at a kindergarten and going to college. That is America's pace.'

'She looks so different. So modern and stylish!'

'It's the hairstyle and the American clothes.'

'Herself at last, unrestrained, in a home of her own. Whom did she marry?'

'A nice St. Lucian – Henry Lewis… She says he is behaving real foolish and spoiling the child. But we haven't spoken of you. Congratulations,' he said; 'that was wonderful news.'

'Thank you. You are looking well. How are you feeling?'

'Just great.'

She got up from her chair and came and sat next to him on the settee. The past enveloped them. And without any warning he felt her warm tender cheek on his. 'You are feeling sorry for me,' he said.

'Shhhhhh! Congratulations,' she whispered and caressed his eyes and forehead and neck and lips with hers; and then what was before a carefully engineered dam, burst within him and he responded as a healthy lion. She was convinced that he could not be ill; it must be some error, some mistake. When they opened their eyes, the sun's last rays were scattering slanting streaks of saffron on the floor.

'Let me light a lamp.'

'Not yet. Don't let us ever part again.'

He listened to the sweet nectar she was offering. Again she spoke, 'Let us get married soon.'

He caressed her forehead, her temples with his lips.

'Marry me,' she whispered.

'Marry me now.' There was an urgency in her voice, as if she felt he would not survive the night.

'You shouldn't say that. It is too tempting. I am not that ill, Sastra.'

'Your illness will leave you.'

He smiled. Here he was struggling with himself, but she was throwing restraint to the wind. Her loveliness overpowered him and her caresses unbridled him. He sensed she was trying to use herself to dam the mouth of his life stream, so that it would not empty itself, reach its end and be lost in the mighty ocean deeps where all things settle. He must not allow her to become a bulwark.

While she was asleep, darkness had come. He had lit the lamp, and its ochre flame transformed their faces into paintings by the old masters: she, comfortably resting in his arms, a haven: he looking at the darkness beyond, thoughtful, pensive, his eyes shining, reflecting his predicament, mirroring his peril.

As she gradually became aware of her surroundings, seeing the ochre light and the room and his shadow on the wall and thinking it might be a dream, she reached out to him and finding him no illusion, again embraced him as if driven by a renewed fervour, saying, 'When?'

Again he tenderly caressed her and when at last satisfied by his lips she nestled closer to him, wishing to curl herself round him, he said, 'My dearest Sastra, you must help me to take the right path for us both.'

'Marry me,' she whispered, kissing his neck and chest. Gently lifting her face with the palm of his hands, he said, 'You must listen, my dearest.'

'I do not wish to listen to reason; it is dull and is without passion. It has been my close companion for too long.'

Neither spoke; all that they had longed for, dared hope for had now been found a thousandfold, and such a find was difficult to comprehend.

He caressed her as tenderly as if she were asleep and then said, 'You must know I cannot marry.'

Seeing she was about to interrupt him, his fingers touched her lips, and then, lifting her soft hands, he cradled his own in them.

'In all societies, a widow with a child...'

'With children?' she suggested.

He frowned, trying to register with her a measure of the sternness of reality, the harshness of life.

'Such a widow... is greatly disadvantaged. Her chances of remarrying in any traditional, conservative society are slim, and in our conservative Hindu community, remarriage is virtually impossible. Sonnets and songs are written on first loves, but who cares for the second love of a widow with child? Which mother encourages her son to marry a widow with child, when so many young and willing brides are in the offing?'

'I would not wish to marry again.' And caressing him with her cheeks she said, 'Who wishes to drink from a cup when she has drunk her fill from a chalice born of light?'

Again they embraced, her words emboldening him, transforming them: two flames in the wind. Later, much later, though comforted by his tenderness, she saw that his initial anguish had increased, and not wishing to prolong his pain, yet troubled that he would behave as the community would wish, as her father would wish, she decided that he must make his decision fully aware of how she really thought and felt.

'I know you wish to tell me that bringing up a child alone, without a father, and on one income will not be easy.'

He was relieved that at last she was seeing their situation clearly. 'My father,' she continued, 'I am sure, thinks as you do, so when, to please you both, Govind and I agree to marry, will you attend my wedding? Will you?'

He said nothing.

'Will you feast with us on the day and rejoice with all the guests? Will you give me and my husband your good wishes, that our marriage may be blessed with many sons and fewer daughters? Will you embrace me and say farewell with dry eyes? And when you return to this house, to this room, will you sit here alone and study the shadows on the wall? Will you dream of me and wish and plead and beg and promise the gods of Time and Youth any sacrifice, if they would but retrace their steps?'

Now she, sitting upright the better to see him, had moved to the chair opposite, for she feared for herself. So she waited; waited for him to speak, but nothing came. His eyes welled and appeared to have narrowed. Again she spoke, 'I would beg the gods unashamedly, I would throw my pride to the wind and visit you at dead of night. Now I ask you, give me my sanity and my pride. Stir my soul and let my spirit fly. Help me, Rabind, to sing and dance and shout and laugh. Help me my dearest to live. Let us decide upon our time, let us say what will be within its span. No more of shadows and longings, let us live our dreams my dearest, help me bring mine forth from the land of ghosts.'

Nothing stirred. They had become a piece of sculpture. No sound, no movement. She had stood outside his fort, shouting and pleading, had asked him to lower the bridge, yet saw nothing but what was in her mind's eye – a dolphin skipping the water, with a slipper, smiling, his eyes sparkling with moisture. These were the eyes before her.

'You are dearer to me than life itself and I hold that to be sacred. How can you speak so openly about what tortures me. Don't you think I am aware of all you have said. Were I thinking only of myself I would have married you a year ago, were that possible. On that river bank – I would have made you my wife. But now to leave you alone so disadvantaged, for I see the world as it is, I find this too difficult to contemplate.' And looking at her he smiled. Oh God! he cried out within, give me the strength to do what is right for her; return her good sense.

And seeing him smiling, but not understanding the turmoil within, she crossed the floor and its slanting shadows and taught him to forget reason, for she offered him the sweetest pleasures of her lips and cheeks and throat and eyes. And he succumbed. And together their spirits soared as one, for they flamed into life not knowing that to love with that consuming fire was also to suffer, to absorb pain, to die.

As he walked her back home, they both appeared as if they had been swimming against the tide for their hair and eyes and skin glowed. He held her hands but seeing a family he knew approaching, released her, not wishing to compromise her lest her father were to refuse him and said, 'It is only right, Sastra, that you should know what form with time my illness will take. I would like you to speak to Capil, I will tell him I wish you to know all that you need to know, that the bitter, the ugly truths of the final stages of this illness be unwrapped and placed before you. If after this...' But she would not allow him to complete his thoughts and placed her fingers on his lips, as if they were children, as if it were the most natural of gestures, of what should be.

'I shall speak to my parents; speak to my father, be

bold; tell him, all… Tell him,' she whispered. 'Don't be afraid, say your wish is mine… I shall do the same.' A sudden gust of wind caught an outstretched branch of bougainvillea of the deepest purple, blowing it so that it fastened on his shirt, restricting his movement. There, before the still-creaking iron gate, he wished her good night, her eyes caressing him as she lifted the thorn-covered branch. He remembered another time when she had welcomed him in the heat of the day, when she had been so shy, so reserved and afraid both of him and of her parents. And wondering where all this goodness came from, trembling at the thought of embracing earth's sweetest joys, his desire grew.

When Rabindranath returned home he was restless. He paced the floor, went out in the garden and strolled without direction. He retraced his steps and sat before his desk. What should he say? The photographs of Purusha and Surinder, Ganesh and Gajraj watched his dilemma. Had he promised Sastra he would speak to her father? Did he say speak? He was not sure. How does one carry on a conversation with a man who is direct, who is suspicious of courtesies, seeing them as an integral part of the duel, a man who wants you to speak your business in a businesslike way.

After a while he decided he would write, the formality of language veiling the hopelessness of his situation. A pen and writing paper rested on his desk, but he did not pick them up. How can I even think of this? What am I really saying to her father when I make such a request?

The photographs of his parents and grandparents continued to smile. And though he wrote under their gaze, he did not see his letter as asking Narayan that the spirit of the Pandes – lit by Ganesh and carried by Gajraj and Surinder – be allowed to live and breathe again when he, Rabindranath, was no more. This was not, the way he was thinking. Before him was only Sastra Narayan.

As he wrote, that shadow of his lost self, alluded to so vividly by Sastra, came and sat beside him; it was stark and gaunt and kept its eyes on the page. On seeing this, Reason, the faculty he long revered, stood up and said, 'You must know it cannot be right to marry and leave her disadvantaged for far more years than your lives together will be. What stresses and strains will she not endure bringing up a family singlehandedly? What constraints would be hers forever in this community?' But the thought of their lives together, even for a day, the possible realisation of so much joy, began to smother this voice. Hope, the resting place of miracles and dreams, that can withstand dormancy, embraced him.

But his close companion Reason was far stronger than he thought; it had been much exercised and well fed, and stood its ground. Then a deep anguish from within him gushed forth; an uncontrollable passion for her leapt from within him, towering high as spring tides. And he wrote as a man driven, and as he wrote, Reason itself began to shrivel until it lay in a far corner, still, diminishing rapidly, evaporating, then no more. Seeing this, he wept bitterly.

Narayan did not approve. He saw it as the madness of youth. My daughter is a young girl, impressionable. May be she feels obligated to him, or his father. It could be hero worship. I know she is sorry for him. I am sorry for him, too; he wrote well, but are these the ingredients for marriage? She tells me they work together well. I am thinking that is not enough; when she hesitates for a while and adds, 'We understand each other', as if she were his advocate and I the prosecutor.

She is making things more difficult for me. What experience of life has Sastra had? She has no idea what she will face after a year or two... All right... perhaps an outside chance of four years. How rapidly will he deteriorate? Does she know the inner rages of a dying man, the frustration, his suspicions as he becomes more and more tired and weary; sick, impotent; all this spilling onto her? And if she... well... if she were to become a mother. Then what? Alone, struggling on ever alone, seen by other men as exploitable, vulnerable, weak! Having to compromise herself, at first just a little, because of the children; that's how it starts; having no one to trust, to trust totally when her mother and I are dead and gone. And all this time alone, alone with the children, overprotective of them and growing old before her time. No one to whom she could unburden herself and not lose her self-worth. My God, how little she understands life! Too protected. Too protected from its ugliness, its living hell. She knows nothing, nothing, of life. Any realistic view of life must be influenced by hard experience and she has none. When I say this to her, she is calmer than I. It is as if she thinks I have to say these things – these are my lines and she must listen.

But Sastra had asked herself, how could one feign love to another: how can I marry Govind. Ma once said faces reflect the souls they mask. What sort of face would I have: a woman moulding her inner feelings to a traditional design? Would my clown's mask fool Govind? My poor father is measuring time as calendars do; how can I say to him that it is the quality of a moment that lifts the human spirit? I will have a lifetime of ecstasy in a moment. I do not want a year or a month; that would be too much... One day... one day I ask. How does a daughter say this to a father, to my father?

Today my daughter is high up on a tree, swaying sweetly on the highest branches. Naturally she will not answer to any call which says, 'Come down to earth.' She tells me she couldn't marry anyone else. I can understand that now. To feel that way now, but time... give herself time; time is what she needs and nature will run its course. Youth and good health and a change from the village will help her overcome all this, this obsession for a former teacher. She is trapped, caught and does not know it.

I cannot say this openly, but I often think if Parvatee had been a more disciplined mother, held her on a shorter rein, this problem would never have raised its head. That college exhibition class is what did it. Little does the community know the sacrifices others make on its behalf...

Govind is right for her, from all points of view – caste, family, religion, character, profession; and there is a friendship of long standing between the families. What must Shakuntala think? She has been patient and understanding. I asked Sastra whether these things stand for nothing. She is quiet and then says Rabindranath's family qualifies too. But I asked her, 'Is his situation the same as Govind's?' I had to ask. I had to bring it in the open – it was harsh, tough, necessary. I am fighting for her tomorrows; she, for the minute, playing its time of the moment.

She sat there. Just sat. I felt she would have stayed there for ever sitting and watching time pass. It was her silence, her vulnerability, her idealism that seemed to be looking at me. Life is not about idealism. It is about judgment, about seeing a situation, assessing it and doing the best under the circumstances.

At last she spoke:

'Pa, how can I marry anyone else when all my waking thoughts would be elsewhere. How can I live this way? How can we expect Govind to accept this? Would it be fair to him? There are all kinds of deaths. Some of us die long before we are buried, though we walk and talk. My marriage to Rabindranath would transform my life into a beautiful, translucent thing, not an ordinary thing. Please speak to him, Pa, try and understand him a little, read his letter again.'

I have noticed her mother is now weakening, she is talking of karma. How can I reason with that? It is the refuge of those unable or unwilling to better their lives, seeking solace. Karma has shackled Parvatee. She is beginning to side a little with Sastra. It is all emotion... it is a comforting thing to do now, to soothe her daughter's emotional distress... but what happens later?

Narayan knew that the present has a force, an immediacy that the future may not comprehend, and so that he might honestly say to the future that he had gone about making this decision in an honourable way, he decided he would go and speak with Rabindranath.

Having declined the offer of refreshments, Narayan said: 'My daughter believes that if I were to know you better, my attitude towards her marrying you would be favourable. You must know I do not believe this. She says so, because she makes your character the pivot of her arguments. To my way of thinking, the very fact that you wish to marry her shows your character in another light. What do you say to that?'

There was a deep canyon of silence between them. Then Rabindranath spoke.

'What can I say, that you do not already know. My affection for Sastra grew when we worked together, our separation has only helped to confirm what I had always wanted – to marry her. I am now in a weakened position, and understandably my request will be seen as selfish and self-centred. I cannot say that I am not thinking of my own happiness when I ask your permission to marry her, but consider my past and judge whether selfishness fuelled my life or that of my parents. Had I known, years ago, that this illness would overpower me, so early in my life, I would have lived differently, conducted myself differently. This affection we have for each other would not have been nurtured.'

'My sole reason for wishing to marry her is that my life would become a joyous, grand thing, not an existence. Had I felt that hers too would not be the same, I would not have written you, for I am constantly aware – believe me it stays with me all the time – that were we to have your permission to marry, I would one day leave her behind; and so marriage would be an unscrupulous thing for me to enter into if I did not think her life with me would be what she too would wish.'

Rabindranath took up his glass of water to drink. Narayan said nothing. He had listened but though Rabindranath's integrity struck him, he was no less unhappy with the idea of marriage. But it was all making him grow weary and he feared his resolve was weakening, feeling that a university education helped a loser, someone with a weak case, to make a good stand.

'The main difference between my life and that of a healthy man,' Rabindranath said, 'is that the latter knows he will not die of an illness, not that he will not die. He could have an accident tomorrow. No one knows when he will die. In my case medical science has made it possible to say roughly how long I should be able to survive the illness. Those unfortunate people who die on the roads every day are in a worse position than myself they and their families are unprepared. But I have been forewarned and this will greatly influence the way I live each moment of each day. This ultimatum has helped me to see life as a small barrel of fine spirit which I will sip and taste and enjoy, glass by glass, day after day, knowing that this liquid light is dropping lower and lower down its cask.'

The fact that Rabindranath was so amiable, even smiling, helped Narayan to speak his mind a little: 'To live your life as if there will be no tomorrow is admirable. These teachings are in the Shastras, but my agreeing to your marrying my daughter would ensure that all her tomorrows, for years to come after your death, will be stressful, painful and sad. I am concerned with the quality of her tomorrows, when you leave.'

Narayan was tempted to say, especially when her alternative is so good, but he knew the prescribed path of courtesy, he knew that there were things that must remain unspoken. Besides, he pondered, what hurts would I have sown, if they decide to go their own way.

'To believe that is to believe in some destiny, in karma, or to believe that people and situations remain static with time. I don't. Sastra will make something worthwhile of her life, wherever she is, with or without me, for she carries with her much courage and an ability to separate the substance of things from its shell.'

To be told that he would have to believe in karma or destiny to say what he said quietly amused Narayan. He would say that, Narayan reflected, still firmly believing that in the context of village life, it was irresponsible for Rabindranath to contemplate marriage. Suddenly

Narayan felt too tired to argue any further, though much of his deepest thoughts he had not expressed and when they parted, each felt he had lost the essence of the argument to the other.

The next morning after Sati and Parvatee had talked late into the night, Narayan was approached by his wife. 'They have decided not to see each other. It is Rabindranath's idea, he thinks the neighbours will begin to talk and Sastra's good name will leave her.'

A week later she returned to him and said, 'If you don't give your blessing, I will have to give mine. They don't have much good time left, don't you see? And we are wasting what little they have, with reasons that do not reach Sastra. What can Rabindranath do? Put yourself in his shoes. What would you do? Tell me, if you were his age, what would you do?'

He said nothing.

As he got up to go, Parvatee said, 'You are her father, you have to be kinder, be more generous, more understanding. What else can you do? Can we live with ourselves if we continue to take this stand? We all know, we have all learnt, "Honour thy father and thy mother". This she is doing. Is there no time when parents, more than anyone else, should honour their child? If it were Sastra who was dying, would you have prevented Rabindranath from marrying her? I am asking myself this question over and over.'

Narayan looked at his wife as if she were a stranger. What could be wrong with this woman? Had she gone mad? A man alone with a child is not burdened. Female members of his family rally round. But a woman alone with a child is a woman alone with feet tied. I shall have to let Sastra know that even well intentioned men would use her vulnerability – a widow's vulnerability – a young mother with child – to their advantage. A madness has captured my daughter and now my wife; and I am weakened, worn down.

That night he sat alone and thought much:

I am sure a time will come, I am sure of it, when I, Narayan, shall regret this decision; a time when I would be sure that there was another way; yet I know full well, I have no choice, no real choice. How can I now, even in a few years time, encourage her to marry Govind, knowing that her thoughts and tender feelings are elsewhere. And when Rabindranath dies and she stands by his mound of earth and weeps, what will she say? What will she think of me? How will I be able to look at her? If the essence of an act has evaporated, it becomes a waste to perform it. My wish that she should marry Govind has become such a thing. God help me to carry out what I must now do with dignity.

The wedding ceremony was performed according to Hindu rites, a quiet family affair, nothing as Shakuntala and Parvatee had once dreamt of; no favoured artist was called to decorate her daughter's face and hands and feet; no dancers were called, no singers, no drummers.

A few of the neighbours spoke of the unconventional haste and the modest nature of the ceremony and wondered; cynical imaginations wove a pattern of intrigue, far removed from the vulnerable truth. Dr. Lall, though, had been overwhelmingly magnanimous in his several gifts to the bride and bridegroom and came over personally to tell them: 'I wish you all that I would have wished myself in these circumstances, and may your craziest hopes and wildest dreams come true.' He tried to smile mischievously, but it was not easy. 'We must

217

keep in touch and, remember, call me at any time of the day and night, even if you only need reassurance, a second opinion. May you know the joy of living.'

Dazed by the incense, the smoke of the pitch-pine, the fragrance of roses and orange-red marigolds, the sombre Sanskrit vows and ancient, melodious chants, Rabindranath and Sastra stood before Narayan and Parvatee, and the older couple blessed their daughter and son-in-law. The pundit arose and did the same, showering sanctifying Sanskrit verses, rice and flowers upon them. Turning to the small gathering he asked that they too bless the couple and pray for their welfare. 'May your goodwill stay with this young husband and wife to the very end, as they set out together.'

Sati and Capil were deeply moved for they had discussed the debilitating side of the illness with Sastra; she had wished to know the worst, as she had promised Rabindranath she would, and had born it bravely. Sati could not keep a dry eye; Shakuntala was unable to attend.

On the night of their wedding, for the first time alone on that long day, they could hardly believe their own good fortune; and just lay there, each absorbing the enchantment, the glow, the loveliness of the other, stilled by an unfathomed joy, softly subdued by the quiet dignity of Narayan and Parvatee and the gracious solemnity of the Vedic rites.

The small red candle fluttered coyly at first, but when blown by the wind began to leap, and Sastra marvelled at the vitality, the beauty of something so ephemeral. Rabindranath came before her and opened the casket, the contents of which he had once shown her, though neither could recall in any detail what they had seen. Now they saw it as husband and wife. An inner moving light; a newly born, dark sapphire sky vibrating, pulsating with the primeval energy of topaz, rich rubies and amethyst; a whole new universe created; a single heartbeat, growing, enlarging; the sky and sea changing places and the emerald earth rising until it was in perfect equilibrium between sea and sky, an equilibrium strengthened by starlight streaks from a fast-fading, crumbling ancient world which affectionately directs its last throbbing flows of energy to this new birth. And, for the first time, they both saw what Ganesh had seen in his lowly mud hut in a far village in India and what Rajkumari and Gajraj, Surinder and Purusha had seen as they made lives for themselves in Trinidad. What they saw was not jewels fixed in some immutable way, but an array of energy, of flames, of lights in movement, in constant flux.

Removing the piece of jewellery from its casket, he crowned her nakedness, which needed no adornment for one so lovely. And there they gave and received of each other so much joy and beauty and delight that Rabindranath knew his short life would be a living poem; and Sastra came to understand that her happiness was to be a bewitching intoxication of joy; painful, yet sadly and deeply stirring. These two flames became one and a solitary candle kept watch.

CHAPTER TWENTY-TWO

A WISH FULFILLED

The years had galloped past for Govind. He was in a bar, seeking solitude, time to reflect. Another beer. This part of London was dull and drab. Through the window he could see a building site – masons, bricklayers– hear a cement mixer grumbling. There was a bus terminus lower down. This part of the East End was not familiar to him, but today he wanted to be away from his fellow students, to be with himself.

The mood at college was one of jollity. The hard slog, the six year stint was over; he had completed his internship and was planning to have a year's experience in Port of Spain General Hospital before going into private practice. He had already applied and been accepted. Capildeo had approved. 'You will need the cooperation of the hospital when you are on your own; it is good to know how it functions – to know people there; besides you get a wonderful opportunity to meet the specialists, the matrons.'

He had not written to Sastra because he had sensed long ago that Rabindranath would take the prize and he did not wish to seem to be pleading, and after a while the many attractions of London, which required no commitment, had absorbed his pain.

Already, he sensed the future, had adjusted himself to

thinking of a stable, enduring, comfortable life – in time a healthy private practice in St. Augustine; marriage, a family: all seemed as natural, inevitable, as the two seasons in Trinidad. And yet he could not shake off a deep feeling of melancholy.

Sati had written – in the same tone as his mother would have done – of medicine being a vocation, a dedication, a calling. Their expectations were so high; he had applied himself, had done remarkably well and was now looking forward to going home.

About his friends at home and the family, he had been kept well informed. Thanks to Sati's letters, he knew of Sastra's marriage to Rabindranath, of their first child, Purusha, named after Rabindranath's mother and that another was on the way. He had news of the hospital and the island wide inoculation of all children with B.C.G. and there was the other Sati – the matchmaker. 'Your mother and I are keeping our eyes open for a suitable bride. As soon as you arrive, we will need to sift through the many enquiries. Already they are forthcoming, and we are having no easy time stemming the tide. It surprises even me how news has spread that you will be home soon. It is as if the wind listens and speaks as it blows.'

She had been like a sister to him, and had it not been for her (he was sure she encouraged his cousin, Capil, to write) it would have been so easy to have lost touch.

He could not but think of Sastra. He was sure that Rabindranath should not have married her; it was not the sort of thing he would have done. He could understand Sastra marrying out of pity, sheer pity; it was what he had come to expect from a young woman with a Hindu upbringing, with its emphasis on the loyalty and devotion of its women folk. Rabindranath should have known better. It was not what he would have done. It was unfair to her. Rabindranath should have understood this. Unpredictable behaviour! People are so unpredictable!

✶ ✶ ✶ ✶ ✶ ✶

As the plane began to descend, to circle round the island, Govind felt his memories reawakening – memories of a happy childhood seeing familiar places with a starry-eyed freshness. There was the forest, there the Northern Range, the bold outline of the East coast, straight as a rule. Where was Manzanilla Beach? He couldn't tell exactly. From this height, the forest appeared more closely knit, compact, and the roads, some of red earth, like deep cuts of a surgeon's knife. Caroni Plain was still there under the empty blue sky and the fierce sun. What a contrast to London! Then he realised that for the first time he was seeing the place of his birth with foreign eyes – it had become an island in the sun, a holiday place.

Then his stomach dropped. The earth came closer and the aircraft touched, bumped and rumbled along the runway, gradually reeling in its energy until it stopped. He was back.

He walked through the Customs shed. His dear old mother was awaiting him. He knew she had prayed and lived for this moment. They embraced and while she tried to fight back her tears, she garlanded him. The same faithful family pundit and friend was there. He too garlanded Govind, having first given thanks to God and welcomed him both in Sanskrit and in Hindi, the first because it is the language of the gods, and the second, so that the small family gathering might understand. Then with a clasp of hands and head bowed, the Pundit took his leave graciously and the two cars sped from the airport.

When they arrived home, many neighbours, young and old, their forefathers once from China, Africa and India, came to meet him and greet him and to observe what changes, if any, had taken place in his demeanour. All agreed that already he was looking like a doctor, that he had grown more handsome. 'The nurses would have the time of their lives trying to concentrate on their work'. They were glad that he was going to be in the hospital, but just in case their child fell ill, was it all right to bring the sick child round? Shakuntala, wiping her eyes, said, 'Of course it is all right. Once you are a doctor, you are on call, even on a Sunday. Sickness doesn't have a time to call.' The neighbours were thrilled with the idea of having a doctor in the street, just next door. He was not at all like those doctors in the hospital. 'You can't speak to them, Govind's mother, they so full of themselves, but our Govind here, this little boy who used to run about the yard, looking for lost cricket balls, is today a doctor...' They just couldn't believe it. They had to tell themselves this over and over 'before it sink in, God be praised... If you leave everything in his hands, you will never regret it... Look at his mother here; that's just what she did. And look how proud she must be feeling today, deep down inside...' '...She was never one for showing off, but she must be feeling really proud...' '...Come to think of it, we all proud, besides she...' And so, in the midst of all this friendly chatter, and to a background of religious and popular Indian film music, everyone called and was feted.

Narayan and Parvatee were there, and later, Rabindranath and Sastra came. Govind was surprised at how well the young couple looked. Purusha was so much like her father. Govind said, 'I am your lost uncle, returned. You are a big girl!' Purusha nodded her head in agreement, delighted to be addressed by a real doctor. 'I can swim,' she said. 'My daddy taught me. Can you swim?'

Govind said, 'No. Will you teach me?' Again she nodded.

Both parents smiled, and Sastra said, 'For a moment I thought she was going to say she can swim better than her mummy.'

'Not any longer,' Rabindranath said, his deep affection for his wife coming through his eyes and voice.

Govind saw this and was uncomfortable. Sastra had bloomed, was radiant and clearly very happy. Rabindranath had a serenity and an inner confidence, a thrust he found puzzling for one in his predicament. Now, Dr. Tiwari, he said to himself, you will have to grow out of this disappointment.

CHAPTER TWENTY-THREE

AND DARKNESS FALLS

Govind, on his way to Maracas Beach, had done all the climbing; now resting high up on a watershed he could see the descent before him – a sheer drop to the sea. He picked up a pebble, hoping to time its fall, threw it, but misjudging the distance, could neither hear its drop nor see its fall.

Here and there, on the outer cliff edge of the sinuously curving mountain road, there were no lights, no iron railings. He stopped the car to take in the panoramic view of where sea and land met: the blue of the dark deep and the grandeur of heights; the salted air and the fresh mountain breezes; the silent watchful clouds tracking across the sky. He sensed the emptiness between him and the stars and the ocean deeps, the stillness, the force of space at the end of the land and the outer infinity above; the earth rising almost perpendicular from one element and piercing the other, clothed by vegetation and scarred by man. A sharp cut deep into the mountain range exposed the tale of its formation for those with eyes to see. 'The same age as the Alps', he hears a classroom voice.

Towering above him were the highest peaks of the Northern Range – rugged, steep – yet he had counted three wooden houses as he climbed. A hermit's life on the mountains? The idea appealed.

From this height the sea looked perfectly smooth, the waves barely perceptible with white ruffles moving irregularly, like lace trimmings, only to be lost, absorbed time and time again without trace in the immensity of the blue.

He could see why some doctors in private practice thought he was naive. Overworked and too conscientious, his time at the Port of Spain General Hospital was not all that he had expected. Stay there two years and build a reputation, he had told himself. Compared to the takings of a thriving practice, his salary was a joke; but was practising medicine a business? His colleagues saw it so. 'Wait till you have a family'. But his mother and Sati talked as if a doctor was a priest, a man with a calling. Was he?

The descent was much quicker than he had thought and he stopped near a clump of coconut trees, seeking to give his car their unstable green shade.

Not yet eleven o'clock, but from Maracas Beach high pitched sounds of pleasure went ahead of their makers. Four children dashed out of a car and ran full speed to the water's edge. The froth and foam caressed their feet but they could only feel the terror and excitement of the wall of water half-threatening, half-welcoming them.

The beach, its peaceful anonymity and the lapping of the waves, sapped his tension until the seascape with its regular distant murmurings lulled him to sleep.

Later, on night duty at the Port of Spain General Hospital, Dr. Chandra Maharaj called:

'Had to phone you to tell you I heard a patient saying that Dr. Tiwari was the healthiest-looking doctor in the compound.'

'It must be the sea air.'

'Haven't seen you properly since you arrived. Three months?'

'We are understaffed.'

'It's a common affliction. How is your mother? Ma was asking.'

'She is well; keeps herself busy…'

'That's good, especially at their age… Come and have lunch with us on Sunday and please bring her; Ma and Pa would be disappointed if you don't. Sati and Capil are coming.'

'Look, I have to cut off now. I may be able to make it. If I can't. I'll let you know.'

'If you're running late, it wouldn't be any trouble to send the car round for your Ma. The old people tend to eat early and retire.'

'I'm looking forward to that style… I must go.'

Then what should have been an automatic renewal of Govind's contract, the second six month period, was turned down by the Administrator. He was told that resources were stretched and priority had to be given to newly qualified internees, large numbers of whom were now returning from abroad. Govind was entirely unprepared for this, had made no alternative arrangements and did not want to have to equip a surgery so early. No one yet knew him outside the hospital, and he was only just beginning to become a recognised face to the old hands of doctors, nurses and matrons – and he had not yet made any valuable contacts with the Hospital Services Department. He had thought that in about two years' time he would have established himself in the hospital and then could have taken his good name with him to build and enhance his private practice.

When Shakuntala first heard this, she could make no

sense of it but later thought it might be God's plan that Govind should start his private practice earlier. As chance would have it, in St. Augustine, obliquely opposite Dr. Capildeo's grand residence and thriving practice, was a rundown, rambling, wooden burnish-brown building, which still had a certain old-fashioned elegance. The owner was willing to let the young doctor have the two front rooms at a nominal rent. He said, 'I could cut the grass and generally upkeep the lawn; as to the windows and doors, Doc, if any needs major repair I'll send a carpenter round, you understand me, Doc?'

Govind nodded.

'Well then, I'll send the boy over some time to cut the grass. Can't let a doctor's place look like a burial ground, right, Doc?' and he beamed. Govind smiled reluctantly. 'Leave it to me, Doc,' he said and his clanking jitney left.

Next door to this brown structure, and opposite Dr. Capildeo's surgery and home, was an equally grand, gracious residence purchased by Chandra Maharaj's parents. Unfortunately for Govind, the close juxtaposition of these two palatial buildings to his own surgery gave passers-by the unwarranted impression that this was the practice of an unsuccessful man, a witch doctor whose medicines did not work.

So disadvantaged, Govind hung his plate and waited. During the first month, few ventured to cross over the road to the new doctor when the old one – Dr. Capildeo – was right there. Those who did were gratified by the bedside manners and the time Dr. Tiwari spent on their cases and so, slowly, by word of mouth, his reputation began to grow. Sati, too, had helped. Having sought and won her husband's approval, she encouraged their younger patients to attend the surgery across the road when time was of the essence. So, little by little, his practice grew and the anxieties of the first month began to fade.

One Sunday afternoon, after lunching with his mother, he decided to call on Sastra. After all, he had not seen her baby son, Jiva, and Capil had said. 'Don't stay too long to make the visit. Don't delay your going.'

What must their life be now, he wondered. She chose him knowing... A fortunate man, to be chosen in spite of... Does he feel his good fortune the way I do... He who has the prize is comforted... but a man without – his dreams are troubled. But now, how does he think now?... Leaving her... exposed... strained beyond the limit... Are his dreams troubled? The pain offers him no choice; I know this. But knowing the pain to come and still to be chosen... And after? Would she be different after? Have I changed too? What did he possess that I lacked? Was it simply to have been there when the pollen fell... Yet, to take by stealth... to misuse the ancient trust of pupil and master. He must have known the seeds he was planting, sowing against me, my family and hers... We were on the same rung – she and I. Our parents asked us to stand too near each other; she did not have to look up to find me... And after? There was the time – at our home on the day of that puja, we were close, becoming closer; I, swinging her above all the shrubs above the frangipani and wild poinsettia. Why couldn't we have fastened our hold? I played by a rule book which blind passion does not read.

He did not yet know that Rabindranath had resigned a month ago from his teaching post as head of the mathematics department; nor that his breathlessness had visibly increased, and his tiredness too; that he was

229

trying his best to keep up appearances, which of late was becoming more and more a losing battle.

Sastra was in the bedroom breast-feeding Jiva. Purusha was swinging her legs on a stool, enjoying a dish of curried crabs and had almost finished what was on her plate. She was attempting to get down from the stool when Rabindranath saw her fall; he expected her to cry, but no sound came as she lay on the floor, face upward, and looking alarmingly still. He tried to get up from his chair, to bear the intense pain of the effort, but found that he could not.

'Sastra!' he cried.

Purusha's pulse was still there, but Sastra could not get her to respond. She lifted the child's head to rest more comfortably on her lap and repeatedly tried to revive her, but the child remained still.

'Call Capil,' Rabindranath said, urgently, afraid that his coming would be too late.

At that moment Govind's car drew up before the house. 'Is anybody home?' he called loudly, copying his mother's custom, before entering.

From where she sat, Sastra cried out, 'Thank God it's you,' and almost laughed in relief. 'Come quickly!'

Seeing the crab shells and the fallen child, Govind took her pulse and hurried out to his car. He gave Purusha an injection, lifted her up and said, 'Show me her bed.' There he sat with her, Sastra anxiously looking on, until Purusha began to stir and open her eyes. Sastra's tears dampened Govind's cheeks as she embraced him.

'She'll be all right now,' he said. 'The injection works fast; but no more shell fish or crabs; her reaction was too severe!'

'But she has had it before.'

'Our bodies are changing all the time.'

'Thank God you came when you did. Could she have survived?'

He shrugged. 'Her reaction was bad. Why depress yourself with the might-have-beens.'

In the sitting room, Rabindranath felt alone and useless. He had heard the whispers and the stillness. It seemed an age.

At last Govind came, leaving Sastra with Purusha. Since the marriage, Govind and Rabindranath had had little opportunity for being together; their long absence and Rabindranath's rapid deterioration now made it difficult for them to be natural with each other. Govind could see the discoloration of the skin, the patches where the internal bleeding was bruising.

'How are you?'

'Better today.'

'The pain, increasing?'

'Not everyday... but the joints...'

'Would you like to increase the dosage?'

'Then I cannot think; sleep comes... prefer to have the day.'

'What does Capil advise?'

'He leaves it to me... I can have more... I know the dosage.'

'And Sastra?'

'_'

'What does she advise?'

'Like a sculptor... she holds... looks... listens, from moment... to moment, to the flakes... chips falling about her... she caresses the stone... Of late guides the medication.'

'How are you feeling?'

'Low… throat… my mouth… excuse me.'

As Sastra waved goodbye to Govind, Dr. Lall's car drew up and he walked rather unsteadily up the path towards her.

'I'm so glad I've caught you in; I'm leaving for good this time round.'

'I thought you were already in Toronto. So good to see you.'

'You're splendid, do you know that? I keep in touch with Capil; Rabindranath is defying the odds.' He smiled warmly. 'I have been coming and going not knowing what to do, but this time I'm sure I wouldn't be back. I've resigned.'

She could see he was very unwell and did not know what to say. She had always liked him, even when many years ago he was courting Sati and she was the little sister to whom he brought sweets.

'Give me your address,' she said. 'I will write. We must keep in touch.'

'I would like that very much. Promise,' he said, grinning as his body swayed backwards.

'I promise,' she said.

That night, Rabindranath was unusually quiet.

'Purusha has responded very well to her medicine,' Sastra said, 'soon she'll be her old self. She looks so much like you.'

'I have a confession to make,' he replied.

'Don't tell me, let me guess. Once upon a time the girls in one of your classes had a crush on you, and you did nothing to discourage them.'

'Yes… that too,' he said.

'Is there something else?'

She waited.

'It is better to tell me; you will feel lighter. Please don't spend time, our precious time, carrying burdens of guilt.'

'Jealous a... little of... Govind, though I have... no reason.'

'You have every reason. Your wife complimenting him and thanking him so warmly – and he's a handsome man and very clever too. I would be in the same position with the charming and delectable Miss Singh.' And as she caressed his hair she whispered, 'I would have gone quite, quite berserk, so you have, as always, a far better control of your emotions than I.'

'Cannot... believe... you would be... jealous of Miss Singh...'

Neither spoke for a while and as she kissed his forehead, he said, 'Have I given you... cause?'

'Well, you are always so pleased to see her.'

'Tell me... you don't... believe this.'

'I can say that but it won't be true.'

'Come, I would... never... have thought... it possible for you... to be jealous.'

'My husband is a handsome, intelligent, loving, generous and fine young man, and I don't believe I'm the only one blessed with the wisdom to see this.'

They held on to each other tightly for they knew that the descent had begun, but they had not anticipated that the gradient would be so steep. Already they were tumbling headlong, bruising each other. And while his hair absorbed her tears, she thought, I am glad he is jealous; it is an emotion with more energy, more fire than sorrow, which weighs him down so.

CHAPTER TWENTY-FOUR

TWO SPIRITS SOAR

Much rain had fallen in the night and the morning was cool. It was five thirty. Rabindranath slept. Sastra, lifting herself gently from his side, went to the back garden. There everything had bathed and was clean. A string of dewdrops hung on the clothes line. Clouds were moving east. Suddenly a gust of wind and she was heavily sprayed by the swaying orange tree. She looked around: the leaves and petals, beaded with water, reminded her of the backs of children playing in the rain. A yellow light came and the grass changed colour. For the first time she observed the firm young shoots on the ornamental hibiscus shrub, its flowers, a morning yellow, raising themselves outwards and upwards. The earth was soft.

That morning she did not want to leave him. But such crises had happened before and he had proved right that he would recover during the day. But of late her premonitions had been coming more often; it could not have been otherwise as she witnessed his gradual wasting away.

Early in their marriage, she had been full of hope, had silently prayed for, cried out for a miracle; had tried everything suggested by well-wishers – keraila juice, fresh garden herbs, roots and leaves and stems; soups and teas made from roots and stems, which he had drunk to please her; and simply prepared vegetarian meals.

They had been able to offer each other the gifts of Purusha and Jiva and together they had played and sung and laughed, listening to the vibrations of life's variety in movement and sound. All this while, time was moving swiftly and silently on. When it came, she knew. This realisation she held but not its acceptance.

Looking back she felt she must have tired him, but he had managed to keep from her, and from himself, his failing strength far far longer than even he had imagined. She wondered how much of this was due to what she recognised as her wishful thinking, her buoyant, open, kind attitude towards the illness. Initially she had treated leukaemia as if it were a living thing that would respond to love, caring and affection.

'You must take the children to swim,' he said, as she returned from the garden. 'How are they coming on?'

'Jiva swims like his father, effortlessly, and enjoys it with all the relish and excitement of childhood. Purusha will too, if she would only relax in the water; she needs to forget her fears, let it be, welcome it.'

'Don't be too hard… it will come.' He smiled and she did too, trying to dam her tears for she had been exactly as Purusha. It had been his gentleness and patience that made her a swimmer, encouraged her fear to evaporate.

'One day she will swim without thinking,' he said, 'and the soft rhythm of the water will part for her.' He paused, tired, and a silence joined them. 'I know she will… I can see her in my mind's eye swimming… with Jiva.'

She sat on the bed and said, 'Do you remember when you recovered my lost slipper?' He made an effort to reach her hands and seeing this, she reached out and held his in both hers. His fingers moved a little in her palm as if he were a new born baby. 'Do you remember,' she said, 'how we sat together on the bank afterwards?' He avoided her gaze and looked past her; his eyes had taken on a distant look.

'You will be late,' he whispered; 'they will miss their lesson.'

'Would you like to sit under the orange tree near the tulsi plant? I shall cover you well.'

'Too much trouble – I'm all right here. You ought to go now.' But she prepared the shade of the orange tree with rugs and blankets and helped him to sit comfortably, and they parted.

After three miles, near the foot of Mount St. Benedict and about to change gear to make the ascent to the swimming pool, she saw him lean over and fall. The picture before her was so vivid that she turned right around and drove faster than she should, saying to the children, 'Daddy is not well, he has grown worse.'

'How do you know, Mummy?' asked Jiva.

'Be quiet, Jiva, Mummy knows and I know too.'

'How do you know, Purusha?'

'I'm not telling.'

'How do you know, Mummy?' he asked again.

'I feel so, Jiva; I may be wrong. I want to be wrong.'

On entering the house, she said, 'Stay here until I call you.'

As she descended the few steps to the garden, it was the angle of his head that was awkward. O God, let him be alive she entreated and skilfully eased him from the fallen chair, resting the upper part of his body softly on her lap, knowing that all this movement was paining him. 'I called you,' he said. 'I wished it. I knew you would come,' he whispered.

236

'Shshhhhh!' she soothed, and then broke down completely, 'Don't leave me Rabind,' she cried.

'I'll never leave you,' he said; 'Where are Purusha and Jiva?'

'Shall I call them?' And he nodded.

She said to them, 'Daddy is not well.'

'We know,' said Purusha, busying herself with crayons. 'Will he get better, Mummy?' asked Jiva.

'Come, he wants to be with you. He has asked for you.' And the two children ran up to their father and Jiva climbed up on his lap and Purusha sat beside him.

'You are the nicest children I know,' he said, but they couldn't hear him.

'Will Daddy get better?' asked Jiva.

'Shshhhh!' said Sastra.

'I am going away,' he said, 'I am so sorry but I have to go.'

'I will come with you, Daddy,' said Jiva. 'Mummy will let me come.'

But Sastra could not answer.

'Will you, Mummy? Will you let me go?'

'Mummy is crying, Jiva,' Purusha said.

'I will always be with you,' he whispered, for his voice was becoming softer, like a shadow's walk and it was difficult to hear him; the energy he needed was fast leaving.

'Now kiss your daddy and go to the house.'

'Can't I stay,' asked Purusha.

'No. Take Jiva.'

And Purusha kissed her father with her moist cheeks, saying, 'I will miss you, Daddy. I will try harder with my swimming.'

And Jiva embraced him. 'I am going with Daddy,' he said to his mother. But she could not hear him.

'I will come with you, Daddy,' Jiva said, burying his head on his father's lap. Their small footsteps left the garden and the wind was silent.

'My dearest Rabindranath,' she said, her tears falling rapidly on his hot, thin, wasted face. 'Oh my dear husband.' She felt the stillness coming; he was struggling, trying to keep it at bay for just a while longer. 'Thank you,' he said. 'Thank you my dearest Sastra... You... are all... and more to me... You were my life's joy.'

And he was calm but her anguish choked her. 'Oh!' she cried out silently. 'Don't leave me, for God's sake don't. Oh God why? Why? For God's sake why? Why did he have to suffer so? Is there a God?' And she opened her mouth to allow the intense pain and the agony and the cry to leave her. Yet he heard no sound, for nothing came from her throat though her tears streamed on and on. And she began to caress his forehead. 'Jiva has your eyes and Purusha your hair,' she said, smiling at him. And a strange peace flowed from him to her and she kissed his eyes and forehead and cheeks and said, 'You have the most beautiful eyes I have ever seen,' and again his fingers moved within hers, and she knew. After, the light left his eyes and she placed both her palms over them as she had first done at the merry-go-round, reliving that pleasure and pain; gently she closed them and wept bitterly, comforting a body fast losing itself, rearranging his hair, Ganesh's hair, Gajraj's hair.

There in the garden, as she watched over his body, a part of Sastra departed too. When they had embraced once more, his spirit left with the passing wind and hers soared too, and only a part returned to her. And as she sat there with him, a woman whose spring had just ended, she wept for him and for his love and for their summer that never would be, and for their song of love and life and hope, and for the great fulfilment that had come with their spring, that comes with spring, and at last she cried bitterly for herself, for her anguish was over-whelming.

Beside his father, Surinder, Rabindranath was laid to rest.

She took a week off work and was restless; visited his grave daily and just sat there the way he had once done on his way to face his first College Exhibition Class. At home she wiped his framed photograph until the glass made clean rubbing sounds, and went through the family album again and again. She avoided the stream. Her memories of him were the memories of her life.

Purusha and Jiva were a comfort to her. Jiva did not comprehend death, but heaven he understood, and spoke of it as a place where he too would one day go and sit on his father's lap. Purusha said little, ate little and quietly mourned her father. She was the first born and the pleasure they had shared remained with her.

Parvatee and Govind, Sati and Capil visited her and gradually came to know the children better. Narayan did too but for him it was never easy. He had not ceased to question himself, on solitary walks and in the quiet of the day. Could there have been another way for Sastra? Now he saw his daughter's life ahead as one daunting uphill struggle and he grieved for her.

The week passed. Sastra returned to school and, in an effort to occupy herself mentally, to lose herself, threw herself with demonic energy into its exacting work. Then Milly's letter came. It was only then she remembered having sent the telegram.

Milly had been on holiday when the news arrived. The five page letter, written in her clear, kind hand, mourned with her; it was as if Milly was with her, comforting, reassuring her. Shared memories were there to be treasured, to strengthen one. Rabindranath, she reminded Sastra, would have wanted her to absorb courage from his short life, not to become choked, paralysed by it. 'Besides,' wrote Milly, 'you know if the spirit lives, as I believe it does, Rabindranath will walk with you whenever you are in need, and will come of his own accord to protect his loved ones. You were both blessed to have loved so much, never tiring of each other, never wishing to part. That was a joyous thing – your life together, like beautiful music; it is the meaning of being.'

The letter tapped deeper griefs yet unopened; and there, sitting on his side of the bed, she began to empty herself of pain, anger, fear and loneliness, the emotions and attitudes which could have so adversely affected the quality of her life and those of her children. It was not easy. Her spirit had been bent low, for despair had come and had tried to find a place to lie.

Her feeling of loss was immense, she felt it would fill up vast barren lands of the arctic and still overflow. At first she wished for solitude so that her thoughts might embrace him, welcomed the vacuum, the emptiness that surrounded her, and there alone relived the joys of their shared life: hearing his whispers, capturing his smile. It is not easy. She holds his spirit. Feels his closeness... Jiva has his eyes... and then the vast emptiness would return.

Her consciousness drifts, blows, is lost. She is not alone. He is everywhere. She cannot concentrate on anything but him, for her mind has learnt where her comfort lies and drifts back to him... back to him... She cannot concentrate on the present. Save me, Rabindranath... Save me from myself, she cries within... a wayward mind... unsteady... I cannot hold anything... O God! Help me! I cannot hold the present, I am slipping back. I will become yesterday... I need to move on... for Jiva, for Purusha... myself too.

The large, daily claims of family life tugged at her time, but still her spirit left the present for the past. In time she decided that her only hope was to leave and make a new start elsewhere. 'Change... a new place with its own shadows and shapes, colours and sounds may help me to heal – may show the path to the present. For Purusha and Jiva I must try harder. Help me, Rabindranath. I am a planet without a sun, whirling in the cold darkness of infinite space alone, drifting. An awesome blackness surrounds me. I fear the gradual crushing of an ice age over me. All around a terrifying vacuum, a gaping terror of space. I look around and around and nothing, there is nothing. Where is the light?'

BOOK FIVE

CHAPTER TWENTY-FIVE

A CHANCE THING

Being a doctor does not reduce an alcoholic's problems. Indeed, having to answer to the name of 'Dr. Lall', and to wear that profession at the clinic in Toronto where he was receiving help, jarred so much that he thought of dropping the title. Only the inconvenience of changing his passport, his cheques and the deeds for his comfortable town flat prevented him.

'I am slowly reforming,' he told himself. 'No external pressure, just a quiet, slow, slumbering existence.' He had a cleaner who came in the mornings – the time he went out to read the newspaper in the park flamboyant in summer, aflame in autumn.

Sastra's letter arrived during the Canadian spring. She wished to come in summer... in the middle of summer. That would give him time to adjust. After lunch he reread the letter in the spring sunshine. It was the tone of the letter he liked. 'Dear Dr. Lall...' What a nice way with a letter. And though he knew this was the customary way to begin, found much pleasure hidden within the word. 'It would be nice for Purusha and Jiva to get to know you better... I am no scientist, so an easy way out for me has been to say, "Ask Dr. Lall when you see him". So, like squirrels, they have been putting away their nutty questions to share with you later.'

Two children with their beautiful, trusting young mother, who didn't understand the jargon of real estate agents, nor those of mortgages and insurances. And what of rising damp, and sharks? She could so easily go under in this rapidly expanding city. Suddenly he had a purpose.

He began to focus on his project in a businesslike way. It was not easy, but to see her happy and the children in good neighbourhood schools were strong incentives. He visited the better residential areas and schools; measured distances between houses and shops and bus routes and trains. He was drained but kept on and on until he was satisfied.

As he travelled to the airport to meet her that morning, on the big, wide straight roads, on the flyovers which still made him uncomfortable, Lall felt as a young child does on Christmas Eve. Unaware of the extent to which Sastra was reading his spirit, he tried to be his old perky self, wear his well-worn mask, but he could not disguise the fact that his hands were unsteady, that he had been very ill, had grown thin. He smiled too often, and she could tell the strain of his inner wretchedness by his eyes, from his voice, his body, his walk; from the way his coat hung.

He guided her along what, to a newcomer, were strange paths pitted with deep crevices, until she found a house she liked and a teaching post in a college. All week she would work until, too tired to leave her desk, she would fall asleep over the night's preparation. Her weekends, she told herself, were Purusha's and Jiva's. He took a while to like his school, until an outgoing Irish teacher, herself a recent arrival, enabled him to settle into his new surroundings. The size of everything made Sastra feel foreign, the houses, so enclosed to her eyes, the schools, the playing fields, and people travelling everywhere in cars. Some things they liked – the local drive-in restaurant, no litter on the streets, the large detached houses, the big shopping centres, and the lines of lights making everywhere dazzling bright. From time to time Sastra would invite Dr. Lall to have Sunday lunch with her and though he ate little, pretending each time he came that he was feeling far better, making a show of his former spirit, nevertheless, even when he was with her, a weary inner sadness stayed with him.

Purusha and Jiva wanted to know about leukaemia and whether the body could have healed itself were it given the right foods and drinks. He spoke softly of the healing capacity of the body, and more softly of the destroyers of the body, mentioning alcohol and cigarettes in passing. He helped them to the belief that their own bodies were marvellous living things. 'No wonder it has taken so long to be perfected,' he would say. 'We need cures from outside ourselves for some things, but for many, many, things the body will repair, and will forgive. Its magnanimity is humbling. Rabindranath brought courage to his illness, a great deal of courage. It isn't an easy thing to have when you know you're "going under".'

First the days and the weeks kept coming, then the months and years flowed past. After a while Sastra knew it was only a matter of time for Dr. Lall. It was at this late hour he began to say, 'If I were a younger man, Sastra, Rabindranath would not have stood a chance.' He said this each time he came, unaware of his repetitions. Sastra never drew this to his attention, to this affectionate man, who, losing his judgment and awareness of self, was fading to a shadow. For she felt that shadows too, though ephemeral, should be acknowledged – it was a way of honouring their origins.

'I am sure of it,' she would say again and again, laughing, wishing to amuse and to comfort.

'So many important things happen by chance, Sastra. Did you know that?'

'Sati could have married you,' she said. It was a spur of the moment thing, something tumbling from a closed cupboard, something she had often thought of, but never allowed expression.

He said nothing; he would not enter that gate she was opening. It seemed too far away in a country lost to him, fading from his map.

'Well,' she continued, 'Capil was always sure of himself, he visited us often and made it difficult for Sati to say anything else but yes.'

He lit a cigarette.

'Well, I am not a brahmin, I didn't want to enter a race knowing I would lose.'

'I never thought you would lack confidence.'

'It is not so, not confidence – a kind of acceptable aggressiveness, an impermeable toughness I lacked. I lost my father at seven. My mother's sensitive, unassuming self and her own modest upbringing became a part of me. I preferred not to have asked than to propose, knowing, believing, I would be rebuffed. It seemed a waste, a foolish thing to try. I felt I wouldn't be at ease with the family, nor Sati with me, if I were turned down, so I did what I did... better to have something than nothing.'

'You waited for my parents to invite you home. You see, Lall, you went about it in an old-fashioned, gracious way, and because of this you lost out to someone who jumped the queue, who broke the conventional rules of etiquette... Pundit Karsi calls it the "modern way".'

'The daring pick up the prizes?'

'This "modern" way was always there. It is the savage spirit in civilised clothes, Lall, it steps on others, moves forward at the expense of the gentle and the decent; weakening, reducing something as fragile as courtesy, as it stamps on it, like wildebeest bellowing the praises of conquest – Rule. Rule.'

'I was born too early. Rabindranath, you know, would have had a difficult time, would not have stood a chance.'

'I agree. Yet, had you decided to run that other race you could have won.'

He did not believe what she said, but a spark within him wanted this opiate.

'Why do you say that?'

She laughed and embraced him; kissing him on the forehead.

'You are nice to be with,' she said; 'that's why.'

'Does... does...' He did not speak further, but she received his thought.

'You must know,' she said, 'you must know we all think you're nice to be with.'

He said nothing.

When the long summer evenings dispersed warmth and light and colour far and wide, they would together sit in the park, beside the lake, on a weathered bench in quiet alcoves, wreathed in green and freshly turning yellows, and stroll side by side each comforting the other, just by being there. When they strolled past shop windows, and saw each other's gentle face imprisoned in the glass, catching a glimpse of each other's longings caught unguarded, they would move on and say some idle word to cover that revelation.

He held out far longer than he himself expected, and grew closer still to her. Purusha and Jiva made it possible for him to feel a part of their family and he was grateful.

They learnt much from him about the healthy workings of the body, and he from them about simple joys. Sometime later in the crematorium, as his simple coffin of sweet pine slowly moved along the conveyor belt into the furnace, it was only her flowers and her tears and two small posies from Purusha and Jiva that saluted him and bade him adieu.

He had helped her to forget her own lonely struggle, had helped her to focus on the day-to-day commitments of family and college. Now she found she was no longer looking forward to returning to Trinidad; for her own part she had lost the desire, though for Lall's sake she would go and leave his ashes in the hospital grounds, as he had asked.

CHAPTER TWENTY-SIX

THE PAST RETURNS

It was a month since Shakuntala died and Parvatee wanted to have this puja in memory of her, for they had drawn close as her end approached.

'The house is now too big for me, Parvatee,' Shakuntala said on one of her visits. 'Govind works all day and comes home late and after that, the night calls begin. Some days he can't even eat in peace; no rest, poor boy. People are coming from all over; last week a lady came all the way from Barrackpore; even I don't know where that is. But I am here today, Parvatee, because I am tired talking to the gardener. You will have to bear with me a little longer.' That is how Shakuntala conducted herself, right up to the last. Her spirit was independent, sensitive to not overstaying, of not becoming an uninvited guest, even with a lifelong friend.

Perhaps it was the incense, the Sanskrit chants and everyone talking about Shakuntala and old Madam Tiwari that made Sati nostalgic. When she returned home she took out the family albums, spread them on the floor and looked for photographs of Govind's ajee and Shakuntala and Sastra. She was also hoping to find photographs of Govind and Sastra, taken before they went abroad.

So much had happened in five years! She thought about Lall, poor Lall, how he and Sastra had been so close, especially at the end. What had happened to him? Drink? In his younger days he'd been so shy in her presence, and so attractive. Then, he neither smoked nor drank. The stresses of hospital doctors were evidently far weightier than even they realised, she thought, and wondered why Govind had declined her invitation to Sastra's homecoming lunch. It was becoming a pattern with him… he was becoming a recluse. She knew Capil suspected her of taking a secret delight in observing how they would behave together, had accused her of 'failing to see the obvious twice'. This was absurd. She knew very well that no young man marries a widow when there are so many young virgin brides asking for his hand, especially when his mother had been Shakuntala. With her, virginity and purity had been one. She had spoken of the womb as if it were a hallowed temple, a sacred, holy place. She had said too that the best opportunities came only once and that no one can push back the hand of time, not even the gods. She had wanted a virgin bride for her son; she would have likened a young, beautiful widow to a nicely laundered sheet, but that was not the same as brand new.

But what, she wondered, did Govind want? No one had asked him. Could he have wished to marry Sastra, the mother of two? Maybe he was so bruised and tired from all that had gone before, that he just allowed himself to be carried along by other people's wishes into the arms of Chandra Maharaj, a brahmin and a medical doctor, ably assisted by her ever-so-charming, wealthy parents, who had sung their finest song at Shakuntala's door.

She was sure Chandra and Govind would become engaged; they had known each other from primary school days. Marriage to Chandra would enable Govind to upgrade his surgery, and the income of two doctors meant that not only a well equipped surgery, but also a good clinic, could all be put together in no time.

Yet she felt that there was some unhappiness in Govind that he was trying to exorcise by burying himself in his work. He was holding a one day surgery in Laventille, only charging the cost price of the medicine and often waiving that too. She knew Capil had warned him that he needed to get the balance right, not go overboard and lose his paying patients.

She thought how nice to see her sister again, she who had grown so close to Lall, staying with him to the end. It was sad that a man as attractive and brilliant as he should end like that. She blushed, for he always held a strange attraction for her. Once or twice she herself had wondered whether agreeing with her parents to marry Capil had not been an involuntary act… a drifting into marriage. Everyone around you sees it as inevitable and then you find that even to question the direction of the current becomes too great a task, never mind changing its course. For a moment she allowed herself to wonder what might have been the consequences of standing against the flow.

Capil came into the room with a tray. 'Thought we could have tea while you show me photographs of the most handsome man in the album.'

'Are you referring to Rabindranath or Dr. Lall?'

'I will say this, you have a unique disability; the obvious never strikes you, especially when it is close by.'

'Very good tea.'

'I met Govind.'

'When is he coming to see us?'

'He is not coming for lunch if that's what you mean. Chandra cannot make it either – one of those impossible days for her in the hospital – but she would like to have Sastra round for dinner and has sent this invitation.'

253

'Has she invited Govind too?'

'I didn't ask.' He smiled. Sati began to wonder whether it was just going to be the two young women catching up on each other's lives. Then Capil said, 'He will be there too.' And now she asked herself whether Chandra was far more calculating than she let on, wanting to observe how those two behaved together before pursuing an official engagement.

'Did you know Mr. Ramsaran is selling the Pande property?'

'You mean his property.'

'Yes. He has been offered the headship of Princess Town Primary.'

'Who will take the college exhibition class?'

'No one on the staff, he says, wishes to take it on.'

As Sati drove her sister home from Piarco Airport, she thought how well Sastra looked, how little she seemed to have aged, in some ways had grown more beautiful. Perhaps it was the cold climates which kept one younger.

Parvatee and Narayan sat around Sati's oval mahogany table for a late lunch and saw the reflection of the new generation: Ayisha and Arjun; Purusha and Jiva; and though Parvatee was content, she could not help thinking how it would have given Shakuntala much inner peace and pleasure to have embraced and fussed over even one grandchild before she died. She recalled how resentful Shakuntala had been in the days after Sastra's wedding. In her heart, Parvatee felt Shakuntala had every right to feel angry. They had all let her down. She herself had promised, had agreed with her for years about Sastra and Govind and then went back on her word. But what could she have done?

'Shakuntala placed her son's wellbeing and her own,' Narayan had said, 'on promises we gave openly.' She looked at Sastra and her children and wondered whether it could have been any different. But Sastra's feelings for Rabindranath had been too intense, raging like a forest fire. Everything had happened so suddenly. Now there was calm, what did her daughter feel? Did she now see it as Narayan had done?

She thought of how Shakuntala had tried, towards the end, to accept Sastra's marriage; but it hadn't been easy. How could it be? She had kept her hurt bottled inside. She felt we were all on the other side. When she remembered what Shakuntala had become in her last month, Parvatee wiped her eyes with her ornhi.

At about half past four Sastra went home with her parents, leaving Purusha and Jiva with Sati, who wanted the four cousins to try and get to know each other better in the short time they had. Before she left, Sastra expressed the wish to visit the Tiwaris' family house, and Sati said she would arrange it.

'I was expecting you. Doctor Govind sent me a message,' said the lean man, when Sastra knocked. 'Once he said Narayan younger daughter, I knew who it was. I know you, beti, but you wouldn't know me. Your father and mother I know well. They know me from long time. Come, I'll open the gate for you. So how is Canada? Over there nicer than here, na?'

'No,' she said. 'Just different.'

'I am sorry the doctor is thinking of selling… just thinking it over, you understand. But you looking nice, beti; like over there agree with you, na?'

'You're looking good yourself,' she said, smiling broadly.

'You wouldn' believe, nobody believes me but I was eighty last week. Yes, eighty years and four days exactly,' he laughed. 'I must say I owe a lot to the Doctor. If anything is going wrong inside,' and he pointed to his chest, 'he will tell me. Whenever he comes here, he asks me – as a matter of fact he tells me when it is time for a check up. Well... so far I have nothing to worry about... The doctor examined me the other day, he said, "Raja, I have nothing to report. You are a young man".' He laughed again, a little self-consciously, 'Well you know that is how the Doctor speaks... So long as he is around, I will be all right; he is a good man, the Doctor... I keeping you back, na? Come, I'll open the house... Dr. Govind comes here now only sometimes.'

Passing clouds hid the sun; the house and the yard were in the shade.

She entered the sitting room and remembered the time when Dr. Lall and Rabindranath were discussing that terrible fire. Had anyone been caught? Was the verdict accidental death? It had come and passed over them.

Here and now there was only stillness, an overpowering stillness permeating everything. The house had become a museum, a meeting place for spirits. She wanted to leave, to go outside.

The sun had come out and the yard was again sunny and bright. In the kitchen there was a silent order. Everything was still in the place allocated by Shakuntala and old Madam Tiwari. It was as if they were just away on a journey and expected back.

But there were no kitchen sounds or smells... no garlic, no pepper sizzling in hot oil; no santoor, no flute, no blowing of the 'sankh' – the spirit of the ocean in its whorl. The chulha was well swept, but there was no warmth, no scent of the forest wood. No voices. No movements. Govind's ajee and Shakuntala could have been but part of a dream – the dream of her youth.

The machan and the swing were still there and the

rich scent of the roses lingered in the air. She sat on the swing and remembered.

Later that evening as she was putting on her lipstick, getting ready to leave for dinner with Chandra and Govind, Sastra found that her palms had become somewhat moist and warm and her fingers trembled ever so slightly as she dressed.

Govind had suggested that they might stop by his mother's house. Sastra hoped that he would not press this. She thought of Chandra Maharaj and heard Sati's voice: 'The past is the past.'

He was punctual. As the car drove off, Parvatee waved, and she recalled a young girl complaining, 'Ma, you're matchmaking,' and Shakuntala had said, 'If only we could get the same people to make up Sastra she would look like Sita's Rama.' Narayan sat beside his wife, blowing and puffing; he had hurriedly climbed up the stairs. 'I just saw Govind and Sastra. Where are they going?'

'Chandra Maharaj has invited her to dinner.'

'Is it a family dinner?'

'I didn't ask that question.'

'I am thinking of selling the property,' Govind said, 'You don't mind if we call in? I need to speak to the gardener.' Sastra said nothing, though she was not entirely at ease. She could not tell why she felt so uneasy, why she felt an anxious expectation. Expecting what?

While Govind went to speak to the gardener, she strolled around the siwala and long mango tree and, without thinking, came and sat where the old lady often did. There was something comforting, some peace resided under this mango tree which shaded the spacious yard. Here, old Madam Tiwari had sat and seen the pain that was awaiting her grandson, her daughter-in-law and herself. Her deep distress, her moral dilemma, she had faced with courage and honesty, but it had weakened the tie that had long bundled her daughter-in-law to her. What followed was a new daily silence. A polite withdrawal by Shakuntala had then encircled her and, in the absence of abundant human warmth and affection, receiving only that which was measured by duty, she drifted. Soon, greatly reduced in spirit, feelings of guilt towards her grandson and her daughter-in-law pressed on her, suffocating her. Later her weary memory dimmed, and she was unable to recall what brought her to this distraught path. It was then she became a *sanyasi*, devoting her last days to prayers, fasting and penance; yet the feeling that she was unworthy of love, of salvation, had visited and stayed with her. And so, Old Madam Tiwari's end, when it finally came, was dignified, but cold, sombre and sad. Denied the passion she had sought for Sastra in her own youth, her spirit had moved ahead of its time, and for this, suffered deeply.

Sastra was lost in thought and it was some moments before she realised that Govind was standing beside her. 'Everything,' she said, 'still looks dry.'

'More rain will come.'

They stood together by the rose bush from which she had chosen a bloom many years ago. Govind was about to say something; she could feel his tension.

'It is the same,' she said, 'the garden, and yet you know deep down within, it isn't. The garden of our youth, the garden I imagined, the one that stays with me is not here.' The now too tall poinsettia shrubs and the shady cluster of cacao trees hung over them. Again he attempted to speak. She bent her head to hold the rose's concentrated scent. And he became a whirlwind, lifting what he had been denied, overwhelming her. And in her need to be comforted, she responded to his embrace, embracing her youth. Her delicious neck and her sweet fullness stirred him and he wanted more from her. His warmth and strength and his affection began to loosen the disciplined yoke of her single parenthood. And he began to pound at her door, hoping that he could turn back the years to the promise of old and she would let him in; but she found herself entangled in a fine mesh; anxious, confused, unable to move, to move with him; unsure; needing time and space to grow again; afraid to be engulfed by this clear, rushing mountain stream. On regaining herself she gently but firmly disentangled herself as if he were an old and trusted friend who for a moment had forgotten himself, and not as a lover parting in sweet sadness.

Govind wondered whether in the manner of her refusal was the desire to be treated not as a widow, but as Rabindranath's wife. As they stood, awkward, apart, she said, 'So much has changed and yet you haven't... I know you will show me the kindness our parents would have wished.'

He was moved by her stoicism. What was this strange, unfathomable attachment to Rabindranath? It seemed unnatural. Had her bereavement taken so great a toll? Would her feelings ever be stirred again, and by whom? Would she ever allow another to break through the tough carapace she had grown. The thought that she could live her life looking for something that could never be recovered made him wish for a moment that Rabindranath could witness what his death had dammed up in her.

'You are still missing him.'

She heard but no sound came from her.

'You should throw off the dead,' he said. 'Rabindranath is dead! Gone! Life is around; offer it a fighting chance...

Nothing stands still. Why do you? Everything that grows withers and we're a part of that... all choices close with time.' And though as a doctor he was used to dealing kindly but professionally with the relatives of the dead, the thought that she could prefer the dead to the living left him with an emptiness that almost swallowed him up. What must these memories be that did not lose their fire, pulse, energy, light, that were still glowing, still with colour, giving succour still, even now? But surely they too would die... All things wither and die. Memories too. Thank God!

The car's headlights swung into Chandra Maharaj's family home, revealing a neat, landscaped garden, with an orchid tree, clematis, spider lily and pepper hibiscus dancing round poles and pyramids on a prettily-kept, well-lit lawn. Chandra Maharaj must have been watching for their arrival, for as soon as the car had pulled up, she was coming through the silver and black terrazzo porch to greet them. Sastra noted the sophisticated taste in dress that drew attention to her fine shoulder bones; Chandra Maharaj was undoubtedly confident, professional and charming. She kissed Sastra affectionately and drew her to sit beside her on the settee. Soon after, Govind discreetly withdrew.

'You are looking well. A bit on the thin side perhaps, but that is to be expected,' Chandra said. 'You have had more than your fair share of sorrow.'

In the grand sitting room, every object was an exhibition, its angle and height, colour, shape and texture carefully, aesthetically chosen. Chandra was used to her guests expressing their admiration in silent awe, or in gasps of pleasure, so when Sastra said matter-of-factly, 'You have a grand place here, Chandra,' she said, 'Do you really think so?'

'It's most impressive.'

'Tell me, what are you doing? Teaching isn't it?'

'Yes.'

'I couldn't, just couldn't teach. It's the patience I don't have... an honourable vocation... never been well paid though. But you always wanted to, I remember.'

'Yes... Do you work full time in the hospital?'

Govind, returning to the room, said, 'She has no choice. The public doesn't yet have confidence in women doctors. Mind you, generally speaking, I think they are better... Chandra, we're starving.'

'I am smelling something really good,' Sastra added.

Chandra appeared amused and left saying, 'Excuse me, I'll just see how things are shaping up in the kitchen. The girls are in charge.'

'You have to excuse Chandra's parents; they retire early.'

'The family has a grand place here.'

'It is all Chandra's doing; her parents leave everything to her. Do you like it?'

'She has pieces here that must be worth quite something.'

'I wouldn't know. I can't relate with these. But then art is subjective, isn't it? – except great art. Chandra says, "I think I know what I like, but not what great art is".'

'What do you like?'

He was uncomfortable with the question. 'I guess I am at ease with simple forms conveying elemental messages... of life... of light, movement, colour.' He hesitated, 'Yes there is another thing... I like to listen to the quiet conversation going on in some paintings.'

'I like to listen too.'

'I don't think that was a fair question.'

'Why?'

'I may like something and not know why.'

261

'I agree; it's a bad habit we all get into, wanting to know the reasons for everything... Yes, the question was unfair, but you gave a good enough reply.'

The meal was sumptuous. Served in silver-engraved glass dishes cradled in baskets or placed on special stands, the warm, distinctive aromas rising from the food reminded Sastra of the feasts at the Tiwaris'. It was full of imaginative choices and when she had casually asked for a soft drink, instead of wine, one of the maids said, 'You could have soursop, mango, tamarind or sorrel. There is also coconut water.'

Govind said little and, by the time the evening drew to a close, both he and Chandra had lit their third cigarette. Chandra, though, rose to the occasion, initiating the conversation, asking about anything that came to her – Toronto and the children, and Dr. Lall's illness and how he had coped, and whether Sastra was thinking of returning to Trinidad. After this, she added a story teller's colouring to accounts of her more idiosyncratic patients in the hospital and this helped them all to relax. Sastra laughed and Chandra smiled. And there was the middle-class problem of maids and gardeners: 'You have to go all the way to the country today to find people you can trust, Sastra, it is not what it used to be when we were at primary school. The town spoils people. I have been very lucky; my two live deep in El Socoro Road in San Juan, but they are like real country girls, they don't answer back. I couldn't take that from anyone; they would have to go.'

When Sastra got up, thanking Chandra for the evening, her hostess said, 'I'll be dropping you back.' And turning to Govind: 'Take the girls home for me, na. I've given them tomorrow off.'

The following day went quickly; her stay was rapidly

coming to an end; it was already half past four and she was leaving early the next day. So far she had resisted the urge to visit her former home, though she had heard it was empty, up for sale again. She was not sure how her parents and sister would regard such a visit; Sati had pointedly said, 'The past is the past'.

But as the afternoon began to fade, a growing excitement to see the house again could not be contained.

There had been times when she couldn't help wondering whether the six years with Rabindranath had been the work of her imagination. But there were Purusha and Jiva – two lively bundles of their love for each other. Of late the longing to visit the house, to walk through it again, renew a close physical contact with it, had intensified, for some things were beginning to fade and she was afraid.

As she sat on the porch with her parents, the house could be seen, and time stood still. It seemed but yesterday when she was in Surinder's class, running about on the playing field at recess, chatting with Govind, Chandra, Francis and Harilall; cycling to the stream, taking Rabindranath's class.

The quiet retreat of the sun in the dying of the day was also affecting Parvatee and Narayan. They talked about when they were younger and stronger; how times had changed, people had changed; it was no longer easy to get the village women to come and help at a katha with the cooking; women were now busier than ever working outside the house – taking in sewing, growing more vegetables for the market, polishing and cleaning more and more. That's how the world is moving – having less and less time for neighbourly helping out. 'So because of that,' Parvatee continued, 'I cannot do anything big any more; besides I don't have the energy, I'm not young now.'

'You have done your part,' Narayan said, 'you have done more than your share to carry this way of life. Now let others help.'

'Mustapha died, you know,' Parvatee said, wiping her eyes; 'he was really very good. The last time he came to do the parathas for me, he supervised the digging of the big chulha two weeks before the katha.'

'No one was as good as he,' Narayan said, 'he was so unassuming, willing to help. His father was not like that. Too tight.'

'Well, what can you expect, Pa, his father belonged to the old school of Hindu-Moslem mistrust.'

'They don't trust us.'

'We don't trust them either, Pa. Mustapha was a fine man; it didn't matter whether he was a Moslem or a Hindu; he was just a fine man.'

'That's true.' Parvatee said, 'I never felt he was a Moslem; he was a good man.'

And then it was that Sastra noticed a light moving in her former home.

'Is anyone in the house at present?' she asked.

'No. You know Ramsaran is selling it,' her father said. 'No use you thinking of buying it back,' he added, noticing how interested she had become. 'We're too old to look after it for you, and you are too far away.'

'I will go and have a look at it,' she said.

'You could get to the back garden through the gate,' Parvatee said, 'but the house is locked.'

'Oh, I only want to walk around.'

She approached the wide, white, iron gate, opening it slowly and was not surprised to hear it creak. It needed repainting; rust from the top hinges had traced its own flow down the paintwork like stray strands of henna-coloured hair.

The grass was up to her knees in places. The rose trees were now spindly and neglected. Oh Milly, she thought, once you made me feel this house, this garden, was part of paradise. The few roses on the branches drooped, their heads bent, ready to fall.

She opened the side gate and entered the back garden. There was the calabash tree, overhanging, needing cutting back; the yellow and white hibiscus fence, a thing of glory at its best, now overgrown, entangled, the orange trees and the tree hibiscus rapidly turning from bronze to blood red under the setting sun; but the tulsi plant, what had happened to it? She tried to work out in her own mind exactly where it would be, where Rabindranath had fallen that day. She was no longer sure. And though she looked, parting the long grass with her hands, searching over a larger area than it could possibly have been – there was nothing. She wondered whether the seeds could have been scattered by the wind, and that somewhere in the long grass or a nearby field, seedlings had become thriving plants. The pleasures of their many strolls across this once sunny, well-kept lawn, the hedge surrounding it alive with yellow and white hibiscus, suddenly came back to her and with it the fragrant scent of tulsi in chanamirit.

That spark again. This time she was sure it had moved, though now it stood still. She thought that the kitchen door, the back entrance, was being eased outwards by the wind. She hesitated, felt a call from within the house, felt drawn by something inside. Slowly she opened the door. Dusk was approaching: the shadows were lighter, longer, leaner. No wind. She passed the chulha, through the kitchen, into the dining room and entered the sitting room.

On the far corner of the wall was a shadow, but no sound. He would have to be standing along the dark corridor hidden from view; she needed to walk to the end of the sitting room, where the corridor opened into it, before she could tell who or what it was. She was surprised to see her own shadow outsize on the opposite wall.

She heard sounds, footsteps approaching, coming nearer, and saw the shadow rising along the wall, about to have its neck bent, then to hover on the ceiling. She inquired softly, 'Rabind, is that you?'

She could feel a strange silence. No steps. A voice held back, suspended by her question. A reply studied. It was as if the substance of the shadow high on the ceiling was caught off-guard, the question never envisaged.

And then from within her and from without her, she heard voices and felt his presence.

'Dearest Sastra, I am bound to you, am here because you willed it so, our spirits inseparable. I come here to release you, where our past dwells, where solemnly with tears we parted. Here too, dearest, our past must rest and not be stirred to resurrect our spring. I come to ask you what I need to have. Release me, dear wife, from the living, for where I am, time moves inexorably on. Allow me, dearest, to rejoin the earth from whence I came. Search here no more, for I am fast becoming lost even to myself, becoming part of everything.

'O joy of my youth, O wandering spirit, may a sweet sleep, a child's contentment be yours. I will it so. Release me too from solemn, silent vows, from nectar-dripping thoughts which cloyed my wings and left me stilled, dying. Bring me strong winds, a rush of rains to beat upon my wings, to cleanse, that I may enter new gates. O kindred spirit, enable me to breathe again, to taste afresh the joys, the miracle of life.'

And the voices subsided and she stood dazed, suspended from time and space and form.

Through the shutters, chinks of light brought abstract shapes and, as she opened wide the doors and windows, the old musty air, too long locked in, escaped; the fast retreating sun rushed in and the shadows left.

The time to leave crept quietly upon the young Pandes and upon their grandparents too. The sun had risen above the horizon and they were all sitting in the shade waiting, when Parvatee saw Dr. Capildeo's car crossing the railway line. The driver stopped before the house and called, 'The doctor sent me. They ready?'

Purusha and Jiva got up and kissed their Nana and Nanee. 'Do not give your mother trouble now,' Parvatee said, 'try and be good children and take care with your school work.' Narayan turned to his youngest grandchild. 'Jiva has to be the man in the house now, and look after his mother and sister.' A blushing Jiva, embarrassed by the enormity of the task, hid behind his mother, pulling at her skirt. 'Purusha,' Narayan continued, 'you are older, so set good standards for Jiva. And when it is holiday time, come and see us. You are a sensible girl; Jiva and you can travel by yourselves if your mother can't leave her work.'

'The stewardess is very good,' said Purusha; 'she will look after us.'

'Purusha saw that on television,' Jiva said, 'but we don't know if it's true.' They ran downstairs to the car and Narayan turned to his daughter and said: 'Remember, this is still your home; with your qualifications and dedication you will always be able to get a job here. You can come back any time. Always remember that. I will miss you. Your mother will miss you even more. You understand what I am saying... Write us often... A letter means a lot.' Sastra hugged her father and the now much older man, completely grey and trembling, was greatly overcome, and when his daughter turned to kiss her mother, he left the room. On returning, he spoke softly to Parvatee: 'Say something to her, she must leave now.'

'What can I say?' Parvatee asked, wiping her eyes, 'I don't want her to leave, I wish she did not have to go. What to say? You speak for me too. Sastra, you were always a blessing to us. Always a good daughter.' And Sastra, overcome by the generosity of her parents, embraced them both, again and again, and with a voice breaking like glass said, 'You are better parents than I deserve.'

Narayan looked away and Parvatee wept, anguish filling her stomach with renewed pain.

Before he started the car, the driver called out to Narayan, 'Well, Boss, we are leaving now.' Purusha and Jiva and Sastra all waved, and Narayan and Parvatee made one last courageous stand, waving until the car sped on its way to the Churchill-Roosevelt Highway.

Later that afternoon as they were having tea, Narayan said, 'It just shows how these birth readings make no sense.' Parvatee said nothing.

She felt differently, but why disagree with her husband, he was a good man, and as what she thought could not irritate him, only what she said, she replied, 'You always had Sastra's interest at heart and she knows it. You do what you think is right. What else is there?'

He got up: 'I don't think I have ever said this before,' he hesitated, 'I am not good at saying some things, but you have been a good mother to the girls and a good wife, no man can ask more.'

And as he walked alone in the dusk, Narayan grieved for his daughter, for her present loneliness and the uncertainties surrounding her. He pictured her standing alone, her slender hands holding the reigns of that fast moving chariot of life with two young children in the back seat, and he couldn't help thinking that the swift turns and twists of the track were too much for one pair of hands.

The flight from Trinidad to Toronto was delayed and by the time the Pande family got a taxi and arrived at their home, everyone was tired and hungry. After hot showers, sandwiches and tea the children went to bed. Sastra sat in the suburban stillness of the night and looked out through the window. She saw the space, the cleanliness, the brightly lit windows. In the taxi she had felt welcomed by the complex neon lights of her local shopping centre and was now at ease even with the fastest moving cars on the highway. Across the city other communities from all parts of the world were establishing and making lives for themselves: Chinese, Jamaicans, Trinidadians, Italians, Greeks, Indians from the subcontinent and Indians like herself from the Caribbean. For all there were choices; they could be part of communities, or they could be whom they pleased. Each choice carried its own cost; now she could not envisage being without the choice. Maybe they were all becoming Canadians.

Looking back to her fortnight in Trinidad, she was glad she had returned, revisited the houses and the gardens, met Govind and Chandra... Yet despite the rich pleasure of being with her family, seeing old friends and dear places, she sensed the truth of Sati's dictum – 'all that was now behind her, all that was of the past'.

As it became darker and quieter, tiredness began to overpower her. She got up and moved from room to room, drawing the curtains one by one as a cherry-cheeked maid had once done on evenings long long ago in Ireland. She was about to draw those of her own bedroom window when it began to rain, the windblown drifts striking against the pane. Through the rolling beads of water, through the glass, she could see the moving apple trees and cherry trees and the night. Two tall pines in the neighbour's garden held her attention; their giant shadows fell obliquely across the lawn. She stood watching, thinking and dreaming, saw her younger self lost, untried, standing on a hillock in the snow in a faraway field in Ireland. Her memory slipped still further back, and a young man, barely eighteen, unsure of himself, walked upright around a classroom. 'And from within you will grow a fine expanse of wings,' she heard his voice, 'light and beautiful and strong. With such wings you will fly to the moon and the stars and the bluest blue of the skies.' Her cheeks were wet, yet she did not feel sad or lonely or lost as she once had, walking with Breugel's 'Hunters in the Snow' in a faraway field in Ireland, and though the task before her was daunting, his spirit came with the wind and she sensed a peace, a strength growing within her.